Stalked by Revenge

Zane Clearwater Mystery
Book 3

Lynn Lipinski

Majestic Content Los Angeles

Dear Readers,

Readers like you mean the world to authors like me. I am electrified and anxious to hear your reactions to the story I have worked on for months in private.

It's hard to know when a novel is done. Most authors I know could tinker with draft manuscripts forever, polishing sentences, changing settings, and shifting plot points to try to match that perfect novel we had in our heads. Acclaimed U.S. author James Faulkner, in a 1956 interview in the *Paris Review*, said "All of us failed to match our dreams of perfection. So I rate us on the basis of our splendid failure to do the impossible."

That impossible feat is using written words to capture the wonder and woe of the human experience, and for mystery authors, to be entertaining and thrilling while doing so. If someone as talented as Faulkner struggled to live up to his own dreams of perfection, I can take comfort at least that my worries place me in very excellent company.

For me, one of the ways I decide I'm done is when I re-read a chapter and think "wow, that's good. Did I write that?" It's a funny moment when I don't recognize my own writing and a testament to just how long it takes to write a novel and what an overwhelming process it is to keep all these fictional lives and worlds going. I hope that as you read *Stalked by Revenge*, you enjoy the story and don't hold it against me that more bad stuff happens to Zane and Lettie.

Lynn

* * *

Find me online:

- Website: https://lynnlipinskibooks.com/
- TikTok: @lynnlipinski
- Facebook: @lynnlipinskiwriter
- Instagram: @lynnlipinskiauthor
- Twitter: @lipinski_lynn
- YouTube: @lynnlipinskiauthor

Praise for Lynn Lipinski and Stalked By Revenge

Lipinski's natural gift for storytelling shines.

— Marci Bolden, author, *Life Without Water*

[Lynn Lipinski's] writing is magnetic, charged with intrigue, elegance, and grit.

— Marina Crouse, writer

If you have not read Lynn Lipinski, you are missing out! Well written, dark, and well thought out!

— Debra, Open Book Posts

Stalked by Revenge will keep thriller and suspense aficionados engaged from beginning to end.

— Pacific Book Review

Compelling family dynamics at the heart...[a] character-rich rural noir.

— BookLife

Like its characters, this mystery is engaging, compelling

— Kirkus Reviews

Trade paperback ISBN: 978-0-9964676-9-8

eBook ISBN: 979-8-9866288-2-0

Library of Congress Control Number: 2023900033

Publisher's Cataloging-in-Publication data

Names: Lipinski, Lynn, author.

Title: Stalked by revenge / Lynn Lipinski.

Series: Zane Clearwater Mystery Series

Description: Los Angeles, CA: Majestic Content Los Angeles, 2023.

Identifiers: LCCN: 2023900033 | ISBN: 978-0-9964676-9-8 (paperback) | 979-8-9866288-2-0 (ebook)

Subjects: LCSH Siblings--Fiction. | Family--Fiction. | Crime--Fiction. | Criminals--Fiction. | Oklahoma--Fiction. | Thriller fiction. | BISAC FICTION / Mystery & Detective / General | FICTION / Thrillers / General | FICTION / Thrillers / Crime

Classification: LCC PS3612 .I75 S83 2023 | DDC 813.6--dc23

Chapter 1
Zane

All Good Things Must

"I've been shot! I need an ambulance!"

The dash-cam footage was black-and-white and grainy, but the audio filled the classroom with crystal clarity. A man's voice, rough with pain, screamed for help into his radio as taillights sped away.

Watching the videos of police officers being ambushed and killed was a weekly ritual in Cal Himmelman's class. Zane Clearwater hated it. Six weeks into Oklahoma's consolidated police training, the videos had gotten easier to watch but the first three shook him to the core. He had seen enough people die up close and personal: his father Jeremiah Doom and that poor sod Wally Zittman at the carnival. Every violent death took him back to the trauma of his father. Two years later, he had just gotten better at moving past it.

Who was he kidding, Zane thought. The videos didn't get

easier to watch. And it didn't get any easier to listen to Himmelman's commentary either.

"Situations change in a heartbeat," Himmelman said. "You're being watched constantly. You can be getting a cup of coffee like that guy was, and people take your measure. Calculate their odds, especially in anti-police neighborhoods like they got in Oklahoma City and Tulsa. Heck, even out in some small towns, there are blocks where you don't know who's watching and who has a gun. It's us against them."

Zane slumped against the hard back of the chair-desk combo. This mentality made him feel like an outsider. He'd been faced with murder charges when his mother died in a mysterious fire and without the help of Detective Angus Pastor, he might have been convicted. He wanted to be a police officer who helped people, not one who wore suspicion like a second skin. He wasn't sure there was a place for him in law enforcement some days.

"Not everyone without a badge is a criminal." The voice came from behind him, but Zane did not have to turn around to know who said it. Devante Flores constantly argued with the instructor and the classmates who bought into the us-versus-them mentality.

"That's true enough," said Himmelman. "But you never know. People are unpredictable. When you walk up to a house to investigate a noise complaint, you don't know who is behind that door and what weapon they have. You've got to be looking for your escape route if things go to hell."

Most of the class nodded along with Himmelman, fully invested. The handful that had hesitations or felt the same as Devante sat quietly.

No bells rang, but Himmelman must have had something better to do because he glanced at the clock and said the magic words. Zane slipped his notebook and pen into his backpack slowly. He was in no hurry to get to the mini-boxing matches that were next on the schedule.

Zane scrolled through the text thread from his sixteen-year-old sister Lettie this morning, re-examining the latest sonogram of his niece in utero. So many hopes and dreams came with that little peanut of a person, curled tight. The baby was a surprise for their family, and he certainly hadn't wanted his baby sister to get pregnant at such a young age, but he'd never call this baby unwanted. He planned to give little peanut and his sister everything he never had and then some. This job with the Skiatook police department was going to make that possible.

The booming voice of Scott, one of their cohort's loudest and most aggressive members, interrupted his thoughts. "Maybe you should have gone to social work school," Scott said, directing his derision at Devante as he often did. His towering frame bumped into Zane as he and his two friends headed for the classroom door, pausing one-by-one to kick at Devante's black boots to mar the glossy shine required for inspections. They laughed and slapped one another's backs like they'd just made comedy gold.

"What a bunch of assholes," Devante said. He bent to pick up his notebook and pen from the floor by his desk as the classroom cleared out.

"Maybe you can land some punches during the boxing matches," Zane said. He felt sorry for Devante, but Devante stood in his own way a lot of the time. The dude had a lot to learn about picking his battles and finding the right time to make his arguments. But Zane could appreciate a hothead. He had those tendencies himself and worked hard to control them. But he could still remember going off on Randy Womack, his old boss at the Tulsa Zoo, and getting fired.

"Not likely. I really don't think those guys understand what going fifty percent means." He was referring to the defensive tactics instructor's admonition that during the boxing matches, the fighters should only exert half of the power they would during a real fight. "Someone's gonna get hurt."

Devante was shorter than most of the class, and in his place, Zane would probably shy away from hand-to-hand combat too. A former high school wrestler, Devante possessed some skills, but mostly after the fight had gone to the ground.

Zane stood up from his seat and glanced at his phone again, surprised to see a voicemail notification pop up. A call must have come through in the few moments since he had last looked at it. They were supposed to keep their phones in their lockers at the academy, but most ignored that order and kept them on silent all day.

He knew it was Old Spice before even really looking because no one else in his life would leave a voicemail. Not even his grandmother did it anymore, saying she preferred texts because he always answered faster.

He listened for a few seconds as Old Spice identified himself as though caller ID didn't exist and then got to the news the Tulsa police detective had called to deliver.

His heart dropped.

"Clyde Doom could get out of prison," the detective said. "I wanted you to know as soon as I heard."

Zane pressed the phone closer to his ear as though it would somehow block the words from entering the world. Just when he thought he and Lettie were safe and on the right track. *Clyde.*

"You coming?" said Devante. Zane stood immobile in the classroom for a few beats longer, then forced himself to move.

"Yeah, right behind you," he said.

The instructor met Zane's eyes across the classroom as Devante exited. "Everything all right? You look like you saw a ghost." Himmelman's observation skills outshined his people skills every day of the week.

Zane shuddered at the memories dredged up by hearing Clyde's name. Acne-cheeked Clyde, Zane's youngest half-brother, usually glassy-eyed from meth. The blotchy, shaky-lined wolf tattoo on his neck. The gun in his hand. Lettie tied up.

He felt trapped. He wanted to get out of the classroom, walk out of the building, go to Lettie, and keep her safe. He managed a few faltering steps toward the door, frozen by foreboding mixed with anger. How was this happening?

Himmelman ran his meaty hand over his balding head and sighed. They were alone in the classroom now and the sound from the hallways had died down as well. Everyone was moving out to the gym.

"I'm not trying to be an asshole, Clearwater. I'm trying to be the little voice in your head that says, 'be careful or you can die out there.' This is a serious job with serious consequences. Not everyone makes it home at the end of their shift."

His words rang true in a way Zane hadn't reckoned with before, but not the way Himmelman meant them.

"I get it," Zane said truthfully. And Himmelman didn't have to try to be an asshole. He made it a lifestyle.

Zane forced his legs to move out of the classroom and toward the building exit, two glass doors emptying onto the winter-white quad. Panic scraped at his stomach. He slowed his breath, counting to five before exhaling it in a visible puff to alleviate his growing fear. As he headed toward the gym behind one or two stragglers, the afternoon sun slipped behind clouds, erasing his shadow. Behind him, he heard the clang and thwack as the wind whipped up the American and Oklahoma State flags on the flagpole at the training center.

Zane hit the call-back button on his phone, finger shaking.

"Zane," Old Spice said.

"How is this possible?"

"The appellate court overturned his conviction and twenty-year sentence. Said the trial judge was sexually harassing the district attorney who prosecuted the case."

"What does that mean?"

Old Spice's gruff voice took on an edgy tone. "It means he gets a new trial. But it also means he might be getting out on bail while he waits for a federal trial because of that McGirt ruling. He's part Cherokee, just like you, and the crime happened in Indian Country when he was a juvenile. Everything's backlogged in the U.S. Attorney's office so who knows when that will happen."

"Is he out now?" Zane said. His voice was hard and clipped and felt like it rose from an anger that threatened to consume him.

"Not yet," Old Spice said. "Now there's a good chance they'll keep him locked up until that new trial. But you never know."

Zane pushed through the front doors of the gym, the smell of floor polish and sweaty socks assaulting his nostrils. The cold air outside had chilled the thin layer of perspiration on his arms and neck, another sign his anxiety still rocketed. His emotions cycled through denial, rage, and fear, and finally settled on the numbness of shock. It would be so easy to run. Probably smarter too. But distance wouldn't deter Clyde's vengeance. And fleeing would just delay the inevitable.

Maybe he wouldn't have to stand his ground. Maybe Clyde would toe the straight line and not try to seek revenge for Zane killing their father and testifying against Clyde and his brother Link in their trial.

Yeah, and maybe Lettie was going to give birth to a magic unicorn.

He changed his clothes and entered the practice gym. A crowd of trainees surrounded a makeshift boxing ring made of crime scene tape and stacked traffic cones. Cue Zane's internal eye-roll. The academy had enough money for a real boxing ring setup. This makeshift one was the defensive arts instructor's idea of a joke. And there was Ryan, standing in the middle of the room like a hillbilly sensei, his tan felt cowboy hat shading his eyes and his short grey mustache and beard. An enormous key ring hung off his belt like an old-fashioned jailer's ring. A few pairs of trainees around him sparred with smiles on their faces, more light-hearted than Zane felt. Laughter and mainly male voices bounced around the high-ceilinged gym, though about ten women were in their cohort. The women tended to take the trainings more seriously, Zane had noticed.

On the far side of the room, two women in the academy's black berets, T-shirts and loose pants engaged in one-on-one combat on blue mats, a snap punch and high knee rise blocked. A few of the instructors hung out on the gymnasium bleachers to watch the show, passing a bag of chips. Zane saw Turner, the copper-headed firearms instructor, glance at him and look away again. Turner said something to the other instructors, each looking at Zane and back again. Maybe the news of Clyde's good fortune and Zane's bad luck traveled fast. Everyone in the academy knew about Zane's past.

"Gather round, people," Ryan said. He was slow on his feet and in the way he talked, but he had a sharpshooter's eye for creating dramatic match-ups. He must have heard the news about Clyde, too, because he called out Zane's name for the first match. Probably thought he was doing Zane a favor by giving him an outlet for his anger.

Fine, Zane thought, grabbing a fresh mouthpiece from Ryan and letting the man lace him into gloves.

"Against Zane today we'll have Big Scott," the instructor said. Zane wavered and sucked his teeth. Scott, the jerk he'd just seen bullying Devante in class, was not just bigger than he was. He was also a dirty fighter, making a hobby of terrorizing weaker trainees.

Scott's posse of smaller bullies stomped their feet and clapped for him. "He'll knock you out at twenty percent!"

"Three minutes," Ryan said. "Don't give it all you got. Just half-effort, got it?"

Scott winked at him, a big comic wink as though mugging for television cameras on one of those old comedy shows with a laugh track. The urge to smack that stupid expression off his face intensified, and he hopped over the crime scene tape, soft blue mats under his feet. Maybe throwing some punches was the right medicine for the moment. And if Big Scott bested him, fine. He had taken plenty of punches in his life; he could take a few more.

Ryan rang the bell. Zane went in fast with a first punch, no time for dancing and ducking. The men traded attacks, Scott's right hook sending Zane reeling. If Big Scott was operating at fifty percent, Zane didn't want to see what his full capacity looked like. He was throwing punches without mercy, a hard look in his eyes. Zane absorbed the punches and let Clyde's face superimpose itself over Scott's sweaty one. Clyde coming for him. Clyde coming for Lettie. No one to stop him. Zane jabbed at Scott's face as if bashing his way out of a burning building. It felt good to let go of some of that anger.

At the end of the three minutes, Zane had fended off the attacks and counterattacks and left Big Scott panting and surprised. He liked being underestimated and wanted to hold on to the feeling of satisfaction that came from surprising an opponent, but the fight had been a hard one and his energy was spent. Getting hit in the head can rattle your brain, he thought. But something in Scott's eyes, that hard meanness, had reminded him of the cruelty of his father and half-brothers. Even on the right side of the law, the capacity for meanness and injustice existed. It was human nature but it also depressed him.

"Good fight, men," Ryan said. "But I think that was more than half-effort. Next match-up, I need you to take that order seriously."

"I did hold back," Scott muttered to Zane as he crossed the mat. "You piece-of-shit lowlife. You don't belong here."

Scott's words were pure loser's bluster, Zane reminded himself, shaking his head as though to loosen them from his brain. He headed for the water fountain, managing a smile or two for Devante and a few of the others who clapped him on the back as though he'd won some title match-up. He didn't want to watch the rest of the fights, but the instructors would expect him to.

He took a deep breath, remembering his resolve. Nothing was going to keep him from his goal of helping people find justice. Nothing. The resolve had grown in him since he had faced the terror of being wrongfully accused of killing his mother, and he was more determined than ever to become a part of the law enforcement community. He had overcome the odds to get hired as an officer-in-training by the Skiatook Police Department, one of the handful of cities that didn't require college coursework, which he didn't have. He had landed in this training program and fought daily to keep his place. His instructors said he had potential and lauded his hard work. But this wasn't just about getting top grades or showing these idiots he wasn't a quitter or not disappointing Old Spice, who had vouched for him.

This was about learning every single skill he could to become a person who could really help people who needed it. Someone who understood the right and the wrong side of the law and could help good people navigate the grey areas in between.

And today, with the news about Clyde, it was about protecting himself, Lettie, and the baby from danger. Again.

With everyone's attention on another match-up in the ring, Zane bent down to grab the backpack he'd left on one of the low bleachers and unzipped the front pocket. Breaking the news to Lettie about Clyde would be best done in person, but he wouldn't get out of training until after nine o'clock this evening. So the phone would have to do.

"I just heard about that criminal who kidnapped your sister getting a new trial," said Cal Himmelman. Zane startled at his voice. The stocky instructor certainly could walk on cat's feet when he didn't want to be noticed. His appearance over Zane's right shoulder felt like an ambush.

"If it's not that McGirt verdict tying our hands, it's good convictions that don't stand because of some technicality," he said. The name McGirt was shorthand for the landmark Supreme Court case decision that held that much of eastern Oklahoma was Indian land. The Supreme Court's ruling complicated how the state could prosecute criminal cases on Indian land and between people of Indian heritage.

Zane and his half-brothers shared Cherokee blood, but to Zane, the ruling seemed like an abstraction, something for the powers-that-be to sort out. He wasn't sure how to even think about it. And anyway, it wasn't why Clyde had gotten a break. A judge who couldn't treat his female co-workers with respect was the reason. Crazy, unintended consequences of #MeToo.

"You're one of us, now, Clearwater. Don't forget that,"

Himmelman said. "We've got your back just like you've got ours, okay?"

Zane didn't feel the connection, really. Himmelman's statement of support came with qualifiers. Everything was a loyalty test. Everything was about creating an us-versus-them mentality that just didn't ring true for all the grey areas Zane knew existed. Still, he needed allies and he wasn't about to alienate Himmelman.

"I appreciate that," he said.

"There's people here who'll help you. You just got to ask. I know Angus Pastor thinks highly of you, and for some of us that's enough."

Zane wondered where that sympathy and support had been for all the weeks leading up to this moment.

"Good," he said. "It's a lot to process right now. I think I'm in shock."

Zane saw the calculation in the other man's eyes. Himmelman sized him up one more time then pressed a business card into Zane's hand.

"My personal cell is on here," he said. "You call me if anything comes up. If you have any questions or anything. I'm retired now and I might be more helpful to you than you think."

It was an oddly cryptic thing for a straight-shooter like Himmelman to say and Zane wasn't sure what to make of it. He ran his finger along the edge of the card. The edges were bent and softened as though the card had sat in a wallet for years without use. He couldn't imagine a world in which he would call Himmelman for help, but he thanked him again for it and slipped it into the cargo pocket of his pants. He reflexively pulled out his phone to glance at the screen only to be surprised by seeing Lettie's name and face on the screen. She was video-calling him. Himmelman tapped the side of his nose. "You oughta take that, I'm guessing," he said. "Even though it's against the rules, I think most will give you a pass today based on what's going on."

Indeed, word had traveled fast through the law enforcement grapevine.

"Zane, can you come home?" Lettie said. Her face was visible only momentarily, in fragments, as she walked through the mobile home Verda had bought for them at the newly renamed Majestic Mobile Home and RV Park in Tulsa. On Zane's phone screen appeared one of Lettie's eyes, opened wide, eyebrow arched. Then her lips, pressed together tight. Then the white ceiling fan turning slowly. Zane's stomach clenched and panic throttled his breathing. Dread descended like a thick fog, making his bones feel leaden, unmanageable. It was Friday morning, and police academy cadets were prohibited from leaving the campus until dismissal at six in the evening.

"What's going on?"

"It's all over Twitter," she said. "Clyde Doom is getting out of prison."

"I was just going to call to tell you," he said.

"But something weird happened. This package came." The phone camera swept to a white plastic envelope. A yellow baby rattle shaped like a lion's head smiled back at Zane.

"Adorable," Zane said, relief slowing his heart even as confusion replaced it. Why would Lettie call him about this?

"It just appeared on the doorstep an hour ago," she said, her eyes widening with fear. "No return address, no card, nothing. A baby rattle in a white envelope with my name on it."

"One of your friends maybe?" Zane said. "A rogue Amazon delivery?"

Hand shaking, she held the camera over the white envelope. Only her name was on it, no address.

"Not from Amazon. And I checked with my friends. I called Maxine at Earth Spells, I checked with Emmaline and her parents, I spoke with Dock Hirsch across the way, I even called Angel's mom. No one dropped a baby rattle off here. Plus, me and Verda have been here all day. A friend would have just knocked at the door." Her words spun faster and faster, reminding Zane of the carnival's gravity ride, spinning so fast that the floor could fall away and riders would be pinned to the walls. He felt pinned to the wall.

"Calm down," Zane said even though he felt nothing like calm inside. "Has anyone been in touch with you recently on social? Anyone who could have just found out you were pregnant? Maybe there's an easy explanation for this. Magnolia, maybe?"

But as soon as he thought of his ex-girlfriend, he remembered her latest post about a new job in St. Louis. Anyway, she had known about Lettie's pregnancy and even donated to his sister's GoFundMe campaign.

"I guess I didn't check with Tiffany, but why would she leave it on the doorstep?"

Hearing his current girlfriend's name brought her face and smile into his mind, a sweet pause in an anxiety-filled day. "Doesn't make sense. She'd be coming over this weekend anyway," Zane said. "One of Verda's friends? What's the name of that man who moved into the place with the carport covered in chicken wire? The one who kind of flirts with Verda?"

"Leon something? I guess I could walk over there and ask," she said. "But Zane, what if it's Clyde somehow? And he knows where we live?"

Lettie's worried face filled the screen, the look in her eyes taking him back to the moment when he saw her tied up and terrified in the Dooms' compound in those insane weeks following his mother's death. The decision he made to pull the trigger on his father, Jeremiah Doom. It was the only decision he could have made. But it was also one that haunted him like an unfriendly ghost every day since. And now the specter had come to life with his half-brother Clyde Doom possibly walking free.

"He's still in prison right now, so it wasn't him directly. Let's take it one step at a time," Zane said. "It's weird all right and it's hard to overlook the timing, but maybe there's a simple explanation for this." He took a deep breath and started to fill Lettie in on what little information he had heard from Old Spice. What he didn't need to tell her was that he would protect her at all costs. She already knew that.

Chapter 2
Zane

Return or Retreat

Driving down the jutted road leading into the Majestic Mobile Home and RV Park was an uncomfortable homecoming. Usually, Zane could put the fire and his mother's death out of his mind enough to feel the customary relief at being home. But with the impending release of Clyde—the son of the man responsible for that fire—and the weird baby rattle story, the Majestic felt unfriendly and cold. Lights in the windows of the mobile homes he passed on the way to their lot seemed threatening, as though the people behind those walls conspired against him. He pushed it out of his head. You could not get through life if fear held you still. If his experiences with soul-crushing terror had taught him anything, it was that you had to focus your attention. Do the next thing.

And for Zane, the next thing was to hold his sister tight.

She made her way carefully down the steps of the mobile home as he pulled into the parking space beside his grandmother's lemon-yellow Cadillac. Lettie was all stomach at eight months pregnant, face flushed and hand brushing at her arm as though she'd walked through a cobweb and was trying to get the sticky webbing off herself. She looked worried, walking slowly toward him. Zane held her longer than usual, kissing the top of her head as he felt her draw in a shaky breath. He had to be strong for her.

Before today's upheaval, their new life with Verda at the Majestic had settled into a comforting routine. Outside of Zane's absence while training at the police academy, the autumn-to-winter months of Lettie's final trimester had been unremarkable. Lettie, her boyfriend Angel, and Zane tag-teamed to keep Verda's hoarding at bay in the three-bedroom unit, sometimes waiting until Verda went to bed then throwing away useless items she had collected. Last week's haul included a broken tricycle, a dirty plastic storage bin, and a stack of ency-clopedias. Life was a steady schedule with Lettie and Angel enrolled in online classes, taking their homework as seriously as they took her pregnancy. Most nights the two of them pored over a book about what to expect when pregnant, half in wonder, half in terror.

The pattern of those days seemed like a sweet memory. Already he was twitching at sounds—a truck rumbling by the entrance to the Majestic too slowly, a leaf skittering in the wind behind them. He squinted at the darkness over Lettie's shoulder—nothing. It would be a long night, he could feel it already, stirred up by shaky thoughts and exhausted from the endless loop of what-if scenarios running through his head since he'd heard the news.

"Come inside, I've got chili on the stove for supper."

Where Lettie had expanded the past eight months with the

baby growing inside her, his grandmother Verda Davis had shrunk, as though caring for them burned twice as many calories a day. As she morphed into a more defined and angular version of herself, her mobility improved, and she rarely needed the cane she had once wielded with great difficulty.

No matter how she transformed, one thing stayed the same: her hugs were still the best. She held her arms out to embrace him, her kind face framed with puffy silver blonde hair and punctuated with a bright-pink-lipstick smile. He fell into her scent cloud of baby powder and lilac and nuzzled her shoulder for a moment like a child might. Lettie's boyfriend Angel stood up from the couch, game controller in hand, telegraphing worry and relief. His eyes rested on Zane like he was Batman coming to the rescue or something, and Zane didn't like how heavy those expectations felt. How many times was a person supposed to have to save his family from danger? When could they just live their lives peacefully? Probably never. Depressing. As if sensing his despair, Angel approached to join the hug and they held tight for a few moments before breaking apart.

What if they left? The thought had occurred to him on the drive from Ada to Tulsa. His anxiety had spiraled out of control: Clyde sent that baby rattle as a message to show them he knew where they lived. Clyde was coming for them. Zane tried to tell himself he was being paranoid but he couldn't help but imagine all of them moving out of harm's way. Not Los Angeles again, like Lettie tried months ago, but maybe somewhere like Texas. A big state, a place to get lost. They had proven themselves to be survivors, but the world seemed destined to make them confirm it again and again. People talked about cats having nine lives. How many lives did Zane and Lettie have? They'd used up two. It wasn't fair. Maybe the smart thing to do was leave.

Zane could tell Verda knew the news because she fussed

longer than usual over the food and drinks. She demanded he taste the chili to see if it had enough salt. It did. She talked to him about the probiotic drink that Lettie had gotten her hooked on and how expensive it was then poured him a shot glass of it so he could taste it. Lemon pepper ginger flavor, tart on his tongue. "Have you seen the price of meat lately? It's downright outrageous. Especially luncheon meat. That president better do something about these prices or he's not going to get reelected, that's for sure. Food prices affect everyone."

Zane took a seat at the table and reached for Verda's hands to pull her into the seat next to him. "Grandma, it'll be all right."

"No one around here sent that rattle," Verda said, her voice low as though talking to herself. "Lettie spent another hour going around asking people if they saw anything or had pictures from those video doorbells, but no one could help."

Lettie and Angel slid into their seats at the table, their eyes lingering over the plates, glasses, and utensils as though they were unrecognizable objects.

"I was thinking maybe we could leave town," Angel said. His words shot silence into the room like a bullet. Zane squeezed Verda's hands before letting them go. For a few moments, everyone made a show of fixing their chili bowl with cheese and chopped onions and sour cream, silverware clinking on porcelain. They had all arrived at the same place mentally about the baby rattle. It was meant as a threat and somehow Clyde was behind it, pulling strings from prison. Zane knew it was circumstantial evidence at best. Clyde wasn't stupid enough to make an overt threat that would reduce his chances of bail.

"I had been thinking of going to Playa del Carmen in Mexico," Lettie said. "Back when I was trying to run away. It's safe, a touristy kind of place, and not too expensive."

"Mexico? Wouldn't we do better in the United States? It's not like we're fugitives from the law," Angel said. "We're running from a criminal. We have the authorities on our side."

"I don't speak Spanish," Verda said. "I don't even like Mexican food that much, other than tacos and nachos." A little smile floated around her lips. She was trying to make light of the situation, or at least lighten the mood. Zane welcomed the shift.

"Grandma, we've got to get you to try taquitos," he said. "And I bet Leon would love to give you some Spanish lessons."

Verda could not help but smile but her reply was stern and sharp. "Zane, Leon is just my friend. I'm too old for—" She stirred her chili some more as though trying to find the right words. "Spanish lessons," she said.

"What about Texas then?" Lettie said. "It's a big state."

He and Lettie were in sync. But hearing her give voice to the notions in his head made him question his own thinking. He played out in his mind what it would mean to leave. They would need new names if they didn't want to be found. Otherwise, they'd be sitting ducks in Texas just as they were here in Tulsa. They'd have to change everything, uproot their whole lives. Even then, there would be no guarantee.

"I know how to get new identities," Lettie said, as though reading his mind. She had swapped her interest in the occult and witchcraft for a deep involvement in the dark arts of hacking. She said she only used the skills for good now, no more credit card fraud. But obviously, she still knew how to work the levers of fake ID cards and bank accounts.

"Surely the police can protect us," Verda said. "Clyde may be mad enough to drown puppies, but surely he doesn't want to wind up locked up for another month of Sundays for committing more crimes. He's a hot-headed young man but he don't want to ruin his life any more than it already is. He just wants to scare us half-witted. It's probably like a game to him. Why he's only a few years older than Lettie."

Zane nodded. If there was one thing he understood from his law enforcement training, it was that the police couldn't prevent crimes that hadn't happened yet. Sure, they deterred some people from breaking laws, and sometimes they were able to act fast enough to stop a crime in progress. When someone wanted to hurt or kill another person, there was little the police could do before the crime happened. A restraining order could create some space, though, keeping Clyde at a distance from them and giving them some peace of mind.

"Verda's right," he said. "Maybe we can get a restraining order."

Lettie stirred her chili, her eyebrows knitted in a skeptical V-shape. "If we're going to stay, then we need to get a better security system than a bunch of nosy neighbors." Her tone was dubious.

Zane didn't like the idea of waiting for trouble to show up on the doorstep any more than Lettie did. But he didn't understand her sometimes. She was smart and hard-working. She had proved herself to be courageous. But she was reckless too. She didn't know how to sit with the uncertainty of life like he did. Goodness knows he had spent enough time trying to get comfortable with it through his sobriety work in Alcoholics Anonymous. Though she had a point that Clyde was something to be feared, he didn't feel like rushing around to make plans to leave was the right choice. Yet. It was something he'd heard the other day at a meeting that came to mind. *There are two paths, one up and one down. We have been given free will to choose either path. We are captains of our souls to this extent only. Once we have chosen the wrong path, we go down and down. But on the right path, we are on the side of good and we have all the power of God's spirit behind us.*

The words swirled in his head, instilling a faith that the right path would yield the right course of action. Fear was an emotion to note but not to act on. Leaving felt like the easiest thing to do but also the hardest. And the hardest to live with. There was dignity in standing your ground, but it didn't mean he didn't feel the fear.

Chapter 3
Zane

Newbie Days

On his first day at the police academy, Zane vowed to be a different kind of student than he had been in high school. He arrived early, took a seat in the front row, notebook and pen open in front of him, ready to write down everything that came from the instructor's mouth.

Scott sat next to him in that first orientation, by design, Zane later realized. Though his usual inclination was to stay silent and suss people out over time, he reminded himself to act differently than he would otherwise. His initial impulses frequently got him into trouble. So he struck up a conversation by introducing himself, unwittingly giving Scott ammo against him he wouldn't be afraid to use as the weeks went on.

"Where are you working?" Scott asked.

"Skiatook PD," Zane said. When Scott looked surprised, Zane overcompensated with more detail. "I don't have any college coursework, so I couldn't get into one of the big departments. A friend of mine at the Tulsa Police put in a good word for me at Skiatook. I got lucky."

It was a miscalculation. Scott told him about how his friend had been trying to get hired at Skiatook and though he smiled and said how lucky Zane was, his eyes hardened. "You must have a good friend over at Tulsa PD," he said. "What did you say your name was?"

Zane knew his notorious past was an Internet search away. His family's travails, starting with his mom's death and leading up to his involvement in the credit card fraud ring at the carnival made the Oklahoma news. It was only a matter of time before his classmates figured it out, but he hadn't thought it would be on the first day.

By noon his classmates were whispering when he walked into the cafeteria. He tried to take a seat next to Scott, but the other man tipped the chair forward. "Saved for non-criminals," he said. Classic bully behavior.

On his second day at the academy, Zane looked back on his first-day naivete with embarrassment. Even his urge to make friends had been wrong. He found a seat at an empty table and was surprised when Devante sat next to him.

"You think school cafeterias breed that kind of behavior?" Devante asked.

"Maybe," Zane said. He was glad for the company but hesitant to fall into a chummy conversation with a stranger again. You never knew what agendas people held in their hearts.

"Law enforcement needs people like you," Devante said. "People who have been through real shit."

Zane laughed a little. Devante seemed like a good guy. He had a wide, kind face, somehow made kinder by his slight lisp that added breath to his pronunciation of the letter "s" in "Scott is a shithead." Over the following weeks through the classes focusing on criminal law, patrol procedures, defensive tactics, traffic enforcement, and accident investigation, Devante spoke up regularly about the need for law enforcement to parse out the grey areas between the good guys and bad guys. He tried to link what they were learning in the class to his and his family's experiences in the tough neighborhoods of Oklahoma City where he grew up. But he sometimes argued his points too strongly, alienating himself from some of his classmates (mostly white and male) who felt like he alternated between talking down to them or unnecessarily provoking them.

Weeks into the program, Devante was still Zane's closest friend at the academy. They made it through the first "hell week" together, learning to keep their eyes on the door, do push-ups on demand, and carry coffee in their left hand so they could grab their gun with their right. Sure, there were a few aggressive loudmouths in the class like Scott, but for the most part, the people in their cohort were humane and diligent, interested in doing a job where they could make a difference. That much was clear by week two when Himmelman walked them through a unit called "Psychological Stressors for Veterans."

"Many people you have to deal with are in a difficult situation," Himmelman said. "They may not be capable of focusing on what you ask them to do or on answering your questions."

He showed them more videos: a veteran pleading for a cop to kill him, another attacking an officer. He told them they needed to be understanding but also protect themselves. He talked about post-traumatic stress disorder or PTSD and how it can change their perspective.

He said he knew an officer who quit his job the first time his life was threatened. "Even if you feel like quitting, try reaching out to someone first about how you're feeling. Getting help is not a sign of weakness," he said. "If you have doubts, talk to someone."

Zane took copious notes as Himmelman went on to talk about people experiencing homelessness who don't want to go to shelters. Finally, after ten days of push-ups and shoe-shining, it felt like they were getting to the topics he really cared about. Himmelman stopped talking for a minute, then closed the book and looked up.

"What made you want to be a cop?" Himmelman said. "After George Floyd was killed, after people took to the streets demanding that governments defund the police. What brought you here? It's not an easy road to get here and it won't be easy once you're in uniform either."

The silence in the room was powerful and the weight of the question seemed to shift his classmates' eyes down to their desks.

Himmelman said that when he used to work as an officer, people respected him and what he did for them. Now people doubted their intentions. Trust had broken down. Maybe Himmelman hadn't always had that "us vs. them" mentality.

Zane and his classmates stared at their notebooks. "No wrong answers," Himmelman said. "Let's take it left to right, starting in the back."

A pale woman with blond hair in a bun stood up with arrow-straight posture from the desk to address the room. "You don't have to stand up, Georgia," Himmelman said. As she sat back down, she talked about wanting to do something more meaningful than a desk job. Something where she could make a difference. "I have my private investigator's license and had a business investigating fraud for insurance companies. That work pays well but it's dull. After the coronavirus pandemic hit, I just re-evaluated everything. Decided I needed a new career," Georgia said.

An Army veteran in the back said he missed the military's camaraderie and hoped to find it in the police force. The woman next to him squinted her bright blue eyes and said she wanted to "pay it forward by helping others." Scott and his buddies repeated one another's words: "I want to take bad people off the street."

Devante talked about his family and rough childhood and how the police were called to his home often. "There were some good officers who truly looked out for me. I want to do the same," he said. "I know some people in my neighborhood think the police are just there to hassle them, but I think we can change that."

A solidly built Black man of about thirty named Traymon nodded along with Devante. "My stepfather and one of my good friends are in law enforcement. And they're great men. There's a lot of good people out there who want to do the right thing."

"People tried to talk me out of it," said a Choctaw woman with slicked-back dark hair and an olive complexion named Keyonna. "My husband is Black, and we have a son. I think I can bring an important perspective, help make a difference if I'm on the police force."

When it came to be Zane's turn, his head emptied out and he forgot all the answers he'd come up with while the others spoke. "You all know I've had some run-ins with the police, more than once," he said. "But that means I know firsthand there are good people in law enforcement. One of them is my friend. And all I know is that it feels good to help other people. We can stand by and do nothing or we can step in and intervene when someone needs us. I don't want to stand by."

Chapter 4
Zane

Predator or Prey

Zane arrived at the training facility at seven o'clock Monday morning, bent on asking Himmelman or one of the other instructors how to get a restraining order quickly. His research online showed it might take as much as three weeks to get a hearing. Anything could happen in three weeks. It only took minutes to find yourself in danger. If they were going to stay in Tulsa and not run, he wanted to take every step he could. He just needed to make sure to present his case with more evidence than a random baby rattle arriving at the door and a gut feeling.

The executive director of the academy was a white man in his late fifties, grey hair like sugar coating on his short black hair. He stood outside his office, scanning the crowd and when his eyes found Zane, he nodded and gestured for him to come closer. Everything about Thurman Flentroy was slow and careful: the way he walked, the sharp creases in his suit, how he took a breath before speaking as though he inhaled the words.

"Let's talk before you start your day," Flentroy said. Zane followed him into his office, a green room with floor-to-ceiling windows overlooking a patch of grass. Zane felt his muscles screw tight, scared of the conversation and what it meant that Flentroy had been waiting for him to appear in the hallway. He'd never seen the man do that before.

"I've been looking at your file," Flentroy said. "You've been an exemplary cadet so far. On time, no absences, applying yourself."

"Thank you, sir," Zane said.

"That makes this conversation hard today," Flentroy said. He went on to explain how he was familiar with Zane's "situation"—his tone draped the word in euphemism. "I had misgivings about you coming in because I'm not much of a believer in redemption. Well, except for our Lord Jesus Christ's redemption, of course. But Angus Pastor and the folks at Skiatook really vouched for you."

Zane fixated on the bits of shredded paper on the floor next to Flentroy's desk, waiting for the man to get to his painful point. He didn't have a clue what was coming but Zane knew it wasn't going to be good. No good conversation ever started out like this one.

"Someone has accused you of dealing methamphetamine," Flentroy said.

The words chilled Zane to the bone. It was quiet in the office except for their voices and the low buzz of the fan in Flentroy's desktop computer.

"Who would do that? It's not true," Zane said. It took everything he had to stay composed and calm.

"I can't say now," Flentroy said but his left hand shifted

over a piece of paper on his desk and Zane wondered if the name was written there. He imagined snatching it from him.

"Okay, well when did this alleged meth selling happen?"

"Back when you had the trouble with your father," Flentroy said.

"I was never charged with anything! Nothing." Zane said. "They were selling meth, but I wasn't. And in case you hadn't heard, my half-brother is getting his conviction overturned. We're worried what he might do if he's out in the free world."

Flentroy nodded like he understood and started talking. A torrent of words about codes of conduct, the need to be truthful in one's application, disciplinary processes, reasonable expectations, notice, fairness, equity, and due process. His mouth pinched like he was sucking food out of his teeth. He continued, talking in circles, everything looping back on itself.

"It's not true," Zane repeated. Life may be full of grey areas, but this wasn't one of them. It was a binary choice, as Lettie liked to say. You either sold meth or you didn't. And he hadn't sold meth to anyone. It was an outlandish lie. He couldn't imagine this coming from any other source than Clyde or his brother Link.

Flentroy didn't say anything.

"This is crazy," Zane said.

"This process needs to play out," Flentroy said. "If you're innocent, then that will come through. You have to trust the process. For the time being, you're suspended here and at Skiatook PD. That is, until some folks investigate this and get it resolved."

Zane felt himself sinking into the chair. Sure, there were processes. But when people looked at you like Director Flentroy was looking at him, you knew it didn't matter about processes. They'd already made up their mind. Process was about appearances, not about changing anyone's mind. Like in a dream, a door was shutting slowly while he tried to run to it, the distance telescoping farther and farther away, his feet in quicksand.

The halls hummed with silence when he pushed out of the director's office. He was glad not to have to make eye contact with anyone. Word would travel fast when he wasn't in class today. He texted Devante with the news, knowing the other cadet wouldn't likely see the message for hours. Cell phone use on campus had to be sneaky instead because of the rules. Then he called Lettie and told her the news, reassuring her it was going to be all right even though he wasn't sure of that at all. In the car, he pulled out the business card that Himmelman gave him and keyed in the number along with a text message. *It's Zane Clearwater. I think I need some help.* He didn't have to wait too long for a response. *Meet me at eleven-thirty at Aldridge's.*

Aldridge Coffee Shop was one of those old-school style diners that a casual visitor might just pass right on by. No fancy sign drew travelers, so the crowd was mainly Ada locals who came for some of the best homestyle cooking around. A stranger dropping by to order a latte or cappuccino would get laughed out of the place. Every table was taken, and several had been shoved together so that a large extended family could sit in one place, from grandparents to babies. He found Himmelman with his crisp starched shirt, ramrod posture, and buzzcut hair easily among the crowd of baseball-capped men, grey-haired couples, and women with messy buns and T-shirts.

"Meet Loris Trapper," Himmelman said, gesturing to the woman sitting next to him. The woman stood up from the table and shook his hand. She wore round brown tinted glasses and the clothes of a hunter: camouflage pants and top, hair pulled back in a severe low bun. Wispy grey hairs circled her face which came to point at her nose. She resembled the small animal that shared her name, the slow loris, which the Tulsa Zoo had acquired a few years ago. But her movements were quick and her military bearing and directness matched Himmelman's. Zane shook off his annoyance that Himmelman didn't come alone. He noticed they had taken the two chairs facing the coffee shop door, a strategic decision to observe everyone coming into the restaurant.

"I heard about your suspension from the academy," she said. "I'm so sorry."

Zane flicked his eyes to Himmelman with a question mark.

"I think Loris can help you with Clyde so I invited her," Himmelman said. "I was telling her about your history with Clyde, and she thinks the best defense is an offense."

"I wanted to talk to you about a restraining order today," Zane said, "before all this happened."

Loris and Himmelman exchanged glances and Zane saw the derision in their eyes. They thought he was being naïve, trying to hide behind a piece of paper. But this was the justice system they had. You couldn't lock someone up because you thought they might hurt you. You had to wait until they committed the crime, the assault. The restraining order was just a first step in a process, he thought, then thought of the frustrating disciplinary process that Flentroy had described. Processes didn't protect you from danger. They just covered other people's butts so they could say they did all they could.

"There are laws to protect you from criminal threats, especially overt ones. You should definitely pursue those," Loris said. "Create a paper trail with the police."

Zane told them about the baby rattle.

"Hard to pin that on him to a judge. But you know what it tells me? It tells me he's a little reckless. The deadliest ones don't give any warning," Loris said. "So, he's giving you warning. You can use that to prepare."

"But what about this witness saying I was selling meth? It's total bullshit. Maybe it's the same person who sent the rattle."

The waitress approached and they paused the conversation to peruse the menu. Aldridge's offered all sorts of chicken, fried and baked; fried catfish; hamburgers; biscuits. Zane ordered the half sandwich and soup, one of the cheaper items on the menu. He wasn't hungry anyway.

Loris took a sip of the sweet tea the waitress plunked down in front of her, leaving a ring of wet on the table. "The question is, what are you willing to do to keep your family safe?"

Keeping his family safe was a central principle in Zane's view of the world. He could barely think of how to convey it fully other than opening his hands and saying, "It's everything." All actions he'd taken pointed to that. Before his mother's death, he'd wanted to break free from his family and navigate the world on his own. But that had been the pipe dream of a teenager still trying to find his own identity. Now he knew that family—whether by blood or by choice—was the bond that made the world run right.

"Okay then. You must make sure he knows you're just as serious as he is. You've got to shift your mindset from prey to predator. And here's my first tip. The best initial response to a predator is neutrality. Don't show fear or anger. What do all predators have in common?"

Zane shrugged. "Aggression?"

"A desire for certainty of success," Himmelman said. "They're opportunists and they want to know they'll succeed before they strike. Come on, Zane, we talked about this in class. How breakdowns in law enforcement motivate bad people to do bad things."

"This Clyde, well, he's already shown some weakness,"

Loris said, "sending a threat. Like I said, the most effective ones don't let you know they're coming. So we've already got the upper hand."

"And it's wise to believe what people tell you, especially when they threaten you," Himmelman said. "Once someone issues a threat, they've started down the path of carrying it out."

The food came, giving Zane a moment to take a breath and try to assimilate what they were telling him. Loris cut into her fried catfish like she hadn't eaten in days while Himmelman slowly tucked his napkin into his shirt collar like a bib.

"Why are you two interested in helping me?"

"Gotta keep this sleazeball off the street," Himmelman said.

"System doesn't always work right," Loris said at the same time.

Zane forced himself to take a bite of the turkey sandwich. Sure, he could adopt a predator's mindset. He wanted to go into law enforcement to protect people against dangerous people and situations. More than that, he wanted to see justice done and people get what they deserve. The problem was, even though he had been trying to do everything right, trouble still reached out and snatched him anyway. He redoubled his resolve: Not only would they not run, but they would defeat Clyde so that he and his brother couldn't come after them again. In six months' time, or however long it took him to get a new trial, Clyde would be firmly behind bars again and Zane would be back at the police academy, cleared of this ridiculous accusation. It was comforting—envisioning a future free of Clyde's threat. His life returned to normal. Whatever normal was.

"What am I supposed to do?"

"The very first thing to do is fortify your home," Loris said.

Chapter 5
Zane

On Point

"Go on back and see what you like," the slouchy, feline-faced girl with long blonde hair said, raising her voice to be heard over the loud barking coming from the pens in the adjacent room.

The animal shelter was raucous, full of life and desperate energy. Zane felt dozens of eyes settle on him, transmitting hope. The pens were filled with mainly large dogs: German shepherds, pit bulls, a rottweiler, a few old Labradors. In the corner a few stalls held a selection of small chihuahuas, dirty white dogs, and a dachshund mix with batwing ears, a motley crew being examined by an earnest couple in blue jeans and cowboy boots.

Zane had not stepped foot into an animal shelter before and found it more heart-wrenching than he'd imagined. It was nothing like the zoo, with its collection of wild animals that made eye contact like equals, sizing you up as friend or foe. Nearly every one of these abandoned or lost dogs looked pitiful, begging for love. He wanted to adopt every last one of them and also run out of the shelter and never come back.

He found their desperation pathetic but soon saw how his own old feelings of abandonment and loss stirred up the powerful emotions he felt in seeing these canine faces, begging to be loved. They repulsed him because they reflected his own image back in a way, desperate for love in the old days from Emmaline, from his father. No matter that he'd slowly built a loving group of family and friends around him. That feeling of unlovability stuck like the smell of dog poop on a shoe. The stench clung to the rubber such that even after washing all the visible traces away, the odor remained. That's how being abandoned and then betrayed by your father felt. It fused itself into your identity and burrowed into your self-esteem.

But Loris's recommendation to get a big dog for security had resonated with him so that was what he came to do. "Get one of the big breeds," she said. "Loud bark."

And there was Ballpoint. He had an almost regal look, his ears perked up and eyes cast downward, like a king looking over his minions from a throne. As Zane approached, Ballpoint unfolded his long legs and came to the edge of the kennel to sniff Zane's outstretched hand.

"The owner died," the feline-faced woman said. She exuded compassion as she scuffed behind Ballpoint's ears. "Nobody in the family could take him. They said that when the man died, he had been training him as a catch dog for hog hunting."

An orphan of sorts, kind of like Zane and Lettie. He chuffed the grey fur along the pit bull's wide jaw and felt the dog press into his hand. A connection.

"What's a catch dog?"

"Just like it sounds," the woman said. "Trained to catch large animals. A dog with a job."

A brave dog, Zane thought, one who knew how to go on the offensive. Yet stretching his rough tongue out to lick Zane's face, as though he sensed Zane's worry. Zane scratched his thick head with his fingers. There was no turning back. Ballpoint was his dog.

He filled out the mandatory forms, paid a hundred dollars for medical testing and vaccines, and signed a pledge not to abuse him or abandon him or let him run wild in the streets. The shelter's demand for assurances struck him as sweet and naïve. As though a signature, ink on paper, could make promises hold true in an uncertain future. He knew good intentions didn't always mean anything and he had the feeling Ballpoint knew that too. But he did plan on taking good care of Ballpoint. He had never had a pet before and was excited to introduce him to his family. Though now he was worried about their reception. Probably all of them would have wanted to come along to pick out the dog. Zane had taken the expedient path and he just had to hope they'd like him as much as he did.

He walked out of the kennel with Ballpoint tethered to his side on a hand-me-down leash. The dog's head only reached midthigh, but Ballpoint was powerful looking, broad-shouldered, seventy-six pounds of muscle and short dove-grey fur. He sent a photo of the dog to Loris with the message: *Step one complete.* Then a second message with a photo of Ballpoint to the group chat with Verda, Lettie, and Angel: *New member of the family.*

Ballpoint hopped in the passenger seat of Zane's car and sat looking forward like a person would. Zane fussed for a moment with the seat belt, trying to figure out how to secure the dog before giving up. He'd just have to drive carefully. Zane was relieved to find Ballpoint to be a calm dog, watchful and still, on the car ride to the Majestic.

He clicked the gear shift into park as Lettie opened the door, a wide smile on her face as she spotted the dog. "Come here, boy!" she shouted as Verda whistled loud enough that Angel clapped his hands over his ears. Zane's eyes scanned their smiles, enjoying the moment enough to briefly forget why he got Ballpoint in the first place.

Ballpoint bounded up the steps to the mobile home like he owned the place, then sniffed Lettie and Verda and Angel each in turn before walking the perimeter of the living room and kitchen. Verda filled a big mixing bowl with tap water, and Ballpoint lapped at it greedily. "We got to get this big boy fed," she said. "How does chicken and sweet potato sound?"

Lettie wrapped her arms around Zane. "You'll be back in the academy soon," she said. "They'll clear all this up." He loved her confidence and sincerity and tried to absorb some of it through her hug. "Everything is going to be okay."

Verda plunked a raw chicken breast in a pot of water and put it on the stove as Ballpoint tracked her every move. Zane filled them in on the advice Himmelman and Loris had given him. "I'm going to need your help with setting up the cameras, Lettie."

"Already on it," she said. "Tiffany had some at the store she's going to let us have cheap."

Mention of his girlfriend's name made him smile even as his anxiety soared. Zane pulled out the notes he had taken during lunch with the two former cops. "Dog, video cameras, outdoor lights by the door that are on from dusk to dawn—"

"That's a good idea," Lettie said. "Though we're under the streetlight so it's not that dark."

"Good point. Now, this other stuff gets harder. A driveway alarm, door, and window braces."

"Have you ever heard of hillbilly security?" Angel said. "You go to the junkyard and get a bunch of old metal like wheels, pipes, air conditioners, and water heaters and place them all around the entry points. Make it noisy for an intruder to come near."

"I'm sure the new owners of the Majestic Mobile Home and RV Park are going to love that look," Zane said. But it wasn't a bad idea.

Ballpoint gave up on waiting for the chicken to cook and explored the mobile home like he owned it. His spirit was curious and alert, his stub tail wagging a joyful beat. It seemed to Zane that the pit bull had forgotten the trauma of his owner's death. And how nice it seemed that a creature could move forward from loss in such a direct, optimistic fashion. Zane would give anything for such a simple attitude instead of being weighed down by all that had come before. But people can be resilient just as dogs can. Suffer, heal, move forward. Onward. Next thing, he told himself, forcing himself back to his to-do list.

"We could head over to the junkyard," he said to Angel. "That hillbilly security idea has me thinking why not?" And it was cheaper than some of the other ideas on the list. Zane got a salary from the Skiatook Police for attending the academy but now that he had been suspended, he assumed the money would vanish too. He had to be wise about how they spent on these security items. He already had enough credit card debt to last a lifetime.

A knock on the door startled them all and elicited a loud bark from Ballpoint.

"Hello, it's me." The voice was Tiffany's honey-tinged drawl.

Zane opened the door to see her smiling face. He threw his arms around her and squeezed hard enough to keep his emotions from swelling out. Relief, joy. Love, even. Maybe. She held him just as tightly and pressed her cheek into his chest. Then she pushed back a bit and kissed him smack on the lips.

"I'm glad you're here," he said, eyeing the plastic bags from the Cell-Phone-Fixit store on Eleventh Street that she managed. She looked beautiful, face flushed and sunglasses holding her bobbed black hair back from her face.

"Me too. Zane, I can't believe all this. It's a nightmare. I don't know what to think." Her eyes crinkled at the edges. She set the bags down and patted Ballpoint who sniffed her as though she was a turkey leg from the carnival.

"Who's this?"

"Meet Ballpoint. Newest member of the family. Meant to be a living security alarm, but I guess he doesn't find you too threatening. In fact, he seems to be drawn to you like a magnet. Kind of like me."

"Dogs love me," Tiffany said, grinning. "Also, I have half of an uneaten protein bar in my pocket." She patted her left hip pocket as though it was proof and Zane grinned back at her. He loved her smile so much he practically got lost in it. They held each other's gaze and something pinged between them. She got him in a way no one had before. Beyond words.

They spent the next two hours setting up the video camera and flood light system, aiming both at the mobile home's only door. Zane and Angel played worker bees while Lettie and Tiffany took the lead in installing the 4K camera with microphone, network video recorder, and software needed to watch the video. Zane felt proud: his sister and his girlfriend were tech geniuses in their element. Plus, it just felt good to do the hands-on work of running the wires and screwing the cameras and lights into the mobile home's exterior. Like his mentor, Ernest Buckskin told him, working outside with his hands was one of the best medicines for his perpetually anxious mind. He fumbled in his pocket for the last screw for the second camera mount and dropped it into the dirt. Frustrated, he started down the ladder when Tiffany appeared. She bent over to pick up the screw and hand it to him.

"So, when is this guy's day in court?" Tiffany said.

"Himmelman called me today, said he heard it was going to be next week," Zane said. "Clyde will stay in prison til then anyway. I'm thinking of going but I don't think I'll be allowed to say anything. I'd just go to let him know I'm watching him."

"Who would bail him out if he even got bail? Isn't his other brother still in prison?"

"I'm sure he has a mother somewhere. And his grandparents, Susie and Dave. Maybe one of them. Susie was there when we testified at Clyde's trial, and I heard she paid for his lawyer that first time around." Zane thought of the Dooms' tiny blue clapboard house outside of Sallisaw where he had gone when he was first looking for his father. Dave's dementia had probably worsened since. It was possible either one of them had passed on, too. They hadn't been young. They were his kin too but they would never forgive Zane for killing Jeremiah. "They're not rich though, so I don't know."

Zane finished screwing in the mount and took a moment to admire his work, perfectly flush and lined up where he wanted it. The camera was very visible. Zane didn't want anything discreet. He wanted Clyde to know he was being watched.

"You're doing a pretty good job at this," Tiffany said. "Maybe I could use you at Cell-Phone-Fixit."

"I'm still technically employed..." Zane stopped.

Tiffany laughed and handed him the camera to place on the mount. "I know you don't want to work at the store."

"It's not that." Zane's mouth was a thin, serious line.

"I'm not trying to be smart. You're worried and rightfully so, and I was trying to lighten the mood. It was stupid. I'll go with you if you want. To see Clyde have his day in court again." She smiled at him, and then, determined, loving, she reached over and tucked a strand of hair behind his ear, sweeping his cheek with her knuckles as she took her hand away.

Zane thought for a few seconds. "I'd feel better if Clyde never even knew you existed, Tiffany."

"Ouch," she said. "And I thought we were getting on so well."

He looked at the camera in his hands, his face a tiny reflection in its beady lens eye. He needed to lighten up. He didn't need to make the situation scarier than it already was. "Obviously I'm too embarrassed of you to have you meeting my *favorite* relatives."

Zane laughed painfully and after a beat, Tiffany laughed too. "Definitely too soon to meet the extended family, you're right," she said. "Don't want to rush it."

He stepped down the ladder to wrap her in a hug. "He'll be a threat to everyone I love."

"Love?" Tiffany's eyes locked on his through her grey sunglasses.

He'd blurted the "L" word out so quickly that it took his brain a minute to catch up with him. He hadn't said it to her before. He had only told one other woman he loved her. Emmaline. It was during that terrible period after his mother's death and it hadn't gone well. Emmaline had replied, "I just don't feel the same way you do. I thought you understood that." Looking at Tiffany now, his stomach stirred up, like water or soup starting to boil, big slow bubbles rising up as he struggled with a fleeting impulse to run away. He meant what he said to her though he wished he had done it with more style. Or picked a better time.

"Yes, love." He let everything else fall away and focused on her. "I love you."

"I love you too," Tiffany said. She took hold of his hand and kissed his fingers. He moved closer, breathing in with her exhale. Across the street, a bug zapper electrocuted an insect with a loud, hissing snap.

"Almost done?" Angel said from the doorway. Tiffany lowered their hands and squeezed his palm before letting go. Angel came out and sat on a lawn chair, aiming his face at the sun. "I think my vitamin D levels are low. I need to get some sun. And hey, Lettie said she's almost done too. Want to drive over to the junkyard?"

"He has this idea for an obstacle course leading to the door," Zane told Tiffany. He clinched the camera into place.

"Not an obstacle course. More like fortress walls made from wheels and old refrigerators and stuff."

"Angel, even the Majestic doesn't let you keep that kind of junk in the yard. They call it blight," Tiffany said. "Tech is the better solution." Tiffany was a digital fangirl. To her, every problem had a solution with an electrical current and binary code. "Video cameras, motion sensors. Deterrents."

"Castle walls and moats worked pretty good for people throughout history." Angel gave Tiffany an impatient look. "Fact."

"It does kind of sound like a solution that kid in *Home Alone* would come up with," said Zane. He envisioned the homes of one of those modern homesteaders living off the grid, an armory of rifles and ammo, a sign that read "this property protected by Smith & Wesson."

"And what's wrong with the *Home Alone* kid's tactics?" Angel said. "They worked."

"In the movies," Zane scoffed. A cloud of gnats gathered at the bottom of the ladder, their bodies and wings whirling around his face. Angel was a good kid. Though his mother's criminal connections had gotten him and Lettie into a credit card fraud ring and lots of trouble, he had stuck by Lettie and Zane and proven his love for his sister. Now, here they were under threat once more, and Angel was just as invested and committed as before.

"Come on, we need to get out of here for a bit. Change of scenery," Angel said.

"Sure, we can go," Zane said. "Let's see what they have. Can't hurt, right, Tiffany?"

"If you say so." Tiffany shrugged. "I'll come with you."

"I don't think you should, Tiffany. It's... I've already asked too much of you."

Tiffany considered what he said and shook her head. He felt a flash of love for her again—what was it about sassy, strong women that grabbed his heart?—but before he could take back his protective words she was on the move.

"I've never been to a junkyard." She shook her key ring. "And I have the store's van."

Chapter 6
Zane

There Goes the Neighborhood

The auto and industrial equipment salvage yard sat on a field filled with scrap metal, old tires, and dismantled auto bodies. They paid the one-dollar entry fee to get in, and Angel led them to a blue-and-white doublewide that served as the office. Inside, a man of medium height, well-muscled, with tattoos all over his shoulders and up and down his arms, was dealing with customers and answering a bedlam of phone calls all at the same time. Zane, Angel, and Tiffany waited until he got around to them. "Yeah, what's up?" he said, eyes lidded as though he could barely stay awake to serve them.

"We're looking for some stuff to lay a trap," Angel said.

"That's a weird request," the guy said, his eyes widening. "A trap for what exactly?"

"An alligator," Tiffany said quickly.

"An alligator," the man repeated as though he'd never heard

the word before. "Well, that's a new one. You're welcome to look around, I guess. Y'all making a movie or something?"

"Something like that," Zane said, stifling a laugh.

"A couple of trucks still have some personal items, fence posts, and chains and stuff in them. Out in the back on the left," he said, popping out from behind the counter to open the door and point. "You might find something in there." The phone called him back behind the counter.

Outside, a cold wind sliced like a knife. Zane had been to junkyards before, but this one was neat and orderly. In the yard were rows and rows of automobile parts, all carefully tagged with white stickers with the make, model, year, and one of those black-and-white square codes. The only similarity to other junkyards was the oil- and grease-stained cement they walked on and the pungent, slightly sweet smell of antifreeze and transmission fluids.

They walked by a set of late-model cars, damaged in collisions, and pulled apart for pieces. In the distance, the junkyard's flattener stood quiet, a forklift next to it holding a wrecked auto body like it was a toy. Behind them in the workshop, a high-pitched whir emerged, the sound of metal on metal. It was nice to be outside but surreal to be wandering around the junkyard in the middle of the day. Every step felt weighted by the heaviness of their purpose.

"Mind if I fire up a livestream?" Angel said, holding his phone. "Just a quick one. Show my followers what the auto junkyard looks like."

Zane shrugged. Angel had been doing daily "lives" of six-plus hours playing video games and talking about getting ready for the baby for the past few months. He'd earned a decent following on the video streaming app Twitch and was trying to figure out how to turn those followers into cash without much luck.

"Hey, what's up, people?" Angel said, holding the phone at arm's length, video aimed at his face. "Got a change of scenery for you today. We're at a junkyard looking for some stuff! Want to come along?" He squinted at the screen, reading comments, and hanging back as Zane and Tiffany kept walking.

"An alligator trap?" Zane said, grabbing Tiffany's hand and steering her clear of a pile of broken glass next to a decayed, rusting pickup truck.

Tiffany laughed. "I didn't know what Angel was going to say to that guy! I just said the first thing that popped into my head. There are alligators in Oklahoma you know. South of here."

"Fast on your feet and full of trivial knowledge," Zane said. "You should go on a game show."

Tiffany kicked at a chunk of red plastic taillight, reflecting on his joke. "I might need to cuz I'm going to need money. I hate to pile on with my problems, but something came up at the store," Tiffany said. Zane knew by her faltering tone that she was trying to sound more upbeat than she felt. "The owner came by, and said the pandemic gutted his finances and he needs to sell the store or close it up. I think I'm gonna be out of a job soon. Korey made it sound real dire."

"Has business been down?" Zane didn't remember her mentioning anything like that.

"Not really. That's what's weird. But Korey's treating it really urgent, like a problem he must solve. I suspect there's something happening underneath it all he's not telling me. But the upshot is I guess I might need a new job. I mean, who's going to buy that place? And would they even be willing to hire me at my salary? I can't take a pay cut."

"Why don't you buy it?"

She paused mid-step next to a gutted Chevrolet van and said, "You're crazy, Zane. That's about as likely as me driving this hunk of junk off the lot. Where would I get that kind of money? My bank account is basically ten dollars and a piece of chewing gum."

"You could get a loan or something. People do that."

"Not people like me and you, Zane. We're not Jeff Bezos or anything. Anyway, I'm saddled with debt. Student loans. That's why I was a Bernie Sanders fan. Thought he was going to wipe it all away."

"You're always telling me to push myself. I didn't think I could get a police job and you just kept believing in me," Zane said. The day he learned he got the Skiatook job, he and Tiffany celebrated with a steak dinner at Golden Corral. They'd been so happy. It almost physically hurt him to think of the hope of that dinner now that everything was in jeopardy.

"I don't know," she said. "I think I'll just start looking for another job."

"What about your dad and Maxine? Maybe they could help out with some money."

"They don't have much either. Dad's retired and Maxine doesn't make that much money with her psychic readings and classes at Earth Spells."

Angel came running up to Zane, holding his phone at arm's length as though it were a snake ready to bite. "Hey, something weird just happened."

"What?" Fear bloomed in Zane's chest.

"I got this message during the livestream," Angel said. "It said, do you like the baby rattle?"

"Who sent it?"

"No one I recognize. Username was PeturbabeArgue. Looked like a throwaway account."

"Are they still there?"

"No, I just, I freaked out. I just shut it down. Like, how would someone on Twitch know where I live?"

"Don't you stream from the Majestic all the time?"

"Yeah, but I'm pretty careful. I don't say where we live other than Tulsa. I mean I'm straightforward about our lives though. I talk about the baby, Lettie, all of that. I probably said sometime that we live in a mobile home. But I never use last names and I don't say the Majestic ever."

"Most of us put enough out there on social for people to figure out our connections with just a little digging," Tiffany said. "Not hard to find you or Lettie and then figure out you're a couple. But maybe we can learn something about Peturbabe-Argue. Find an IP address or something. Hey, maybe this person's just a fan and has nothing to do with Clyde Doom."

Skepticism lifted Zane's eyebrows high, but Tiffany's words seemed to give Angel the barest threads of hope to cling to. "I can send a message to say thank you and see what they say," he said. "If this person's just a random fan, they're gonna think it's weird how I shut down the livestream."

"And if they are connected to Clyde then they're going to know you're scared," Zane said. "Just be cool in the follow-up. Act like nothing's concerning you. Like you just want to say thanks properly or something. Say the livestream glitched. People blame everything on glitches."

Angel nodded. "While I was walking around back there, I found something we can use." He pointed to a white 1989 Chevrolet truck with its hood popped, its fat Remington tires still intact but at a weird angle that suggested a broken axle. Zane peered into the cab. The steering wheel and most of the dash were missing though the long bench seat was intact.

"Nice truck in its day," Zane said. Probably a bad accident had landed it here. People usually kept a truck like this for as long as they could keep it running.

"They literally have an alligator trap," Angel said. "Or some kind of animal trap."

"You're kidding," Tiffany said. She rose onto her tiptoes to peer into the truck. Zane's hand found its way to her warm back and felt its way down to the curve of her waist. She turned and kissed him on the cheek.

The long oval trap, studded with screwheads, rested on a velveteen car seat perched inside the truck's bed. Zane dropped his hand from Tiffany's warm back and ran his finger lightly over the sturdy hook and the metal chain coiled beside the trap like a snake. The trap had a nasty spring jaw that looked like it could take off a man's leg.

Angel returned to Zane's side, breathless from making a quick circuit around the adjacent trucks in hopes of another alligator trap bonanza.

"It's the only one I found though," Angel said.

"Better than anything that *Home Alone* kid ever had," Zane said. "Don't put this on the livestream, Angel. We want there to be some surprises."

Chapter 7
Zane

Lights, Camera...

The next morning, Zane and Ballpoint walked around the perimeter of the mobile home, inspecting the security system. Four floodlights and bullet cameras pointed at every inch of the metal box they lived in. In keeping with Angel's hillbilly security idea, a border of old car wheels and tires formed an obstacle course for anyone trying to draw near, making it difficult to find quiet footing underneath the trailer's windows. The pit bull wiggled with joy for the excursion, bumping his head excitedly into Zane's thigh as they walked, tentatively pulling on the leash.

Anxiety was a cold hard knot in Zane's stomach as he waited for Loris to arrive, but it still made him smile to watch Ballpoint prancing around the space, as delicate in footing as those dancing horses that had come to Tulsa last year. The dog found a branch and picked it up with his teeth and shook with excitement. The slightest thing delighted Ballpoint.

"Looks like a busy time for you."

Leon's voice from across the road startled him. The man opened the door to his old blue Hyundai, threw a brown grocery bag on the passenger seat, and swung it shut again.

"Worried about security, huh? Verda was telling me someone bad may be after you." About the same age as Verda, Leon was lanky with thick salt-and-pepper hair, side-parted and glistening. Old-fashioned hair cream froze his comb-tracks in place like the grooves on a vinyl record.

"Yeah, we've got some stuff going on."

Ballpoint pulled at the leash, anxious to sniff Leon's outstretched hand. The other man scuffed behind the dog's ears, earning a grateful lick.

"You let me know if I can help," Leon said. "I've had some experience with bad people, back in Ecuador. I know neighbors need to come together. I'll be late for work if I don't leave now but I gave Verda my number, you know, just in case you all need anything."

"That's good," Zane said, smiling to hear the two had finally exchanged phone numbers. Zane wasn't always too quick to pick up on romantic signals, but these two had been circling a courtship for months. You'd think it was Victorian times and Verda was the woman in that movie *Pride and Prejudice*.

A car engine rumbling turned three sets of eyes down the road they stood in. The vehicle was moving slowly and almost stopped when it came into view of the two men and the dog. Then it picked up pace, and the driver signaled to turn into Zane's driveway, even though no cars were behind it. Zane watched the angular yellow signal blinking, the brown Suburban cut into the driveway.

"Friend of yours?" Leon said.

Loris shut the SUV door and waved at Zane. When she stepped toward them, it appeared as though she was carrying a gun on her hip, but he blinked and saw she merely had her phone strapped to her belt.

"Loris, hey," he said. He introduced her to Leon and Ballpoint and they parted ways: Leon off to work and the remaining three headed toward the trailer to walk the perimeter. Zane felt something very primitive and strange, a whooshing feeling in his stomach and chest, and hands. Their home looked so vulnerable, even with the cameras and lights. It was basically a tin can on a concrete slab. He looked at Loris, expecting to see a look of disbelief on her face, but she was nodding with approval instead.

"The tires are an unusual touch. Did you put them here for this or were they already here?"

"It was my sister's boyfriend's idea. We call it hillbilly security."

"Camera and light placement look good," Loris said. "Looks like you got all the angles covered. Are those Axis cameras?"

"I think so," Zane said. "My girlfriend got them. She works in electronics."

"She knows what she's doing. Axis is the absolute apex of digital cameras, very reliable," Loris said. "The lights aren't on motion sensors, correct?"

"Correct. On all the time if we want them to be," Zane said when he walked through the trailer door. He was behind Loris and Ballpoint, who pulled forward smelling the bacon Verda cooked on the stove.

Lettie sat at the kitchen table, staring into the laptop screen. Her focus was so deep sometimes she seemed to go into another dimension. But after a few moments, she broke the stare-down with the computer screen and stood up. A tight smile spread over her face when she saw them. "You must be Loris."

"Good morning."

Zane did the introductions, and everyone shook hands like it was some kind of business meeting. It felt strange to have Loris there in the mobile home with her immaculate, pressed black pants and shirt and polished leather belt and shoes.

"What are these walls made of anyway? Not drywall," she said, pushing on the thin wall. "Oh, I do feel a stud in there, that's good."

"I think the drywall just has a vinyl coating on it," Verda said. "That's what they told me when I bought the place."

Zane went to the kitchen counter to pour a cup of coffee. "Lettie can show you the command center here on her laptop. It's pretty impressive."

Loris smiled. "May I have a cup of coffee, too?"

"I'll get it for you," Verda said. "We're all just so wound up we're forgetting our manners."

Zane looked up to meet his grandmother's eyes. Disapproval. An echo of his mother's same look when he forgot basic manners like saying please and thank you. He felt like a little boy as he mouthed the word "sorry" at her.

Loris came to stand behind the laptop with Lettie, who started in on a technical rundown: dedicated NVR, POE switches, IP cameras, and network ports. He got lost easily in the nerd talk but Loris seemed to lap it up. Verda brought a platter of eggs and bacon to the table, and he made himself a plate. Oil pooled in the bacon's ruffled edges and it made him hungry.

"It's good: the video is crisp and easy to view. I can zoom in. The audio works," Loris said. "Good job."

Ballpoint nuzzled into Loris' leg. Zane rolled his eyes.

"Your dog isn't exactly fierce in personality," she said. "But he's imposing looking anyway. What's the story with your neighbors? Are you friendly with them?"

Zane was about to answer when Verda started twisting at her hair like an eight-year-old girl and said, "Oh, yes, the man across the way is very helpful to us and keeps an eye out. He brings us meat when he barbecues sometimes."

Zane caught Lettie's eye and they smiled at one another. Verda was smitten with Leon, that much was clear. He couldn't resist teasing her. "Leon said you two exchanged phone numbers."

Verda giggled and blushed some more and protested way too much that they had only swapped numbers for practical reasons. No one in the room was fooled, Zane was pretty sure, but they all let her off the hook with smiles. If nothing else, her delight at the mention of his name lightened and brightened the mood in the trailer. It even gave Loris a smile.

Angel burst out of the bedroom he shared with Lettie in baggy sweatpants and a Tokyo Ghoul T-shirt. "Just got another message from PeturbabeArgue on Twitch," he said in a low voice, as though the livestream was still running and he didn't want them to hear.

"He's been casting all night," Lettie said.

"What on earth?" Loris said.

"He's trying to build a subscriber base on Twitch," Lettie said. "It's a full-time job."

"Like playing video games?" Loris looked skeptical.

Verda cut to the chase. "People pay money to watch him play video games and talk about his life," she said. "Damnedest thing I've ever heard of."

"PeturbabeArgue showed up in the messages again, saying that I didn't answer the question of whether I liked the baby rattle. So, I asked them if I knew them and said that I wanted to thank them properly. That's when it got creepier. They're like, don't worry, you will."

"That's it," Lettie said. Her fingers made loud, fast-clicking noises on her laptop keyboard. "Let me see if I can get an IP address for PeturbabeArgue. They've got an email address in here, but it looks like a throwaway Google one, created just for this because it has the same username, PeturbabeArgue."

"Screenshot those messages for me," Loris said.

"Okay," Angel said. "It's kind of freaking me out though, this person." He went back into the bedroom and shut the door.

"It can't be Clyde Doom," Loris said. "The only Internet access he gets in prison is through video visitation, email, and music players."

"I'm sending an email now," Lettie said. "If this person replies, I might be able to trace the IP address from there. What should I say?"

"Something innocuous enough," Loris said. "Thank you, do we know you? Your username isn't familiar to me. That kind of thing. Don't let them know you're scared or worried."

"Yeah, thanks for giving me a totally not creepy gift," Lettie said, voice dripping with sarcasm. She typed another flurry of words. "I should clarify here: if they're a regular person, I should be able to get the IP address but if they know anything about privacy and security, they'll have the IP address as private."

"Maybe we can turn the tables on them," Verda said. "Go leave a restraining order or bag of flaming dog poop on their doorstep."

"An IP address isn't a physical address, Grandma. Tracing emails isn't always that precise, but maybe, Grandma. Sometimes it just gives us the location of the last server it went through before dropping in the email box," Lettie said. "I don't think we should provoke them with a bag of flaming dog poop though."

Verda waved her comment off with a grumble.

Ballpoint dropped one of his tennis balls—already slobbery after just one day—on the floor before Loris. She picked it up without flinching and tossed it. Her aim was off and the ball bounced into the box containing the alligator trap they had found at the junkyard. Ballpoint followed it like a lightning bolt and sniffed around inside the box gingerly.

"Careful there," Zane said.

"What is this?" Loris' voice was slightly muffled as she bent over the box by the door containing the alligator trap. Loris ran her fingers lightly over its serrated edge.

"Animal trap," Zane said.

"Yes, I see that. Why do you have it?"

"We found it along with the wheels and tires and stuff. Brought it back."

"Zane, you need to be serious here. You've got a good start with the lights and the cameras. The obstacle course, I don't know but it might not be that bad of an idea. Until your neighbors complain. And Ballpoint, well, I guess we'll see how he performs. So far, I think he might just lick an intruder to death."

"I thought you said it was about being a deterrent. I mean, we don't have time to train a killer dog here. Clyde's arraignment is soon."

"Yes, I know. So, let's go get you some guns. Lettie, text us what you find out about PeturbabeArgue," Loris said. Zane felt dazed, his mind back in the anxiety loop thinking about the reality of needing guns. He saw Lettie staring back at Loris. Neither he nor his sister took orders well, but Lettie nodded after just a moment's hesitation. They both knew Loris was there to help them and it didn't make sense to antagonize her over stupid stuff.

The annual gun and knife show always drew a big crowd in Tulsa. Loris, Zane, and Verda rode in silence through Tulsa's streets, the atmosphere between them vibrating with a sense of anticipation and purpose. They arrived at the Tulsa Fairplex, a mammoth structure as big as a football field. A long line of people waited to go in, and cars crammed into the vast parking lot. Verda had insisted on coming, and Zane was glad for her company. Her presence lightened the mood a bit with Loris, who was as serious as a heart attack most of the time.

Entering was a slow process of paying an admission of ten dollars, and Loris showing her personal weapon, then unloading it, followed by desk staff tagging it. They slipped on those disposable plastic identity bracelets like the ones patients wear at the hospital and bypassed the greeters and food carts to get into the exhibit hall.

Zane had been to gun and knife shows before with his friends in school, but he had forgotten how weaponized the crowd was. More than two-thirds of the people they passed were armed. Pistols on belt holsters, rifles slung across shoulders. And the politeness. Seemed like in an atmosphere where most people had weapons, good manners were essential.

Loris cut through the crowd of gun show looky-loos dazzled by the gun and knife displays. Tables and booths and stalls sold mostly guns but also ammunition, army surplus, tasers, stun guns, knives, Civil War paraphernalia, flags, patriotic items, and comical signs: *My alarm tells me you're in my house. My gun tells me not for long; Burglars please carry ID so we can notify next of kin; If you're found here at night, you'll be found here in the morning.* The space smelled of wood polish, cleaning oil, and the bite of singed steel and gunpowder.

The snippets of gun-show connoisseur talk Zane overheard as they walked were as impenetrable to him as Lettie and Tiffany's techie jargon. He thought he knew a fair amount about guns, but he couldn't parse out half of what he heard as Loris led them through the grid. She had a particular gun seller in mind and wasn't one to be distracted by the wares on display or the howdies and check-this-outs coming from different booths. Still, he felt comfortable at the gun show, surrounded by weaponry. People defended their homes successfully. He could do it too.

Authorized dealers sat within the confines of six sectioned-off areas. Inside the enclosures sat scowling men at smaller tables, filling out applications for background checks while staff members and customers fumbled with computer tablets and credit cards. These were the registered guns, Zane knew. But Loris kept walking until they arrived at a private seller's booth.

"Loris, good to see you," the guy behind the booth said. His beard and flannel shirt were sprinkled with powdered sugar from the doughnut he held close to his face. He had a stack of battered guns and tarnished magazines and parts lined up on the table in front of him. "I got a Beretta nine-millimeter you might like."

Loris shook her head. "Not shopping for me today."

She did some quick introductions—the man's name was Judge—and Verda pointed at a forty-five-caliber gun. "We used to have one of these for shooting snakes," she said. "Had some nasty rattlesnakes around our place in Okmulgee for a time."

"You know how to shoot a gun, Grandma?"

"Of course, Zane," she said. "Any good country girl of my age knows how to do that. It's like making biscuits or plucking a chicken. Practical skills. We didn't grow up spending all our time in chat rooms."

"We're looking for a shotgun and pistol for my friend here. Personal protection," Loris said.

"I got a shotgun already," Verda said. "I think it's still under the bed unless one of you kids took it. What type you looking for?"

Zane stared at his grandmother in surprise. How had she not mentioned that she owned a gun? And that it was under the bed?

"I thought y'all were looking for something different than my old Browning Auto 5," she said. "Like an AR-9 or something." Zane's mouth almost fell open. His sweet grandmother was dropping gun lingo like the most avid gun nuts he met at the police academy. No wonder she'd been so interested in coming to the gun show. He thought it was to keep him company, but really, it was kind of her hobby. He texted Lettie: *It turns out grandma's into guns* with a shrug emoji.

Loris hefted a gun made of wood and stainless steel as though feeling the weight of it and asked Verda if she also happened to have a pistol laying around under the bed. "You could save Zane here a couple hundred bucks."

"Just the shotgun," Verda said. "We had that forty-five I mentioned for shooting snakes, but I gave it our neighbor's boy when I sold the house in Okmulgee."

A man with a resigned scowl approached Loris. "I got someone I want to introduce you to real quick," he said. "Some new business maybe for you. Not my kind of thing."

Loris gave Zane a quick look. "Judge here can show you some pistols, and I'll be right back. Sounds like your grandma may have some opinions too."

Zane held the Sig Sauer that Judge pulled out of a crate, enjoying the feel of it. They used a similar kind of gun at the police academy firing range, and it felt solid and good in his hands.

"How do you know Loris now?" Judge asked. "You find her online or something?"

"This instructor at the police academy introduced me to her."

The man nodded and leaned in, seeming eager to share some information with Zane and Verda. "Y'all are too young to remember this, I'm sure, but I'll ask anyway," he said with a wink. "Ever heard of the Julia Jefferson case?"

Verda scrunched up her face as though trying to squeeze the memory out. "Was that the young woman killed seven days after her wedding? Stabbed in her back?"

"Yup, but she was beaten too. She was the one living in Eureka Springs and that murder was right around 1998, I think," he said.

"1998? Now, what kind of wool do you think you're pulling over my eyes to say I'm too young to remember that?"

"I call it like I see it," the gun dealer said. He had a wolf's smile on his face, all teeth.

Zane cringed. His grandmother and the gun dealer were flirting. It was as awkward as a fart in an elevator.

"Anyway, Julia was that young woman's sister."

"They thought the husband did it but then he had some alibi," Verda said. "I remember that. Did they ever solve that one?"

"No, you know, they didn't. The thinking after a while was it was a serial killer," the man said. "But Loris wasn't so sure of that. The way Julia was beaten made it seem like someone really hated her. Someone who would have known her personally. Anyway, that's what got Loris into investigating. She joined the police force but didn't make it too long."

Zane's curiosity rose. He hadn't asked too many questions about why Loris had wanted to help him because he didn't want to pry. And he needed the help. But understanding her motivations better might make him feel more at ease with accepting her help, however freely she offered it and however much Himmelman vouched for her. He knew better than anyone that most things had a price.

"What happened there? How long did she serve as an officer?"

"Aww, it's just—" Judge's voice faltered, marking the return of Loris to the group. "You don't see these three-twenty models for less than five hundred dollars, but because you know Loris, I can let you have it for four-fifty. I got one in coyote tan too if you're interested."

"No, black is good," Zane said.

"It's in good shape. I've fired it myself. Reliable, never jams. I'll throw in an extra mag and a box of shells."

Zane nodded. Having the gun would make him feel safer so it was worth the expense even though he could feel his meager savings draining away once again.

"I'll take the coyote tan one," Verda said, fumbling in her purse for the wallet. "The grip's awful nice. Maybe you can give us a good deal."

Two guns then. The firepower felt reassuring. Zane felt a buzz of power and strength just from being armed. His posture straightened, and he felt his pulse quicken. Loris smiled over her phone, her thumbs banging out a text to someone.

"You need to get to the gun range to fire those weapons and get real comfortable with them," she said.

"Sounds like fun actually," Verda said.

Chapter 8
Lettie

Chop Logic

Lettie knew she had a logical mind. She didn't mean logical as in common sense, though she had that too. Her brain worked in a mathematical, computer-talk way. The art of reasoning, of setting up propositions and proofs with arguments. She had been flying through the coursework in the mathematical logic class she took through her online high school. And one particular if-then statement had been spinning in her head for the past few days.

If Clyde Doom gets out of prison, then he will hurt us. Therefore, it follows if Clyde Doom stays in prison, he cannot hurt us. That logical conclusion was one she had relied upon since Clyde and his brother Link kidnapped her and took her to that awful cabin. Their faces regularly appeared in her nightmares, and her first thought upon waking was often, those men are in prison. That means they can't hurt me.

The existence and actions of PeturbabeArgue flew in the face of Lettie's carefully crafted reassurance. The logical construct *If Clyde Doom stays in prison, then he can't hurt us* had morphed from a rock-solid proof into an unsettling new if-then statement. If Clyde Doom stays in prison, then he finds someone outside prison to hurt us. Who was PeturbabeArgue and why were they willing to act on his behalf? How far would they go? She urgently wanted to find out who this person was so she could better calculate the risk. Was this another member of the Doom family suddenly appearing on the scene, Clyde's mother perhaps? A business transaction? A romantic relationship? She absently touched her belly, the life within. The only way to give her mind any rest was to obtain more data points.

So she snooped and snooped online. She neglected her coursework and ran down every online rabbit hole she could find for PeturbabeArgue, working on what little she had: a Twitch username and the Google email account by the same name. She checked every social media platform she could think of for similar usernames or usernames associated with that email: Twitter, Instagram, TikTok, Facebook, Discord, Telegram, YouTube, SnapChat, WeChat, Vimeo, Parler, and Reddit. Nothing. She checked the banking apps too: Venmo and Zelle. She ran searches on Google and DuckDuckGo against the email address. She put the email in the database of data breaches to see if it showed up. Nothing.

Any Google search resulted in a series of websites advertising services to find people for free. Most were pay-to-play, Lettie knew, and not worth the money. They typically searched the free state and federal agency databases a smart web user could find with a little digging at usa.gov. Drop into the Oklahoma state databases and you could search Oklahoma criminal records or look up an inmate's name to find out where he or she was incarcerated. Spokeo and Pipl did offer reverse email searches for money, but she was determined to get as much as she could for free. After all, good hackers didn't have to pay for information, right?

She considered calling that FBI agent Melanie Strom to ask for help. The FBI's powerful data mining tools would undoubtedly get results a lot faster than Lettie and Google, but she doubted Strom would help. Even though she had been super-helpful as Lettie's contact during the whole credit-card-fraud trouble, she was too much of a rules-follower to break any protocols to help Lettie now. The other agent, Doug Oliphant, was just an ass. If only Peturbabe-Argue would reply to Angel's email so she could fish out some data.

The smell of tomato soup filled the bedroom despite the shut door. She wondered what else Verda was cooking. She could hear Angel's steady stream of chatter for his Twitch livestream through the thin mobile home walls. Lettie thought she felt her stomach gurgle. Food. She must be hungry.

Head cocked, she shuffled into the kitchen. Verda stood in front of the counter, buttering slices of white bread while the cast-iron skillet pre-heated.

"Cold winter day calls for tomato soup and cheese sandwiches," Verda said.

"Smells good."

Verda smiled, tickling Lettie's stomach. The sound of a car driving by perked Verda up. She glanced out the window, toward Leon's empty driveway, as the car drove right by. Grandma definitely had a crush, Lettie thought.

"Can I help?"

"Naw, just give me a minute, and I'll get it ready for you," Verda said.

Her stomach whirlpooled again. She slid both hands over the roundness, rubbing absently. Verda's eyes followed her movements, then, as if thinking it was too intrusive for her to watch, she turned her attention back to the skillet.

Lettie wandered over to the living room window that faced onto the dry wash that was Mingo Creek, staring at a spot on the glass that resembled a ghost hovering over the bleached grass.

There it was again. Little flutters of faint but rhythmic tics, like a tiny drumbeat. Was the baby having a seizure? Was something wrong with its heart?

She choked up, tightening her grip on her belly, holding her breath.

The flutters stopped.

Whoa. The baby just had hiccups, she thought.

She smiled and kept the information to herself for a moment, wanting to soak in the miracle of it all without having to make the experience part of Angel's Twitch stream. She had gotten comfortable broadcasting parts of her life and her pregnancy to the world through Angel's stream. But the dark presence of PeturbabeArgue cast a menacing shadow over Angel's blathering on about video games. And it scared her to death. She needed to find out who this person was before Clyde Doom's bail hearing. She was sure they were connected and uncovering those connections would allow her to prove Clyde was a threat to them.

Clyde Doom could not get out on bail. She wouldn't let that happen.

The quest completion sound for Witcher blasted out of the television speakers. She turned from the window to face Angel on the couch.

"Tired?" Angel said, looking at her.

She turned to face him. "I'm okay. Maybe just a little hungry."

"Got that ice cream and bologna craving again?"

She smiled wickedly, remembering the surprisingly good taste of the salty meat with the creamy sweetness of the ice cream, but the baby started bongo-playing with her belly. She rubbed her stomach but held the fact back, revolted at the idea of PeturbabeArgue seeing the intimate details of her life.

"What is it?" Angel said. "I turned the stream off."

"Nothing," Lettie said, turning back to the window. "Just my back hurting and a little baby bongo. Extra-wide load."

Angel came up behind her, his palm—warm and firm— sliding over her backbone with a gentle pressure. Lettie felt a shiver fly through her.

"Cold?" he said.

"No, just feels good." It did feel pleasant, but she couldn't shake the awful feeling of strangers watching them. With bad intent. The foreboding stole the joy from Angel's touch.

"Have you seen our friend PeturbabeArgue today?" she whispered.

"There's an email from them," he whispered back. "I forwarded it to you."

"I need to see the full original, with all the header data," she said. "Give me your email login."

It felt strange to ask Angel for access to his email. They shared a lot of things: a bed, a baby, a life, but Lettie believed in providing as much data privacy as possible. So much of their lives were online and it was important to have places that weren't open to the world's scrutiny. But to Angel's credit, he didn't hesitate, just nodded, and headed over to his laptop to retrieve the password from his encrypted password keeper.

"I'll text it to you."

Five minutes later, she was back in her room, chewing on the sandwich her grandmother had made and looking at the enormous slab of monospaced typewriter font that comprised the email header text. It was their first serious clue into who

PeturbabeArgue was. Email applications hid this text documenting the origin and path an email took before arriving at its final destination, but Lettie knew that she might be able to glean the important information from it. PeturbabeArgue's IP address, for example, was a unique number assigned to every device that connected to the Internet. IP stood for Internet Protocol. Maybe PeturbabeArgue's Internet service provider and which email client they used. The golden goose would be finding PeturbabeArgue's location.

Email headers are read chronologically from the bottom up. Scanning the text was like talking to a computer but Lettie focused in on the X-headers mixed into the message info and server relay headers. X-headers were fields added to the header text as the email moved through the Internet from Peturbabe-Argue to Angel. It wasn't too hard to hide an IP address so Lettie had her doubts as her eyes found the X-originating-email field pointing to peturbabeargue@gmail.com.

She stopped chewing the cheese sandwich when she saw it: X-originating-IP followed by a series of nine numbers. An IP address.

She highlighted the numbers 192.168.1.25 on her screen, and cut and paste them into an IP address lookup site.

Dead end. It simply led her to the location of Google's corporate headquarters in Mountain View, California. That's what happened when people sent emails from web-based email interfaces or when they scrubbed their outgoing messages with an SMTP service. Frustrating.

Lettie grabbed the spoon and started slurping the tomato soup, letting it burn her tongue and the back of her throat but not stopping. The pain was a wake-up call to her brain.

She pulled up Twitch on her phone and found Peturbabe-Argue's profile. She clicked on the profile image of a woman with brown hair, her face turned away. Only serious, earnest people used their own photos in their account profiles. Most people who wanted to be anonymous used avatars or logos or photos they snagged from someone else's profile or somewhere on the interwebs.

Still, a reverse image search couldn't hurt, to see if PeturbabeArgue had other accounts using it. Most of the search engines could search by image files as well as text. She uploaded the profile image to a website called TinEye which specialized in reverse image searches.

A couple pages of results came up, but the first one was tantalizing. A Pinterest account by someone named Belladonna_xaxa held the photo in a collection called "Hair Color."

Her adrenaline spiked as she clicked on the profile. The baby, sensing her rising emotions, gave her two sharp kicks to the ribs and shifted onto her bladder. "Not now, honey," she said.

This person's Pinterest collections were well-organized and well-tended, including topic boards on dinner ideas, cute cats, and home organization tips. Several boards were devoted to wedding topics: dresses, flowers, and rings. Shiny diamonds on manicured hands, smiling women in white gowns, creamy white lilies, and roses and pink hydrangeas.

Angel had wanted to get married as soon as he heard about the baby, but she had held him off. She was not sure she could take the dual-lifelong commitment of the baby they were going to raise as well as marriage. These smiling men and women in their wedding best, smiling and leaning into one another, faces flushed, soft lighting. She scrolled through the photos of dresses, slinky silks, and puffy gowns, one with a bride's bouquet sailing into the air while the bride posed, her belly flat, her breasts high. All of these women with their shiny hair and creamy skin, white teeth between wide smiles, red and pink lips with eyes so bright and faces so happy. They were the women who went to brunch with their friends and had a little too much wine, the ones who came home and made low-sugar brownies and worried about frizz in their hair in the Oklahoma humidity. Women who did things in traditional order: first high school, then college, then a family. Women who were luckier and maybe even smarter than Lettie in some ways, genetics and family dictating a better, softer life for them than she had experienced. Women who were nowhere near Lettie's age but would never feel as old as Lettie did, eight months pregnant and fearful of a violent man's vengeance.

She clicked on a Pinterest post that Belladonna_xaxa had saved about a man's wedding ring made of meteorite, which she had never heard of. The ring looked cool. A dark stone with light-colored specks connected by a fine interweaving of lines. It would be cool to wear a ring that may have once been part of a shooting star before it entered the Earth's atmosphere and fell kerplunk in some distant valley. Maybe someone had wished upon it as it fell. She used to do that when she was younger.

Belladonna_xaxa's comment on the pin made her jaw drop.

"My fiancé Clyde would love a ring like this."

Clyde. Not a common name. Had she stumbled onto one of PeturbabeArgue's real accounts? The connection was hard to ignore. She scanned Belladonna_xaxa's follower list, looking for Clyde's name or any other Doom connection. Nothing.

But Belladonna_xaxa had an Instagram account but no name associated with it. Her bio just had the name B E L L A D O N N A and a rabbit emoji. Scrolling through her photo feed was gratuitous booby and butt selfies, workout selfies, lots of filters, quotes about living the good life. Her in a tight dress and stilettos decorating a Christmas tree. Her face was obscured in every shot by her blonde-tipped, black-rooted hair or the camera angle. The photos were mostly interiors with no sense of the city or area in which they were shot.

A close-up of Belladonna's eyebrows tagged a waxing and microblading studio which marketed its services with images of its clients. In Tulsa. Heart beating fast, Lettie scanned their feed until she found the matching photo, cross-posted to their account. The caption read: Donna's eyebrows will be perfect for her upcoming wedding! *Love After Lockup*, you gotta check them out! They're the perfect love story for you!

Her heart lunged. *Love After Lock-up?* The reality television show highlighted couples who got together while one was in prison and then tried to make their romance work in the regular world. Clyde had a girlfriend who got her eyebrows done in Tulsa.

She did another reverse image search with the eyebrows photo, this time targeting Facebook. Facebook made people use their real names to establish accounts so if PeturbabeArgue/Belladonna_xaxa/Donna had an FB account, Lettie would have her name. Simple as that.

Her eyes flicked from the laptop screen to the mirrored monitor, scanning the list of image search results against the original photo. A perfect match. She clicked on the Facebook link and found her.

Donna Lancaster. Wagoner High School graduate. Lettie clicked on the profile picture and looked their enemy in the face. She was a white woman with dark hair and large green eyeglasses framing blue eyes. A small mole near the right corner of her full lower lip. She wore a camouflage T-shirt and seemed to be sitting in a coffee house. Seventy-five people had liked the photo and the comments on it were a series of "So pretty" "beautiful" and "love you."

She didn't look like a big threat and Lettie took a shaky breath of relief. She was also completely and utterly findable.

"Angel! Grandma!" she shouted. "Guess who I found!"

Chapter 9
Zane

Target Audience

Zane shook off the nightmares that plagued him all night and stretched his arms toward the mobile home's low ceiling. A grey-and-white muscular ball of fur pounded into the room and started licking his face.

"Ballpoint!" He grabbed the pit bull by the neck and nuzzled the dog's soft ears. Seven in the morning and five at night were Ballpoint's peak activity hours, which happened to coincide with his mealtimes. Ballpoint tumbled after him into the kitchen.

"Morning," Lettie said. "How did you sleep?"

He rubbed at a kink in his shoulder. "Okay. It's kind of a relief to find out who sent that rattle."

Lettie nodded. "Yeah, good to put a face on it. I was thinking today, maybe I'll come with you to the firing range."

"I thought you were worried about the loud sounds hurting

the baby's hearing," Zane said. "And the lead particles from the bullets getting absorbed by your skin."

"Little one here will undoubtedly let me know if the sounds are too loud. My body provides some muffling. And I've been thinking about it. We will be outdoors, and a lot of the concerns about noise and lead exposure are within indoor firing ranges. I can wear one of the face masks and a long-sleeved shirt and gloves for protection."

"It's up to you, Lettie. You're the one who makes decisions for the baby. You scared me with all that stuff about the tiny lead particles you might inhale and poison the baby."

"Hopefully this will be the only day in my life I shoot a gun," she said. "But I think I need to know how to do it."

The four of them loaded into the car and rode the expressway and long country roads out of Tulsa following directions Loris had given them. Angel started streaming the road trip, pitching it as a nature hike to his followers. Now that they knew who PeturbabeArgue was, Zane felt more in control, even with the arraignment looming. He half-listened to Angel's monologue on the merits of rural Sonic cherry limeades versus the Tulsa version with less irritation than usual. The kid could talk the bark off an oak tree.

Thirty minutes later, they reached the pothole-ridden driveway of Loris' Uncle Brian and Aunt Tracy, marked with a mailbox reading "The Trappers." Surrounded by two hundred acres of flat-as-a-pancake land shielded from the road by a phalanx of trees planted for privacy not beauty, the land looked barren, and the pond looked cold and forbidding. The rural Trapper family enjoyed complete privacy. The sound of gunfire in the middle of the day would draw no attention what-soever. Zane parked in the shade under a sycamore next to

Loris' Suburban. She still sat inside her vehicle, talking to someone on the phone with the engine running until Zane caught her eye. She held up one finger to ask for more time.

"Reminds me a bit of one of my childhood friends' places," Verda said. "She had a pony I just loved."

"Being out in the sticks like this makes me nervous," Lettie said.

Angel flicked through his phone. "There's a hospital just ten miles from here if that's what you're worried about."

"Hmm," Lettie said. Zane knew what was making her nervous and it wasn't the hospital. It was thinking about the Dooms taking her to a place out in the country like this. It was thinking about the past trauma and the specter of future trauma. They weren't here to shoot guns for fun.

Loris sprang out of the Suburban. "Leave your guns in the trunk while we go say hi to my people."

"Nice property they've got here," Verda said. "Is the pond stocked?"

"Sometimes they put catfish in there, but I don't know," Loris said.

"I feel like we're supposed to keep our hands where they can see them and not make any sudden moves," Lettie said, eyeing up the security camera which had swiveled to follow their movements.

"Not a bad idea whenever you step onto anyone's property," Loris said as she approached the screen door.

"Hey, y'all it's me," she called.

"Are these your father's relatives or your mother's?" Angel asked.

"Uncle Brian is my dad's brother. What do you want to know that for?"

But the sudden appearance of the couple abbreviated any response.

"Jiminy Cricket, Loris Ann, you know better than to knock." Aunt Tracy wrapped her thin arms around Loris and squeezed. "It's been a minute, child."

Uncle Brian loomed over the aunt's shoulder. He was a little shorter than Zane, with dark hair and a permanent frown etched into his forehead. He noogied the top of Loris' head, then they hugged. Zane was surprised by the silliness of their greeting. After all, Loris was a grown woman and a serious one at that. Families were strange.

"What's up, Uncle Brian? You got that pond full of fish?"

"Yes, and we got some tasty catfish for lunch if y'all are interested later. Thanks for paying country folks a call."

Zane stepped inside and glanced around the room. On the sideboard, a dozen framed photos showed smiling faces, weddings, babies. An eight-by-ten frame decorated in a silver and blue pattern held a wedding photo that looked like it held the place of honor for decades. A black ribbon draped the top, falling along either side of a young bride's portrait, a crown and veil on her head, and creamy white lilies in her hands. Julia Johnson, Zane thought. The woman who was murdered the week after her wedding, frozen in time as she looked on a happy day. Every family had its sadness, he thought.

Uncle Brian turned his attention to Zane and his family. "Here's a motley crew all right," he said, taking their measure with his long gaze.

Aunt Tracy looked at Lettie's belly, swollen with child, hard to miss in the small living room. "Looks like you're carrying low," she said.

Zane and Angel gave her the once-over as though seeing her pregnancy for the first time. The mound of child in her stomach did look like it was lower on her pelvis than before.

"What does that mean?" Zane asked.

"Some people say that means I'm carrying a boy," Lettie said. "But there's no scientific proof of that."

"The ultrasound says it's a girl though," Verda offered.

"You'll find out soon enough." Aunt Tracy took a step toward Lettie, her hand in the air as if she wanted to pat Lettie's belly. Lettie stepped back. It was weird how many people wanted to touch Lettie now that she was pregnant, Zane thought. His sister hated it and Aunt Tracy seemed to think better of the impulse.

"You don't mind if we get going with the training, now do you? Is it okay if we shoot some targets in the north pasture? These good folks want some pointers."

Aunt Tracy and Uncle Brian exchanged a glance that seemed to ask why a grandmother and two teens, one phone-obsessed and the other extremely pregnant, might need firearm lessons. But they didn't voice it. They were the kind of country people who minded their own business for the most part, at least when it came to guns.

"Of course," said Uncle Brian. "Nothing happening on that land but what the wind blows. There's a bunch of soda and beer cans in the barn." Turning to Zane, Uncle Brian said, "If anyone can give marksman lessons, it's my niece. Her cousins called her Barreleyes for years. Too bad she was too tender-hearted for hunting. Loris Ann could have kept us in wild turkey and venison for years."

"We better get started." Loris touched Zane's sleeve and headed for the door. "Thanks for the trip down memory lane."

"Don't you leave without stopping back by for lunch," Aunt Tracy hollered through the screen. "We want to give you and that baby some of the freshest fish in Wagoner County."

Opening the Suburban's back hatch, Loris picked a gun from her assortment and handed it to Angel. "This is what you're going to shoot today—a forty-caliber Mini Glock.

Medium weight, not a lot of recoil, but it has plenty of stopping power." She selected a second weapon. "Lettie, you take this nine-millimeter Glock. Standard issue for Tulsa Police." She grabbed an AR-15 rifle from its case and shut the hatch door.

Lettie examined the gun carefully. "Feels like death in my hands."

"It's not loaded, but keep the barrel pointed at the ground. Never joke around with a firearm. Plenty of fools have shot themselves or their friends with supposedly unloaded weapons."

"Got it," Lettie said.

Zane opened the trunk to retrieve the two guns they bought at the gun show for him and Verda.

"Watch your step along the way. Remember, this is a farm."

When they reached the barn, empty of livestock except for the smell, Loris pointed at the overflowing bucket of cans. "Grab those targets, okay, Angel? And no livestreaming."

"I was just shooting video is all," he said.

"Put the phone away," Loris said. "Let's just live in the moment."

Angel slipped the phone back into his pocket and grabbed the bucket's handle.

"It's really beautiful out here," Verda said. "Does all this land belong to them?"

"Up to that fence there. It's beautiful all right but they struggle to make a living farming. They joke it's their expensive hobby."

She pointed to a chain link fence about a baseball throw away. "That fence isn't the property line. It's to keep livestock back from the drop-off to the basin. Uncle Brian built a shelf on it for target practice. We'll shoot downhill and there's a steep embankment on either side. Stray shots won't go anywhere. You can set up the cans while I load the guns."

"Does someone clean up the bullets?" Lettie asked. "So deer and squirrels and whatever wildlife there are doesn't lick them or eat them?"

"I can't say I know for sure what Uncle Brian does about that, but I can tell you that I bought Remington's leadless ammo because of little one there." She pointed at Lettie's round belly.

As though satisfied with the answer, Lettie joined Angel for the walk down the slope to line up two dozen cans. When they returned, Loris reviewed basic safety instructions and then aimed her weapon at the fence. She fired nine shots at the row of cans and then gestured for Zane to do the same thing. The gun sent a jolt from his hands and wrists and into his torso, adrenaline rushing. "Your turn, Angel and Lettie. Try to duplicate my manner and interval between shots."

"Um, what?" Lettie said.

"Just do what I did, as best you can," Loris said.

Angel lifted the weapon, took aim, and pulled the trigger nine times, both hands wrapped around the gun. He didn't flinch or blink or do a single thing wrong. The same couldn't be said for Lettie, whose head snapped back at the first blast. She looked back at Loris, the gun's muzzle pointed to the sky. "It's so loud," she said.

"Hold it tight," Loris said. "Try again. It's loaded with blanks."

"That's why no one hit anything," Verda said. "I was wondering if I would have to show you all how it's done."

"I wanted you to get accustomed to the recoil and sound of discharge. And also, in case any little varmints were in those weeds, they're long gone by now."

"That's nice now, Loris. Your uncle did say you were tender-hearted for God's creatures," Verda said.

"Why is it so loud if these are blanks?" Lettie asked.

"Is the baby kicking?" Zane felt a sharp new worry for the fragile life inside his sister.

"She jumps every time I shoot," Lettie said. "It's kinda funny."

"Blanks are still a projectile, usually wads of paper or cotton, so there's definitely a crack with every shot," Loris said.

Loris loaded live ammo in her clip and told Zane and Verda to do the same for themselves and Lettie and Angel. Verda met Zane's gaze for a moment with a smile, then turned and fired. The first nine aluminum cans fell from their perch.

"All righty, Grandma! You sure do know how to shoot," Angel said. "God, I wish I could stream this."

"You take that phone out, kid, and I'll string you up for target practice," Loris said. "Now it's your turn, Zane."

Zane stepped up, aimed, and fired. Four cans down out of twenty-four. Not so easy.

"Guess no one's going to be calling me Barreleyes today," Zane said.

"Watch it now, friend," Loris said with a smile. "I may aim to protect Bambi and Thumper out here, but I can't say the same for anyone who calls me Barreleyes these days. Always hated that nickname. And don't even think of calling me Loris Ann. That honor is reserved for relatives over the age of sixty."

"Let me try," Angel said. He stepped up, aimed, fired and nine cans toppled one by one.

"You've never shot a gun before?" Loris said with her eyes narrowed. "Tell the truth."

"I've never fired a real weapon but I've fired tons on video games like Modern Warfare and Resident Evil. You know, the military uses video games to train soldiers. Simulations really work to train for real skills. I'm kind of impressed it worked for me though."

"You've definitely got the skills," Loris said.

"I've played some of those games," Lettie said. Zane could see her competitive spirit rising. She wanted to show Angel she could shoot too.

She put her feet in a wide stance and bent her knees as though preparing for the recoil she knew would come. But her result was the same as what she got when the clip was full of blanks. "How can that be? Angel and Grandma make it look so easy."

"Nothing in life is easy. We're going to move up to twenty feet and use that upturned log to brace your arm. Lettie, you have to keep your arm steady when you fire, or you won't hit a barn, let alone a moving target," Loris said.

"You'll get the hang of it," Verda said.

"Come on, Zane, you too," Loris said. "Looks like the police academy didn't teach you everything about shooting a gun properly. When you can both hit nine out of nine, we'll move back again. Eventually, you'll be able to keep your arm steady without bracing it."

"All in one morning?" Lettie's forehead furrowed.

"Nope but it's a start today. We can come back here another time too if you want," Loris said.

"Let's see where we get today," Lettie said.

"I get it," Loris said. "These are special circumstances. Besides, you might be taking a chance with my relatives."

Lettie watched as Loris reloaded her gun. "What kind of chance? They seem nice."

"They are. They'll graciously welcome you back, invite you to supper on Sunday, and maybe even send you home with a chess pie. Then one day they'll be telling you how the baby needs to live out in the country, and they got a room all set up for y'all. Uncle Brian may have a shotgun and a preacher to make sure you and Angel get married."

Lettie hooted with laughter. "People only do things like that on television. Anyway, they're your relatives, not mine."

"It's not the worst idea," Verda said. She patted her shotgun. "Lettie, you might either want to improve your aim or your hundred-yard dash. I know Angel wouldn't run from no preacher so he's no protection to you here."

"Everyone ought to mind their own business," Lettie said, popping her hands onto her hips and reminding Zane of his mother.

Chapter 10
Verda

Bright Spot

Verda stood outside the Majestic Mobile Home Park office and watched the brisk wind skitter dry leaves on the dormant grass, a dark loud version of the snowflakes that threatened to fall from the thick clouds above. Soon the city streets would be icy, and she'd stop driving then until they thawed. She didn't like driving in the city and certainly wasn't going to take chances on icy roads.

She clutched the mail in one hand, the other wrapped around Ballpoint's thick leash. He was a good dog on a leash, with no pulling or whining. Lucky for him, because she wouldn't take him on these little mailbox jaunts if he was going to tug her along. She'd just got to where she didn't need the cane anymore for stability, thanks to losing that extra twenty pounds and getting more exercise. She wasn't about to risk her newfound vim and vigor with a broken hip courtesy of an overeager dog. When you're in the last third of your life, you have to take care not to get injured. One slip and then you were bedridden, and it was all downhill from there.

She shushed the ideas out of her head. They had more imminent worries than a potential accident. She didn't want to think too much about Clyde either. She had just gotten these grandkids in her life two years ago and she wasn't about to lose them like she lost her daughter Lily.

"Let's go home," she said to Ballpoint. They trotted together up the gravel road and went through their home-coming pattern, quickly becoming a routine. Ballpoint waited at the door for her to wet a paper towel at the sink and use it to wipe his paws, one at a time before he came onto the carpet. She was hot now from the exercise and hung up her coat before settling down to look at the mail. With that awful baby rattle incident, she wanted to make sure she looked through any mail or packages coming to the house first before Zane or Lettie could see them. It was the least she could do and thankfully nothing too sinister seemed to lurk in the mail.

The colorful flyers from the grocery stores beckoned. Who would have the lowest prices for paper towels and chicken this week? She liked the idea of finding the best prices and didn't mind going to different stores. Bargain hunting was her number one hobby. But before she had a chance to dive into the ads, an official-looking envelope from the Internal Revenue Service slipped out of his hiding place between the Aldi and hardware store flyers. It sent a flurry of anxiety into her stomach. Her husband had always been the one to handle the taxes. Of course, Osbert had been gone for years, but she still feared dealing with authorities like that. As though they'd find out she had no idea what she was doing.

But the letter wasn't addressed to her, or Zane, or Lettie, or

Angel. It was addressed to Leon Garcia, the man who lived in the home across the way.

Verda's heart hippity-hopped when she saw his name. She found herself back on her feet and out the door, practically bursting with energy to give him the mail. She wondered if shooting the guns today had given her a confidence boost. She had forgotten how powerful it felt to shoot the rifle and hit her marks. Not bad for a sixty-three-year-old woman.

Leon answered the door quickly, dressed in his knife-creased dark jeans and a flannel shirt. She could almost feel his gaze running over her body and then her face. She ran her hands along the sides of her jeans, wondering if she should have thrown on a coat over her grey V-neck sweater. It is a universal truth that as women get older and grayer, people start to look past them. Sometimes it seemed they didn't even see her at all. So when someone paid her that kind of attention, it was intense. Her heart stuttered under his gaze.

"We got a piece of your mail. Looked important so I rushed over."

"I'm always happy to see you, Verda. You don't need a reason." He smiled, and Verda thought it was like the tough, wizened exterior of him cracked and a bit of the bright-eyed, playful young man inside peeked out. Didn't everyone have that younger version of themselves tucked away? She knew she did.

"Do you want to come in? I just made a bowl of popcorn and opened a beer. I'll share with you." His voice was warm and soft like caramel.

"Oh, sure, I could use something to tide me over." She stepped inside only to start sweating immediately after entering his neat mobile home. Dampness collected between her eyebrows and in the creases of her neck. She thought of Osbert, sitting on the screened-in porch in Okmulgee, in the summer, katydids singing. Her mother bringing them both iced tea and then leaving them to make awkward conversation. Their first date. A supervised one, at her house. She had been so young then.

She shook the memories away and tried to ground herself in Leon's home. She looked at the fake fireplace with the big television tuned to Fox News above it, at the olive-green leather sofa that was too large for the space, the computer and printer that were clearly permanent residents on the kitchen table. On the television, an older grey-haired man in a dark overcoat stood in front of the White House, talking. She hated watching the news these days.

He went into the kitchen, grabbed a beer out of the refrigerator, and gestured for her to join him on the couch.

"Nothing wrong with a little day drinking," she said. "I like a beer now and again, but after all Zane's trouble trying to give up drinking, we don't keep any in the house."

"You don't have to drive home, so why not?" He gave her a glittering smile, revealing the kind of white, straight teeth seen in commercials for dentists or teeth-whitening products.

He asked her a few questions about Zane and Lettie, and she answered them, skirting around the details of where their parents were. It was a silly deception, and she knew it. Word traveled fast around the Majestic and surely everyone knew Zane and Lettie's back story by now. But bless his heart, Leon didn't press her for details. They talked a little bit more about the baby rattle. Half a beer later, she felt more comfortable around him.

"Any kids or grandkids for you?"

"I have a daughter but we're not close."

"No grandkids then?"

"Not that I know of."

"Too bad. There are no words to describe the happiness of

holding your baby's baby. After all the years of sprained ankles, permission slips, textbooks getting lost, worrying about boys and sex, and drinking and pot, being a grandmother is a breeze. And I'm about to be a great-grandma. Imagine that. It's not what I would have wanted for Lettie at this age, but it's where we are."

While Verda was trying to remember a joke, she heard about having grandchildren first or instead of kids, Leon leaned over and gently turned her face to meet his, and then he bent his head to touch his lips to hers.

It had been a long, long time since a man had kissed her and her body responded fast, sealing off any doubts she had about her attraction to him or his to hers. They had chemistry and she wanted to touch him, to feel the warmth of his skin under her hands. She placed one hand on his arm and the other on his chest, noting with pleasure the formation of firm muscles underneath the flannel shirt. Leon kept himself in shape. And underneath it all, she felt the thump, thump of his heart. She ran one hand down the length of his torso, stopping to lightly rest on his belt buckle. The sexual tension between them sizzled. His hand cupped the back of her neck and pressed her into him in a more heated kiss, their tongues moving in time for a few beats before he pulled away.

They were both out of breath when he pressed his forehead to hers.

"Sorry, I've been wanting to do that for a while," he said. "You're a sexy woman."

"You certainly make me feel that way."

"I'd like to take you out on a proper date sometime," he said. "Really get to know you, Verda."

"I'd like that too."

"I'm not a perfect man. I've made some mistakes, but I hope you can look past those and see the real me."

She wanted to put him at ease. "We've all made mistakes, Leon. You don't get to be our age without them. My daughter ran away, and I didn't find her. I didn't look hard enough. I wasn't there for her when she needed me, can you imagine such a thing?" She stopped talking, worried she had said too much too soon in her haste to make him feel comfortable with her.

"You can tell me anything, and I won't hold it against you." She hoped he meant it and didn't say it just to be kind.

"Some of my mistakes kill me inside. But I keep moving forward."

He nodded like he agreed, but something was off like a sadness cloaked his soul. He had said something about not knowing if he had a grandchild. Just like she and Osbert had been estranged from their daughter Lily and didn't know about Zane and Lettie. Maybe she and Leon had more in common than an attraction and a residence at the Majestic Mobile Home Park. Only time would tell. And she was interested in finding out. Wasn't life a funny thing? Always a balance between the good and the bad, the new and the old, beginnings and endings.

She left the warmth of Leon's home and immediately got chills as she stepped outside. The wind was chilly and the sky was grey, but what set her body to shiver wasn't the cold air.

A skinny woman in her mid-twenties was standing in front of their home, wearing big suede shapeless boots, her jean-clad legs as skinny as a spider's. Her breath plumed frostily in the air, her face shaded by the hood of her green puffer jacket.

"Are you Verda Davis?"

A damp wind ruffled through Verda's hair. She walked toward the woman, a feeling so black and forbidding running through her spine. Verda didn't recognize her as a neighbor and the woman didn't have the paperwork busyness of a petition signature gatherer or a door-to-door salesperson.

Verda nodded her head once. "What can I do for you?"

The woman lowered her hood, revealing dark-rooted hair with blonde tips. Back in Verda's day showing dark roots like that would have been seen as embarrassing, maybe even low-class. Women were so much more inventive and freer with their hair these days. But nothing about this woman inclined Verda to make small talk or compliments. A sinister energy pulsed off her.

"You all sure have a lot of video cameras. Scared of something?"

Her words reached inside Verda and stole the heat from her blood. That hair. The woman who had sent that baby rattle had hair like that, at least on the photos Lettie had found of her online.

"What do you want?"

"Do you really know your grandson Zane? You know he spent time in juvie, right? For assault? And he totally helped his brothers selling meth. He's not who you think he is."

"He is exactly who I think he is and you don't know what you're talking about," Verda said. "You're the person who left that rattle, aren't you?" Verda's hammering heart knocked loose a flood of adrenaline that made her feel strong enough to lift a car. "Get out of here and don't come back."

"What are you going to do, call the police?"

Verda walked past the woman in a long, angry stride, turning to face her when she got to the front steps of the mobile home.

"I don't call the police to solve my problems," Verda said. "So why don't you go on and leave now because the next time I come out, I'll have my shotgun."

Chapter 11
Zane

Check Yourself

The woman had to be stopped. Zane was overcome by the urgent feeling that he had to strike back fast. That night, he and Angel went to the house where Lettie thought Donna Lancaster aka PeturbabeArgue aka Belladonna_xaxa lived in Tulsa. As he drove Interstate 169 south, Zane tried to keep his anger in check as he thought about what Lettie had uncovered about the woman and how she had forged a connection with Clyde Doom after he had been put in prison.

"I don't get the attraction," he said. "Does she think she could change him or save him? Does she get off on his brutality?"

Angel kept his eyes on his phone and shook his head. The car's heater pumped the smell of burning dust into the vehicle.

"Dude, you're not livestreaming this, are you?" Zane said, irritated.

"No. I'm with you. I don't get it. I was looking up this condition called hybristophilia. Fancy word for women who are sexually attracted to men known for awful crimes. Bonnie and Clyde syndrome. Apparently, there are enough of them to get a psychiatric condition and a Wikipedia page named for it."

"All right, so what's the deal?" Zane asked. He knew Lettie hadn't found any evidence that Donna was religious in any demonstrable way, so he doubted she was trying to bring him onto the path of righteousness.

Angel started reading from his phone: "Passive hybristophiliacs avoid crime and tend to delude themselves into thinking their lover is innocent or that he'd never hurt them. Aggressive ones get their engines revving at the idea of a rough, murderous thug. They often are complicit in their lovers' crimes and will help them hide bodies or destroy evidence."

Zane thought about the kind of woman who would leave a threatening baby rattle for a pregnant girl then show up and try to bully a grandmother and figured Donna belonged in the latter category. Aggressive. Plotting. Dangerous. Anxiety tempered the angry impatience that had got his butt in the car and on the way to Donna's home. Now he felt doubt with an edge of paranoia. He'd had an idea they would confront her; show her they weren't scared. But maybe this direct approach wasn't a good idea.

The night sky was starting to arrive; spills and pushes of black coming over the trees and behind power lines and poles, cloaking the finer details of the landscape. Angel turned his attention back to the phone. The guy had an addiction, Zane thought. He couldn't stop looking at it for more than a minute at a time. As the orange-yellow streetlights flickered on, Zane clicked through the radio stations to find something other than commercials. He finally landed on a classic rock station and let the Pink Floyd song "Comfortably Numb" fill the car.

"From what I can tell, she seems like basically a regular person," Angel said. "I'm sure she could do better than a man in prison."

"Who knows why people do what they do."

More misgivings about confronting Donna flooded Zane's brain. Their plan had felt more righteous and certain after hearing about Verda's encounter. Now that they were close, their idea to confront the woman felt incomplete. What if she had a weapon? What if she told Clyde they threatened her, and he got angrier? They really hadn't thought this through well enough, but stress and fear didn't always make people sharper. That's why in police training they would talk about relying on muscle memory and drills to take the right actions under stress. Here they were, about to escalate a situation that was already volatile.

Still, he kept driving, keeping a small and possibly delusional hope alive that their appearance would intimidate her. He exited the expressway and turned onto 31st Street. Traffic clotted around the shopping centers and chain restaurants occupying the corners of every major intersection. Light glared from the giant and mostly empty parking lots. Vast generic blocks containing Papa John's Pizza, Walmart, Braum's Ice Cream, Wingstop, Charlie's Chicken, check-cashing stores, and auto-parts stores. All beckoning with bright signs, some blinking, begging for attention.

PeturbabeArgue's block was composed of smallish one-family ranch-style houses built in the 1970s. All of them were made of reddish-brown brick, with faded grey rooftops, bins for recycled materials, and trash lined up along the curbs near old-fashioned mailboxes on posts. A few FOR SALE and SOLD signs dotted the landscape.

Most of the yards were versions of winter-white grass with scattered leaves under trees with bare branches, illuminated by yellow streetlamps and porch lights. It was a working-class neighborhood, that much was clear from the work trucks parked in most of the driveways touting plumbing or electrical or roofing services. A dark arcade of curving trees presided over faded or forgotten toys in the yards, and a Toyota pick-up truck sat on blocks in one driveway, obviously dead. Most of the houses needed something, paint or roofing or weeding, but the residents were probably too tired from doing this kind of work all day to apply themselves to their own home improvements. Or maybe they were renters, ready to move on to the next.

During the dinner hour, the street was empty of life, people either dozing in front of the television or mad-scrolling their phones. Everyone alone in their boxy houses, boxy rooms.

"That's the one," Angel said, pointing at a brown house flanked by two tall trees, its every window blank with closed, yellowing miniblinds.

Zane drove down to the end of the block, turned into someone else's driveway, scraping the front of his car along the curb with a too-sharp turn. He backed out into the street, crunching the bottom of the car again, and parked behind an old camper.

This was crazy, but he'd felt driven to come. He'd had enough of sitting around waiting for something to happen. He wanted to strike back. Classic rock on the car radio—Led Zeppelin blasting—*been a long time since I rock-n-rolled.* He tasted his fury again. It agreed with him—the anger fed a rough power. He clicked off the ignition, the song from the radio still in his ears.

"Do you want to go right up to her house?" Angel said.

Zane's hand was already on the car's door handle, pushing the door open, feet out of the car before he could think anymore. The familiar red tide of anger pushed him forward to another confrontation. He took a deep breath, trying to push it down.

"I guess that's a yes," he heard Angel say as he ran to catch up to Zane.

Outside, the sky was full of bald, smooth clouds that reflected the streetlights. Beside him, Angel's face, normally genial and curious, took on a kind of recklessness, as he jogged to keep up with Zane's quick pace. "Is the plan that there is no plan?" he said.

Zane just grunted and walked down the block. At the end of PeturbabeArgue's driveway, the door to the garage was closed, an older Ford F-150 truck parked in front of it. Somewhere to the right of the house, a forlorn cricket rubbed its wings to make music for a mate.

He knocked at the beat-up screen door; the inside door was cracked open despite the cold weather outside. Through the screen, he could see just a sliver of the television on in the living room, sound turned low.

He knocked again, harder, angrier. "Hello?" he said. "We're looking for Donna?"

A little buzz went through the air. Someone was there, hesitating. Thinking.

"Donna, this is Zane Clearwater," he said. "I want to talk to you." The truck gave him pause now. Was that Donna's older brother, father, other boyfriend? Someone who would rise to protect her? Stupidly, he hadn't calculated Donna being in the house with someone. Another person could complicate things. Zane fought the urge to run.

"This is Angel from Twitch. We're just interested in speaking to you for a moment."

"I've dialed 911 and I just need to hit the call button," a thin, reedy voice called out from somewhere inside the house.

"It's creepy when someone just comes to your house, isn't it?" Zane couldn't resist the taunt, but it earned him a jab in the ribs from Angel.

"Look, just come to the door," Angel said. "We're not here to hurt you. Just talk to you. We want to understand."

The smell of warm chocolate brownies floated out the screen door toward them and as Zane's ears strained to hear Donna's actions, he could make out the clicking sound of a manual kitchen timer clocking out the seconds. Tick tick tick. Somehow this calmed him.

A creak of couch springs, and light soft steps on carpet. She pulled open the door and then backed about six feet away from the screen, phone in her hand. "All I have to do is press call," she said, raising the phone to show them the lighted screen though it was too far for Zane to read.

Zane found himself wishing he had thought to bring that awful baby rattle so he could open the screen door and toss it at this woman. She stood there like a trembling statue.

"We just want to know more about you. How you're connected to Clyde Doom," Zane said, forcing himself to keep his voice calm.

"Clyde who?" She was skinnier than in the photos Lettie had found, and a smile played around her hollow cheeks when Angel said Clyde's name. Her hair was half dark brown and half blonde, with a demarcation happening around her shoulders. Zane felt the urge to scissor-chop the blonde off in an act of desperate symmetry. A worn Christmas sweatshirt topped with wrinkled sweatpants. She wasn't expecting visitors and maybe she was the only one home after all.

From the kitchen, the timer trilled, shrieky and sharp. They all jumped, the gulf between them temporarily bridged in mutual startle followed by tiny smiles. No threat here. Just something cooking.

"Hold on," she said. "Let me take something out of the oven."

They stood there while she clattered in the kitchen. Zane grew more certain that she was alone as no one emerged for a freshly baked brownie or to see what all the fuss was about at the front door. Maybe the truck was hers, Zane thought.

"You're coming on too strong," Angel said in a low voice. "We're just here to gather information, okay? See what she knows about Clyde and any plans he might have. Get a sense of who she is."

She came to the other side of the screen door after a few minutes, close enough for Zane to see the spidery clots of her mascara-laden eyelashes and the small brown mole like a comma on her chin. In her right hand, she held a paper towel on which sat two brownie squares, crumbling at the edges from being cut too warm. She opened the door with her left hand and stepped outside. She was smiling. Zane didn't buy the friendliness. Had she poisoned the brownies? The witch of the Hansel and Gretel story came to mind.

"Those look great," Angel said, his hand sliding out. But she held the brownies close to her stomach and didn't offer them. She had a curdled quality to her, as though she was used to being disappointed. Her grey sweatpants bagged at the knees. Angel slid his hand into his pocket, fiddling with his phone.

"I like to bake," she said, gesturing with slender white fingers punctuated with chipped yellow nail polish and a thin gold ring with diamond chips on her left hand. She looked at them like they were hungry orphans on the doorstep, victims to be tempted, then terrorized.

Was she crazy? Zane wondered.

"Smells like you're good at it," Angel said. They stood on the porch frosted in chalky light, breath forming moist clouds, watching one another like boys in the schoolyard, circling before landing a punch.

"So you found me," she finally said. "Good for you." At that, she extended the brownies to Angel, who took them into his hand and gestured to Zane. Zane shook his head. If Angel wanted to eat this lady's brownies, more power to him. He'd take a pass.

"You covered your tracks pretty good, but we figured it out," Angel said, breaking off a corner of one of the brownies and popping it into his mouth.

"Clyde's not going to like that you found me," she said. "How did you do it? Just so I know for next time."

"We're not going to tell you that," Zane snapped. "What's your connection to Clyde?"

"I'm his fiancée." Her eyes widened, chin lifted, sharp with pride. She raised her left hand, knuckles toward them as though seeking a compliment for her cheap diamond-chip ring.

Zane tried to think of the word Angel had used in the car to describe the women who liked men in prison. Hybrid-something? Hubris? Hybristophiliac. The passive ones felt sorry for the pathetic creature trapped in a cage and wanted to change him. That was not Donna's vibe. She was definitely in the other camp. The ones who got off on the violence. Even the way she said Clyde wouldn't like that they found her was more a boast than a threat. Well, maybe a boast and a threat. Why had they come here? He asked himself again. To send a message of strength and courage. Asking for her to back off, to try to see things from their perspective would only repulse her or worse, empower her.

"Stay away from my family," Zane said, envisioning Clyde standing behind this woman, a storm waiting to start.

"You ain't no cop," Donna said.

"What is that supposed to mean?" Zane said.

"It means you can't tell me what to do," she said.

It chilled him to think of what she knew and didn't know about him. He wasn't someone who shared a lot on social media but maybe Angel did. That stupid Twitch stream. All that time to fill. Had Angel told the world Zane had been at the police academy?

Then it hit him. This woman had contacted the Skiatook Police and told them that Zane had been dealing meth. He didn't care if she did it for Clyde or just because she liked the chaos. The world held its breath, like the yellow silence before a tornado. Zane tasted that dark rage again, felt the itch for violence, just like old times. Just like when he used to drink. Just like his father.

She was teacup-sized trouble, borrowing a dishonorable cause that wasn't hers but acting like she owned it. He watched her shift from her footing, place her hands on her hips. Brown eyes harder than a bullet. Her dumb Christmas sweatshirt in January. The phrase "feeling jolly" across her chest. Each letter a different color. He wanted to grab her until she yelped. He wanted to smack the smile from her face. These were terrible impulses, he hated them. Be calm. Take a breath.

"We're human, just like you," Angel said. His voice was an echo of a peaceful time. "A family like your family."

She smirked at this. "You don't know my family."

"You don't know us either, really," Angel said.

"Yes, I do. I know you live in a shitty trailer park by Mingo Creek." Her eyes met Zane's, cold and hard. "I know you drive that white Corolla you thought you were so sly to park down there. I know you spent time in juvenile hall like I told your grandma. I know you killed your father and testified against your brothers."

"Because my father killed my mother and he was going to kill me," Zane said. "Clyde tell you that?"

Donna's face didn't change. She didn't seem to care. Zane looked at the mole on her chin, and noticed it had a small point on it. More of a period than a comma. He was sure that she was the person who had told the Skiatook PD he had sold meth, but to bring it up now seemed pointless. She would see it as a sign of weakness. There was nothing more to do or say here.

"Let's go," Zane said. Angel still held in his hand the napkin with the remaining brownie. Zane couldn't believe the guy had eaten this wacko's food. He knocked the brownie to the ground, where it broke into dark clumps. The ants were going to love this.

She tilted her head back, exposing her neck and an arrogant grin. "I'll tell Clyde you stopped by," she said. Angel bent down as though to pick up the napkin and brownie bits, but Zane jerked his arm.

"Tell him I'll see him at the arraignment," Zane said.

Chapter 12
Zane

Sister Act

"I don't think it was the worst mistake," Loris said, her voice sounding slightly underwater due to a bad cellular connection. "A show of strength. Sometimes I like to think, what would Tony Soprano do?"

Zane made a non-committal noise. The television gangster would probably kill Donna and Clyde, Zane thought. Loris worried him sometimes. What was her motivation for helping him and how far would she go? Still, she had come highly recommended by Cal Himmelman and she was the only one, really, who was going out of her way to help him do something, anything other than wait for Clyde's release. Even his friend Old Spice had told him there was nothing to do but see what happened. It wasn't comforting.

"You're going to the arraignment, right? You and Lettie both?"

"Yes, of course." Any opportunity he had to speak out about Clyde and what he did to his sister, he was going to take. Their testimony at that hearing could make the difference between this devil getting released into the world or staying in prison to wait for his new trial.

"Good. That will show him you're not scared. You've got to look him right in the eyes and let him know you won't back down."

"Sure," Zane said. *Surreal* came to mind. He could still remember sitting in the witness stand for the trials of Clyde and his brother Link not that long ago. He and Lettie had been in the room when both of their verdicts were read. Guilty. Guilty. It had given him a sense of relief and peace to think of them behind bars for dozens of years. Never had he imagined one of them would have his conviction overturned.

Now he knew the truth. He would never really be at peace with the violence they had brought to his life. To Lettie's life. To their mother's life. Ernest Buckskin, his mentor and friend, had told him that time would reveal the narrative of his life so he could make sense of it. Accept it. But to this day he still grieved for his loss: his mother's life cut short, his father's threats, and the horrible moment when he had to shoot his father. What would his life have been if none of that happened? His rage simmered.

He jolted down the Majestic's bumpy road, his car's headlights bouncing off the foggy night air like a mirror. The new owners might have renamed the place, but this old gravel road remained tangible evidence of its shabby trailer park past.

"Talk later," he said to Loris. "We're home now."

Angel unsnapped his seatbelt. "Just so you know, Lettie says Emmaline is there. She came by to drop off the crib set she made for the baby."

Finally, a pleasant surprise instead of a scary one, Zane

thought. Having Emmaline back in Tulsa, living at the Majestic with her parents once again, gave him comfort. She was, after all, one of his oldest friends. He knew she wasn't satisfied with her dull, small existence in Tulsa but even she would admit her Los Angeles phase hadn't been a good one. She hadn't yet given up her dreams of becoming reality-show famous, but for now, she was content enough sewing pageant dresses and dance competition outfits for the bevy of moms and daughters who loved her creations.

The only downside was Tiffany's jealousy whenever Emmaline's name came up. In a whirl of full disclosure, he had told Tiffany about his past "friends with benefits" relationship with Emmaline. That knowledge set her on a possessive bent any time she heard he and Emmaline had hung out. It combined dangerously with Tiffany's intuition that Emmaline had developed latent feelings for Zane. It was an unexpected edge of Tiffany, this insecurity. The same kind of insecurity that kept her from seeing the possibilities of owning the Cell-Phone-Fixit store instead of just working at it.

What Tiffany didn't realize was that making her happy and keeping her in his life was more important to him than almost anything else. His depth of feeling for her threw him off balance. It was as though the fear and anxiety embedded in Clyde's impending release made his priorities clear.

He trailed Angel into their home, which resembled a lit-up shoebox in the foggy night. Inside, Lettie was stretched out on the floor, stomach balling toward the ceiling. Emmaline kneeled on the floor next to her, hand rubbing Lettie's stomach as if she was conjuring images from a crystal ball. Ballpoint sat next to her like a sentinel.

Angel nearly dropped his phone. "Is it time?"

"Time for what?" Lettie said, as though this was the most normal position in the world. Emmaline leaned into Ballpoint's shoulder and smiled. Her long blonde locks gave the dog the look of wearing a fringe necklace.

"What are you doing on the floor?" Zane said.

There was a mischievous look on both Emmaline's and Lettie's faces. Even Ballpoint seemed in on it. What was running through their minds? Zane saw his grandmother in the kitchen, smiling at them, and felt calmer.

"Oo-oh," Emmaline said, eyes widening. "I felt it."

"What?" Angel said.

For a moment, it looked as if they weren't going to let him on the secret. Then Lettie relented. "The baby's really moving tonight. Dancing around like crazy."

Zane and Angel kneeled on the floor at her side and laid hands on her belly too. Lettie smiled. She wanted to share the moment. Zane placed his palm over her stomach, filling his hand with another life. His niece. "I don't feel anything."

"Just wait."

They sat in the same position for what seemed like an eternity. Zane felt the blood flowing through his fingers, felt a slight thud from his own pulse. Somehow it felt right, to sit quietly in awe of this little life waiting to be born.

There. A series of kicks like an angry heartbeat. "Damn, I feel it!" Zane said.

"Don't cuss in front of the baby."

He grinned. "Sorry, Mom."

He and his sister locked gazes for a moment, unspoken words zapping the space between them, as he kept his hand on her stomach. He would do anything to protect his sister and this baby.

Lettie struggled to her elbows, forcing them all to remove their hands. "Show's over. I think the baby's done amusing us for the night."

"Zane, what's up?" Emmaline leaned over, wrapped an arm

around him, and squeezed. "This is such scary news about Clyde. Lettie was just telling me how you went over to this woman's house who has been threatening you."

"His fiancée," Angel said. "Little diamond ring and everything."

Zane saw a flash of tension between Angel and his sister. He knew Angel wanted to get married, but Lettie kept putting the brakes on it, rightly so, in his mind. They both still had so much growing up to do and he didn't see why two people absolutely had to be married to raise a baby, though he certainly understood why it helped.

"What was she like?" Lettie said.

"Kooky," Angel said.

"Reminded me of the hyenas at the zoo," Zane said. "Disturbing smile, weird laugh, shifty eyes. I don't think we got anywhere with her really but at least we showed we're not scared of her."

"Speaking of, are you going to get your zoo job back?" Emmaline said.

"What I want is to get my Skiatook PD job back." Her question irritated him. Like she had already given up on him, sent him back to his dead-end janitorial job in her mind.

"Emmaline had an idea," Lettie said. "She thinks we ought to contact the media about Clyde's conviction. Get people talking about it, maybe put some pressure on before the arraignment."

"I don't want to go through all that again," Zane said, remembering the news vans and reporters and cameras camped outside the courthouse during the first trials. Sometimes showing up at their apartment, aggressively shouting questions.

"Jeez, Zane. What's worse? A few nosy reporters asking questions or this animal getting released into the world to do who-knows-what?" Emmaline asked, going into bulldozer mode.

He loved Emmaline like a sister, but she really lacked the sensitivity gene. He half-wondered if she thought of inviting the news cameras to get herself some notoriety for whatever her latest scheme was. That's what Tiffany would probably think, anyway.

"You really don't get it sometimes," Zane said, his voice sharpened with the slightest trace of an edge.

Emmaline leaned against the wall where the kitchen cabinets met the living area. Lettie and Angel exchanged another glance and then in unspoken unison, went to go plop on the couch.

"What I get is that you need some ideas, and I have a pretty good one," Emmaline said. "Something a little less violent than the guns and some sort of booby trap set up outside the door. I mean, what is all that crap? Lettie said something about an alligator trap?"

He took a deep breath. He did not want to fight with Emmaline. It was a reflex from a stressful day and the thought of inviting reporters into his mess of a life was repugnant to him. He simply did not share Emmaline's desire to be front-and-center of the show all the time, crying out "look at me, look at me" every day on Instagram and Snapchat. Still, she was a friend. She was trying to help. In her own way.

"We're just trying some strategies. We'd be here all night if I tried to explain it all. And you're right. We should be willing to try anything. Everything. I'm just stressed."

"I get it. I do. It's perfectly normal to feel that way. But think about it. Right now, no one is paying that much attention to this Clyde Doom situation but you and Lettie and this kooky girlfriend. Maybe whatever remnants of family Clyde has outside of prison. You can get real people on your side by talking about what's happening and what it means to you."

Zane wanted to roll his eyes. "I don't like airing all that stuff. Zane Clearwater, juvenile delinquent, shot his father and now he fears the revenge of his half-brother. Ugh."

"If you don't take the stage, then you leave it open for Clyde to create the narrative," Emmaline said. "You've got to act first."

Verda threaded the space between the kitchen table and Emmaline to bring Zane a glass of water. "Take a moment," she said. "I think Emmaline has a good point. You're just nervous about it, aren't you?"

He took the water, sloshing slightly in the glass.

Nervous was putting it mildly. Hour by hour, night after night, he had spent most of his days and nights reliving those worst moments of his life and imagining fresh horrors to come in the form of Clyde Doom. What he could have done to not put Lettie in danger. What he could have done not to have to shoot his father in self-defense. Visions of his father slumped against the truck door, all that blood, tormented him. He had learned how to push the memories into a place in his mind that was safe, but the trick didn't always work.

"You all right, son?" Verda asked.

"Sorry. Yes. It's just a lot. It's been a long day. I heard your question. Of course, I'm nervous. I've been nervous and angry and frustrated and terrified since we got this news about Clyde."

Lettie and Angel chose that moment to return to the group standing by the kitchen. "Remember that Kristy Diguchi?" Lettie asked. The reporter from KTUL-TV who covered Mom's death and the trial? I still see her on television, showing up with her camera crew to crime scenes. Maybe we could call her. Offer to talk to her." Ballpoint punctuated her statement with a loud yawn.

Emmaline bounced from one foot to another. "I think it's a great idea. Zane, are you good with this?"

He sighed. "Yes, if it helps put some pressure on the prosecutors and the judge to keep Clyde in jail. Do whatever you have to, though I should let Loris know. It's opposite-world to what I want to do. But sometimes I don't have the best instincts."

Zane suddenly felt overwhelmed. The trip to Donna's had been emotionally exhausting, and that was only the first confrontation with her and Clyde he would have to face.

"It was big news, so I'm sure she'll remember and understand the importance," Emmaline said. "Zane, are you going to be okay talking to her?"

Zane thought about it. He didn't like being in front of the camera, even when it was just Angel shooting video for his channels, and at the police academy, they had stressed how important it was to keep your life as private as possible to avoid the wrong kind of people from finding out you were in law enforcement. But this was an extraordinary circumstance. Hadn't law enforcement turned its back on him, placing him on suspension on the word of some "anonymous" source, probably named Donna, who clearly has connections to the man he put in jail? Come on.

"I'll do it," he said.

Emmaline reached over to squeeze his arm. "It's going to be the right choice," she said. "We can get people on our side and make sure Clyde continues to pay for what he did."

"Then we can all get on with our lives. Concentrate on raising that baby and finding better days," Verda said.

"Yes, when Clyde is"—he had almost made a slip of the tongue and said "dead" but caught himself—"returned to prison." Yes, that sounded more acceptable. And he had avoided dwelling on what would happen if there was an ultimate showdown. But there was no doubt in his mind that he would do what he had to do. Anything to keep Lettie and the baby safe.

His anger at Donna, at Clyde, at his father, at the situation seethed below the surface. He thought about the five stages of grief he had talked about with Ernest. Denial, anger, bargaining, depression, and acceptance. Ernest had told him it was not a linear progression but instead like eating a stew with many ingredients. Sometimes you tasted denial, another time you got a bite of depression. He tasted anger often, though. It seemed he would never get past it. He could tuck it away in his head, as he had been doing, but it never left. Until he got Clyde behind bars for good, that anger would simmer under the surface, tinged with fear.

At that very moment, Lettie crumpled, gripping her lower belly.

Verda and Angel rushed to flank her, Verda stroking her hair, and Angel rubbing her arms. Four sets of wide eyes, five, really, counting Ballpoint, stared at her as she tried to recover. After a few excruciatingly long moments, she righted herself.

"That's got to be a contraction," she said.

"What was it like?" Angel said. "Are you sure? Shouldn't we call the doctor or something?"

"I'd be so scared," Emmaline said.

Zane threw a dirty look at Emmaline. Why did people always want to focus on the negative aspects of childbirth in front of Lettie? Like she wasn't scared enough. He'd seen women at the grocery store approaching her with delivery stories, being in labor for four days, begging to die. Pain so dreadful they nearly bit their tongues off. Made him want to smack them upside the head sometimes because he could see how it affected Lettie.

Angel must have been thinking the same thing. "It won't be so bad," Angel said. "Remember that television show *Teen Mom* we were watching? One of the girls was shopping at the mall when her contractions began. They whisked her to the hospital, and she nearly birthed that baby in the car. It seemed to happen in the blink of an eye."

"If those teen moms can do it, so can you," Zane said. "Still, do you have your overnight bag packed?"

Lettie nodded. Just then, she crumpled again in pain.

"I think it's time."

Chapter 13
Lettie

And Then Some

No one had told her the pain would be a ripping sensation, tearing through her pelvis, through her hips, reverberating up her spine. She held her breath until it eased, aware of everyone's eyes upon her. She dreaded the idea of her water breaking here on the carpet, in front of everyone, like a child who had wet herself.

"I think it's go time," Angel said, his voice calm but urgent. Verda guided her to a chair and sat her down. Ballpoint licked her hand as though trying to comfort her. She needed the reassurances. Her baby was coming, and she did not feel ready.

Another pain, stronger than before, caused her to suck in her breath and grit her teeth.

Why, she wondered, did this have to happen before Clyde Doom's arraignment? She had so wanted to have that unanswered question—would he be released on bail?—resolved before she brought this precious new life into the world. Maybe they should have left Tulsa. It had been her first instinct and now she regretted the decision to stay. They should be far, far away from this terrible man and his terrible girlfriend. Had she really thought shooting guns was going to help? The loud noises had probably startled the baby, brought the labor on sooner.

"We don't have a name for the baby yet," she said.

"Don't worry about that now," Verda said. "It will come."

"We can't put "No Name Baby" on the birth certificate," Lettie said. Tears pushed at her eyes and a sob caught in her throat. She was going to be a terrible mother.

"I'll get that list we were working on," Angel said. "It's going to be okay, Lettie." His sweet face, worry for her stitched all over it, calmed her down.

She walked to the car, pain-free for the moment, neck thrown back to look at the stars moving in the heavens. They looked large and near and radiant in the cold night air as if they moved on some celestial purpose unknown to the earthbound. Wheeling to their next post in the sky, no account given to the billions of eyes watching, to the dramas and pains of people like her. If billions of women have given birth to healthy babies, then it can't be so difficult, she thought.

Settled into the front seat of Zane's car, three towels protecting the seat in case her water broke, Lettie listened to the names Angel read during a lull in the pain. Esmé. Celeste. Tanya. The names sounded kind of silly, overly fancy. Trying too hard.

Sitting in the backseat next to Verda, Angel reached forward to stroke her arm.

"What if the ultrasound is wrong? What if it's a boy? We don't have any boy names picked out. What about August or Dylan?" Angel sounded worried.

"Those sound like the names celebrities pick," Lettie said. "We need something simpler. Authentic like us."

"Crystal? Because you like crystals?"

"Ugh, remember Crystal in fourth-period history? I can't name the baby after her."

Another round of pain, deep and hard, left her feeling queasy. She rolled down the window and rested her head on the sill, breathing in the cold air until the nausea passed. The heavy, dull ache in her low back stuck around though.

"The baby's going to be a Capricorn," Lettie said. "I'd kind of been hoping for an Aquarius baby."

"What's the difference?" Zane asked.

"Capricorns are hard-working, ambitious, practical. Aquarius is intelligent, quirky, independent."

"They both sound good to me," Angel said.

"We've got enough independent spirits in this family," Verda said. "Hard-working and practical sound like good characteristics to me. Your mama was an Aquarius."

Lettie knew she was lucky to have her grandmother and brother and Angel with her as she went into labor. But she wanted her mother with her more than ever. Even though it had been two years since her mother passed, she thought about her every day and knew how excited she would have been about the baby. Even if she was also disappointed with Lettie for the unplanned pregnancy. Sure, there were going to be lots of things she would do differently than her mom did. But just being pregnant at a young age had already given her a lot of perspective into what her mother had faced. Pregnant, scared of Jeremiah Doom, chased out of her parent's home, left to have the baby on her own. She couldn't even imagine how scary that must have been to be so alone.

A female dog used to live at the Majestic, back when her mother was alive. A stray dog that had a litter in some hidden lair and Lettie would see it ranging and foraging for them, lurking low, savage, and afraid, remembering and mistrusting humans. Melancholy, emaciated, but enough of a provider for her young. Lettie's own mother must have had days like that. She understood the instinct, knew she would do anything to keep this baby safe.

Verda's voice broke her reverie. "I've always liked the name Flora," her grandmother said. Zane and Lettie exchanged a quizzical glance. "Or for a boy, what about Leo?"

"Leo sounds powerful and regal," Angel said. "It also sounds like Leon though."

The next pain nearly made her black out.

She didn't know how long she was out or if the lights of the hospital were real or a dream. She drifted in and out, now being wheeled through bright halls, people smiling at her as the pain consumed her body. Pain radiating from her back to her ribs, framing her pelvis.

She saw Angel's face, worried, telling her she was beautiful and strong.

In a bed, in the hands of strangers, serious but sometimes smiling. "It's your time, mama," someone said.

She panicked. "Where's Angel? Where's Angel?"

"He's washing up," the nurse said, brown eyes over blue mask.

"Does he have the list of names?"

Angel came into the room, wearing a paper gown over his clothes, reminding her in a silly way of the Minions from that cartoon. She started laughing. "Who's your favorite minion, Angel? Stuart? Kevin?"

"Phil," he said. "We're not naming our child after a Minion, Lettie. You're delirious."

Then Lettie's body coiled, propelling her forward into as much of a sitting position as she could find on the hospital bed.

She braced herself, imagining herself as a hard shell ready to meet and survive the next wave of pain. She gritted her teeth to suppress the scream rising from her depths, from the tearing sensation inside her. She held against it, a seashell withstanding gale-force winds and pounding surf, enduring. When the pain finally ebbed, she crumpled against the pillows, breathing as though she had been drowning.

"Labor is not usually so fast for a first-time mom," someone said. "It's usually like half a day or more."

"I can't take this for a half day," Lettie said, panicking.

"I don't think you're going to have to," a masked and gloved woman said. "You're at six centimeters. Do you want the epidural?"

"Yes!" Lettie couldn't remember a thing about what the centimeter information meant from all the books she read about labor other than the words "labor is an emotional and uncontrollable process." It certainly was. And if she had hours and hours of this to go, she needed relief.

It seemed like two years passed, punctuated by nearly unbearable contractions, like the devil's version of menstrual cramps, before the anesthesiologist arrived in the room. "Don't move," he said.

"I'll do my best," Lettie spat out. "What with the white-heat pain in my abdomen and all."

Angel stroked her hair, and she brushed his hand aside. "Not now," she said.

The epidural burned as the medicine went into her spine. "What fresh hell?" she said. "That HURTS."

"You should feel the effects in about fifteen minutes," he said, scampering out of the room as though Lettie was a bomb about to explode.

But Lettie finally had a stroke of luck. The pain relief started showing up at the five-minute mark, first softening the edges of the crashing pain waves and holding back its gale-force winds. Then nothing but numb. The pain just stopped. Lettie pushed down on her belly and couldn't feel a thing. If the epidural were a person, she'd want to marry it, she thought. Giving birth felt doable and she was ready to have the baby out of her.

And three hours later, out came a baby girl.

Lettie lay on the bed like a beached whale, feeling like someone had gutted her. She squinted against the light as she blinked her eyes into focus. Angel held the tiny body now, shrunken and dark inside a white swaddle. After the birth, the baby had laid on her stomach, their hearts pulsing in tie, their mutual dependence on one another still intact. And Lettie's new purpose was born.

Exhausted and overwhelmed and emotional, she tried to calm herself by thinking logically. On the car ride here, she had thought "If billions of women give birth, then it must not be so difficult." Now that she had passed through the experience, she knew it was difficult but doable. So her trepidation at the next chapter of taking this baby home and caring for her was more of the same. If billions of women take care of newborn babies without harming them, then I should be able to do it too. Yes, there was ambiguity. She knew nothing in the real world behaved according to logic. As her teacher said, we can try to use logic to build arguments about the real world to help us understand but there is always uncertainty. There are always surprises.

"It's funny," Verda said. "Osbert and I were going to name your mother after my own mother. Her name was Amaryllis.

But when I held my baby daughter in my arms, the name just didn't feel right. Too heavy for that lightweight little thing. So at the very last minute, I said to Osbert, let's call her Lily."

"They're both pretty names," Angel said. "I like Rose too and Dahlia."

"Amaryllis," Lettie said. "Isn't there a Greek myth about an Amaryllis? Look it up!"

Zane tore his eyes away from his beautiful baby niece's tiny face and pulled his phone out of his pocket.

"Google says something about amaryllis flowers springing up from the blood of the nymph Amaryllis, who was madly in love with the handsome shepherd Alteo. That beautiful flower helped her win his heart," Zane said. He held up his phone to show a bright red flower that looked like a lily to Lettie.

"Let me hold her," Lettie said to Angel, stretching her arms out for the tiny baby. She brought her to rest against her stomach, then reached out and brushed the cheek of her daughter. The baby blinked at her, silent, her mouth open wide. Lettie smiled into those eyes, loving the way it made her feel to see the baby's round face and tiny eyebrows and nostrils flaring. This little baby was a nexus of pure love, filling the room and their hearts with a sense of unity and a desire to do nothing more than protect this tiny life. Through her daughter she felt newly connected not just to her mother, but also to her grandmother and great-grandmother. To all her ancestors, a long chain of women bringing and nurturing life, linked to the chain of love surrounding her in the hospital room. She felt strength from that chain.

And then she knew what to name her. "Amaryllis Lily," she said to Angel, who nodded. A sparkling name of beauty and legacy. A name for a girl who would stand out like a star, like the flower's shape. A girl who would rise with strength and determination on a strong stalk.

"Your name is Amaryllis Lily," Lettie said. It was a bit of a mouthful as she said it out loud a second time. "Maybe Milly for short."

"It's important that you rest," Zane said. "Maybe we should leave you a bit."

There was something in his tone, Lettie thought, that reintroduced the threat of Clyde Doom that had ruled every breath leading up to today. His specter silently entered the room and sat on the bed. Lettie clutched the baby tighter. The fear that had iced her blood since they heard about Clyde's overturned conviction returned with a rush, multiplied a hundred times, unfathomable. She closed her eyes, understanding nothing more than that she would do anything to protect this child. She pressed her lips into her daughter's forehead, whispering "I've got you, Milly. I've got you."

Chapter 14
Zane

Guiding Force

It was four-thirty in the morning and Ballpoint was at the side of Zane's bed, shifting from paw to paw and making tiny whining noises. Zane came to consciousness slowly, mind muddled in a dream about visitors as Ballpoint's anxiety manifested.

"What's wrong, Ballpoint?"

He flipped the covers off and swung his legs to the floor. It was cool in the bedroom, and in the dark, he slipped on sweatpants and a hoodie and led the dog out the door. The dry, chilly wind bit as it shook through the trees, stirring branches and making the trunks creak, sweeping dust across the road. Outside the radius of the outdoor floodlights, a gust whipped at the stiff blue tarp covering Leon's barbecue. Ballpoint went to do his business on a winter-white patch of weeds. Along the edges of the ground cover, frost caught a few beams of the light and gleamed like white crystals. Zane breathed in the cool, sweet air.

Usually, Ballpoint had no trouble waiting to do his business until seven a.m. This four o'clock urge was unusual. Zane scanned the surroundings, looking for anything out of place. Nothing stirred except for a lone tractor-trailer on the highway in the distance.

"Maybe you shouldn't have drank that bowl of water before bed," he said to Ballpoint as the dog returned to his side.

He and Ballpoint headed back up the stairs and into the dark mobile home. He paused at the threshold, thinking he heard the murmur of low voices from behind Verda's closed door. It wasn't like her to sleep with the television or radio on. Maybe she was restless like him and Ballpoint. If she wanted company, she would come out.

Ballpoint hesitated in the kitchen, looking at the plastic container where they stored his food.

"It's too early for breakfast," Zane said. "Come on, you can sleep in my room."

Zane flopped onto the bed and patted the mattress to let Ballpoint know he could join him. The dog curled up at the edge, his warm rump resting against Zane's feet. His solid presence was like a rock to lean against.

Lettie and Angel were still at the hospital but were supposed to come home today with little Amaryllis Lily. He tried to focus on the happy moments of yesterday's birth. He had been exhilarated beyond anything he had ever known. Half laughing and half crying, he held that tiny living baby for the first time in his two hands, feeling her fragility. "I'm Uncle Zane," he'd whispered in her ear. "I'm always going to be here for you."

Rubbing his eyes to stop the sentimental tears that threatened to spill, Zane realized there was no hope of returning to sleep. But he was exhausted. Ballpoint was fussy and kept rising and repositioning himself on the covers. Zane turned onto his back, burrowing his head into the pillow, and stared up at the ceiling. If he couldn't quiet his mind, he could at least quiet his body. What was it about these early hours that triggered anxiety? As though the dawn of a new day couldn't arrive without a rehashing of the prior day's worries. As if those predawn moments broke open any semblance of calm or control and revealed it to be nothing more than a façade laid on top of dread.

Clyde Doom's face appeared before him, bringing with it a fierce anger that prickled through his hair. His mind unlocked memories he didn't want to relive. He remembered Clyde's eyes on him that fateful day at JV's bar when Zane met his father, Jeremiah, for the first time. Clyde's shaved head, his skinny neck tattooed with a wobbly outline of a cartoonish wolf. Crooked teeth. It embarrassed Zane now to think about how much he wanted to be part of their family. He'd gotten drunk and even chased after some poor tweaker with his half-brothers. It seemed so desperate now, the way he'd given in to alcohol and wanted to please them all. So eager to make that relationship work and they knew it. They exploited it, and he was the fool all along.

Then they had tested his bond with Lettie. That was when he knew these men were no family to him but would turn against him. And they did. Even now, after all this time had passed, the knowledge left him empty and hard inside, like a brown beetle's shell. He was not sure what hurt more, their betrayal or the shame of his overeager foolishness. The anger and hatred encircled him like a jeering mob, and he plotted his revenge. First, his testimony at the arraignment, ensuring this creep stayed behind bars while he waited for his new trial. Then he would expose this Donna Lancaster for the liar she was. The depth of his anger scared him. He wanted to ruin them both. He felt the red-hot fury build on itself like a tornado, whirling and whipping his mind through scenarios where he was vindicated, where those who opposed him were smited in a biblical way. The righteousness added to the anger.

A sigh from Ballpoint jerked him back to the present. He remembered a conversation with Ernest before the trials had begun for Clyde and his brother Link.

"You're linked to them along the web of human connection," Ernest had said. "Do you see that bright red anger running toward you? Do you see how it makes you angry and you send more of this fury back? It's a feedback loop and it keeps you strongly bonded to them. They're not going to stop it. Only you can."

"I'm right to be angry," Zane had replied.

"Yes. But I'm sure you've heard that saying from the Christians: Love your enemy. This feedback loop is why it works. Instead of returning anger, if you can return love, the feedback loop is neutralized."

Love. Zane thought it was ridiculous at the time, but he didn't share that with Ernest. And he would admit that once Link and Clyde were in prison, it was easier to soften that anger with some understanding. His half-brothers were raised with violence. It was all they knew. They probably wanted to please their father. Hell, Clyde was just eighteen when all that happened.

But understanding was hard to come by when Clyde had the chance to be out in the world again. And his intentions for revenge were clear enough thanks to Donna Lancaster.

He heard a bedroom door open with a whoosh and the sound of heavy footsteps walking fast. Then the front door opened and shut, very softly but loud enough to prick both Zane's ears and Ballpoint's. He and the dog even exchanged glances. Had Grandma had a visitor? He felt the creases relax a little in his face as he smiled. Had it been Leon?

He automatically reached for his phone to share his suspicions with Lettie but thought better of it before typing the text message. He didn't want to wake her up if she was getting much-needed sleep. And maybe it was best left for Verda to tell them when she was ready. It's not like they hadn't seen it coming all this time. But if Verda was keeping it on the downlow, who was he to spill the tea, as Lettie would say?

He hit the Twitch app to see if Angel happened to be awake and streaming from the hospital room. The possibility seemed remote, but there he was, talking softly into the camera from what looked like a hospital hallway.

"Hey Zane, what are you doing up so early?" Angel said with a wave into the camera.

Dog got me up, Zane typed.

"What a day, huh? I'm a dad and I've got to tell you there is no sweeter feeling in the world. This little baby girl." Angel went on like that for a while, his face close to the camera. The overhead lighting made his eyes look sunken, but his mouth was stretched into a permanent smile. He didn't even look worried at all about his responsibilities. Just happy. The viewer comments were a series of hearts and flowers streaming by.

Then a ping as one of the viewers tagged Zane in a comment.

PeturbabeArgue: *Can't sleep because you're worried about something?*

What was wrong with this woman?

Angel stopped talking mid-sentence, eyes darting for a moment. Zane knew he had seen the comment too. But Angel started talking again, his radio-show host chatter resuming with his thoughts on how old children should be before playing video games.

Just excited, Zane typed. *Thanks for asking.* He wasn't going to let her know his heart thudded so hard he could feel it in the back of his throat.

PeturbabeArgue: *If you're worried about doing something in a few days, maybe you should skip it.*

Was she threatening them? Zane screen-shotted her words. Maybe he could use them to show this guy was still a danger, pulling strings from prison with his loyal girlfriend.

I'm never worried when I know I'm doing the right thing, Zane typed, hands shaking more with anger than fear.

...

So much to worry about tho...

This bitch, Zane thought. He screen-shotted her words again.

"I can hear mama waking up in there," Angel said. "I'm gonna shut the livestream down now to give her some post-labor privacy. I'm sure y'all understand."

The comments and hearts and emojis from the dozens of watchers kept flowing until the screen went abruptly black. This livestream has ended, the screen said.

Zane's phone started ringing and Angel's face appeared again, this time on a video call just to Zane.

"What the hell is wrong with her?"

"I grabbed photos of it. Maybe we can show it to the police, get them to see how Clyde's threatening us from prison. Use it as proof they shouldn't give him bail."

"That's a great idea. I have the video of the livestream too we can use," Angel said. "I'm so sorry I said your name on there, I just wasn't thinking. She wouldn't have known you were on there unless I did that."

"I can't believe she's still haunting your streams like that under that same damn username," Zane said.

"Yeah," Angel said.

Silence settled between them for a moment and Zane watched as Angel started pacing down the hallway.

"Remember when we talked about just leaving town? I wish we had done that," Angel said. "I should have pushed harder."

"Running from problems never works right, Angel. They attach themselves to you like a parasite. You never get free," Zane said.

"My mom's in Branson these days. Maybe we could go stay with her."

"Is she still with that new carnival group?" By which Zane really meant: is she still selling her body for money?

"Yes, but she is working the ticket counter and helping at one of the food concessions," Angel said.

Zane didn't buy the story, but he could see Angel did.

"Listen, we need to stick it out. I've done it before. Lettie has done it before. We have to stand up for what's right. The threats and fear are greatest when they think they can stop you. Once Clyde's denied bail, once Clyde's retried and reconvicted, you'll see. People like Donna just fold up like a paper tiger."

Zane let the raw anger he felt at Donna and Clyde carry his conviction. He could see that Angel's face had changed again, settling into resignation, and he ran his fingers through his hair.

"I hope so. We've got this baby to worry about now too," he said.

"I know."

The silence between them returned, heavier and louder this time with all the worries and fears and dread laden in it. There wasn't anything else to say. He felt a tiny choke in his throat as if he were about to cry.

"Give Lettie a hug for me and tell her I'll come pick you guys up today," Zane said. He wasn't sure he had ever in his entire life asked someone to give a hug for him but he felt emotional. Angel reacted like it was a normal request anyway and said he would. They hung up the call and Zane rolled over onto his side, tossing the phone far from him as though it was a snake that might bite.

He unspooled the miniblinds of the window by the bed to look for the rising light of the new day. He saw the stark, tall outline of a winter's bare tree scratching at the gray sky and heard the twitter and song of tiny, nervous birds camouflaged in the twisted network of branches. Another day. When things look bleak and hopeless, all you can do is the next thing. Get out of bed. Eat breakfast. You had to keep moving forward or everything was lost.

Chapter 15
Verda

Soft Spots

She lay in bed after Leon left, reliving the impromptu date they had. He'd come over with a gift for the baby and found her alone, tending to Ballpoint while the others were at the hospital.

"I wish I could offer you a celebratory glass of champagne or a cigar, but we don't have either."

"I don't have champagne but I do still have some beer. Should I go get it?"

She said yes to the beer and then yes to dinner at the Outback Steakhouse and then there they were, in her bedroom, making out like fifteen-year-olds when the parents were away. She didn't know if it was the hubbub of the hospital and the baby, the nail-biting anxiety of the Clyde Doom debacle and his bonkers lady friend Donna, or that it had been probably ten years since she'd been with a man, but she put all her reservations aside and let her body run the show. She was proud she'd still remembered a few tricks. That old axiom about not forgetting how to ride a bicycle did apply, apparently.

She shrank back into the comfort of her pillow, pulling the covers up to her chin. She could still smell him on the sheets, a chocolatey-musk saltiness that brought back the sweet, warm, tentative moments as well as the hotter, more intense ones. She was going to have that morning afterglow tomorrow, no doubt about it. She just hoped Zane and Lettie didn't notice. She also uttered a quick prayer asking God's forgiveness for the fornication, but it felt insincere because she didn't quite feel sorry about it.

Leon had mentioned his mistakes before and now she thought she knew what they were. Tonight she had traced her fingers around the thick, rough black line drawing of a fish tattooed onto his back. It was a simple drawing, the kind that they teach you to draw in Bible school, a long oval with a triangle at the end for the tail. She remembered drawing them to illustrate that Bible story in which Jesus turned two fishes and five loaves of bread into enough to feed a multitude.

"I got that tattoo in prison."

"I wondered." She had noticed it was done in black ink, a straightforward outline with no color, design, or shading like she saw on a lot of arms and legs in the summertime. Seemed like everyone got a tattoo these days. She liked how young people these days expressed themselves so freely with tattoos, hair color, the way they dressed. They seemed so full of life and potential.

"Do you think less of me now? That you know I was in prison?"

"What did you do?"

"It was in Ecuador. It was politically motivated. I don't like to talk about it."

Leaning back, she widened her eyes. "Why the fish?"

Before he could answer, the sound of a car door slamming right outside the home caused them to stop talking. She bolted out of bed and pulled on her pajama bottoms and a loose-fitting T-shirt and then sat on the bed. They both were silent as they heard Zane open the door, greet Ballpoint, and start messing around in the kitchen.

"Shhh," she said with a smile. Again, she felt like a teenager sneaking around, and the thought made her want to giggle.

When Zane had finally gone into his room and closed the door, she asked Leon again about the fish.

"You know that story of Jonah in the Bible? How he's swallowed by a large whale and cries out for God in his despair? That's how I felt in prison."

"I thought the symbol stood for Jesus feeding the multitudes."

"That's the thing about symbols. They mean what you want them to mean."

He ran his fingertips down her arm, kissing the spots where gooseflesh appeared.

"Don't get us started again," she whispered, her lips finding his. "Zane's home."

"I can be quiet as a church mouse."

"This old bed can't."

They pulled apart again and Leon lay next to her, idly playing with a strand of her hair. "I like that you don't dye your hair."

"I've been silver since I was fifty. Never wanted to go to all that trouble."

"You're beautiful to me." His eyes promised her he meant it.

. . .

Verda had to admit that she felt better knowing Leon was looking out for her. The relief she experienced by having him around was almost enough to make her swoon like a Southern belle. For the first time in a very long time, she felt like she had someone she could lean on. Yes, she could depend on Zane and Lettie, and Angel for most things, but those bonds were different. She could be more of herself with Leon—her full self—and it wasn't just because of the sex. He seemed like a sturdy rock to her. In a way, he reminded her of Osbert.

So what if he had been jailed in Ecuador? She didn't know much about the politics there but from his descriptions, the country seemed volatile and violent at that time. As she got older, she saw how thin the line was between patriotism and revolution and what people would do to hold on to power. Who was she to judge what Leon had done years ago?

What she knew was that being with Leon made her heart ache with something more than just lust. There was something deeper, more elemental to it. She wasn't ready to call it love or anything like that, but maybe it was an intimate connection born out of loneliness and a desire to share the pains and joys of growing old with someone who understood. They both needed someone to talk to, someone to listen, and they gave each other that. And more.

Chapter 16
Zane

Raising Up

Zane and Tiffany sat at the counter of the diner, watching the waitress pour coffee into two white mugs.

"I want to be there for you," Tiffany said. She chewed on her bottom lip for a moment, and it made him want to lean over and kiss her.

"I do not want you anywhere near these people," Zane said. "I don't want Clyde and his crazy girlfriend to see you or know you."

"Zane, there's pics of us all over my Insta. How do you think they don't know about me? About us?" Her full, dark eyebrows spiked with skepticism.

She had a point, but Zane couldn't shake this feeling of foreboding he had. He didn't want Tiffany at Clyde's arraignment. Maybe also in part, he didn't want her to see him scared. He decided to change the topic.

"So what's going on with Cell-Phone-Fixit? When's the owner closing it up?"

Tiffany tore open two sugar packets at the same time and dumped them into the coffee. To his relief, she took the conversational bait and hit pause on the argument. "It's crazy lately. Korey has been in every day so far this week, taking over the office. I've been having to set my laptop on the counter in the front of the store and do my shift scheduling and time approvals from there."

"Have you given any more thought to trying to buy the store?"

"Oh, Zane," she said, eyes narrowed. "That's just dreaming. I have been putting some resumes out there. Applied for a few jobs. People say that it's a job-seekers market but I'm not getting that vibe too much. I applied for an assistant manager job at the Golden Corral, but they didn't call back. Probably want someone with food service experience."

"Is business still good? Customers are still coming in?"

She nodded. "That's still the weird thing. From what I can tell, it's still a viable business, customers streaming in with broken screens and laptops that don't start and the usual stuff."

"Have you asked Korey what the story is?"

"Yeah, he just said the same old thing about COVID straining his finances and he needs to sell the store or close it up," she told him as she took another sip of coffee. "Asked me if I knew anyone who wanted to buy it so I told him about your idea that I should."

Zane nodded. "What did he say?"

"He asked if I was serious and I said no, that I couldn't raise hundreds of thousands of dollars. He laughed at me. Said he was just looking for sixty thousand. I told him that might as well be sixty million as far as my bank account was concerned."

Sixty thousand was a bit more than his starting salary was going to be at Skiatook. But Zane had to admit, the amount seemed more reasonable than he thought it would be.

"Look, I don't know much about business. How much money do you think that store brings in a month?"

"Somewhere between seven and nine grand. Depends."

Math wasn't Zane's strong suit, so he pulled out his phone and opened the calculator app. "Seven thousand times twelve months is eighty-four thousand," he said. "You'd make that investment back in a year if I'm doing the math right."

"You don't know *anything* about business," Tiffany teased. "You gotta put all the expenses in too. The store's lease, electric bill, credit card processing, Internet service, website, marketing. There's a lot that goes into it. Not to mention my salary and whatever the owner takes."

"Okay, right," Zane asked the waitress for a pen and a fresh napkin. "So what do you think the lease costs?"

"I think it's like two thousand a month," she said. "See what I mean? Two thousand times twelve—" She laughed. "Put that in your calculator."

"Twenty-four thousand a year, plus another say two hundred a month for Internet, utilities—"

"More like four or five hundred," she said.

"Okay fine," Zane said. "Look, I think it pencils out. It's a risk because it's not a sure thing like finding a job and getting a salary, but you've got a ton of hustle. You'd put in more time than the owner ever did. You'd probably build it up really well. And I could help you out and I bet Lettie and Angel would want to too."

"You sound like Korey. He was very encouraging. He said I should try to get a small business loan and he would help me with the paperwork. But I turned him down. It's so scary! I'd owe tens of thousands of dollars. What if it didn't work out?"

It took everything Zane had not to reach out and shake some courage and sense into her. Couldn't she see that the only thing holding her back was fear? Why couldn't she believe in herself like he believed in her?

They watched as the waitress slung their breakfast plates on the counter in front of them. Oatmeal and fruit for Tiffany, a spinach omelet with toast, and hashbrowns for Zane. She poured milk and sugar into the oatmeal while he slathered his omelet with ketchup and hot sauce, and they were quiet for a moment as they took their first bites. Tiffany tucked her short dark hair behind her ears, revealing her adorable tiny earlobes adorned with simple gold stud earrings. If they had been alone, he might have leaned over and nibbled on the one closest to him instead of his breakfast.

"Fear is a funny thing," Zane said. "I remember the first fight I got into in elementary school. I was so scared of getting hit. I thought it must be the worst feeling, getting hit in the face. And what if I didn't land a punch? What if I looked like a fool? I avoided that kid and that fight for two days, skulking around the school, staying late, or leaving early. Anything to not get cornered by him. Then one day, he was waiting for me outside. I had no choice. We stood there looking at one another, then he swung and connected with my jaw. And I remember thinking, oh is that all it is to be hit?"

Tiffany's smile tilted up on one side, showing her perfectly straight white teeth. "Who won?"

"Not important."

"That means not you." She laughed.

"Yeah, well, I landed a few punches, but he definitely bested me. But I'm trying to tell you something different. I'm trying to tell you about how you can't let fear hold you back by whispering all these 'what if' situations to you. All it does is keep you feeling small and afraid to really live like you want to."

A lock of hair swung free from her ear as she turned to him. "You are the bravest person I know, Zane. I don't know how you do it."

"The thing is that fear never goes away," he said. "You just step up to fight it every day. Some days better than others."

"I wish you would let me come to Clyde's bail hearing with you," she said. "I'm tougher than you think. I'm not made of glass."

He smiled. Tiffany was relentless, like a bee after a flower. But that was one fear he was not going to disregard. It was fine if that loony Donna Lancaster cyber-stalked them and knew about Tiffany. But Zane didn't even want Clyde's eyes on her. Bad enough that Lettie would need to go and testify.

"You've got to understand," he said. "I know you want to come but trust me, it's better this way. Please."

To his relief, she nodded. "I am coming with you to this press conference thing Emmaline has organized though."

Zane wanted to turn the car around when he saw the white van emblazoned with the Channel 8 logo and slogan "We're Tulsa" parked in front of the mobile home where he lived. A cameraman stood next to the van, setting up a camera tripod. To the left, Emmaline stood talking to a black-haired woman. Undoubtedly Kristy Diguchi, the same reporter who had covered his mother's death after the fire. He remembered her as aggressive and fake sympathetic. On the few occasions he watched local news, he switched channels whenever she came on, no matter the story. He hated the memories she triggered, especially of the footage she ran on television of him being whisked away in a police car. It made him look guilty and the news station hadn't helped by running "Son taken for questioning in mother's death" on the screen.

Emmaline had tried to get other reporters to come out, but only Kristy had bitten as far as he could see.

Tiffany yanked the sunshield down and reapplied lipstick in the tiny mirror. "I thought maybe Emmaline would be wearing one of her pageant gowns for the publicity."

"Down, girl," Zane said. "She's no threat to you." His fingers slid up her neck, curving around the back of her head. He brushed his lips gently over her mouth, careful of the newly applied lipstick. She lifted her chin, parting her lips, all the while her eyes stayed connected to his.

A scratchy thump on the car window broke the spell. Ballpoint's face pressed against the driver's side window, a tiny string of drool hanging out of his wide, smiling mouth. His tail beat faster than windshield wipers on high.

Kristy Diguchi swiveled toward them, holding a big black microphone with the KTUL logo affixed to the front. She wore a bright red mask across her nose and mouth. It matched her tight red dress peeking out beneath a long wool coat and made Zane think of the glossy Los Angeles weather reporters he remembered watching on his brief trip there to find his sister. Maybe that was what Kristy aspired to: day after day of reporting on temperatures always in the 70s and sunny, instead of standing in a mobile home park retelling the story of the man who killed his father in self-defense. But the look on her face told him otherwise. She loved the drama of this. Her love for her job was written all over her face.

Anxiety followed Zane out of the car and over to where Emmaline and Kristy stood between the cameraman's tripod and his home. He ran his fingers over Ballpoint's head, forcing a smile onto his face. He placed himself like a buffer between

Tiffany and Emmaline, reached for his girlfriend's hand, and gave it a squeeze.

"Thanks for coming," he said, extending a hand toward Kristy.

"I'd rather not," she said. "I try to limit my exposure since I come into contact with so many people. Too many germs. You understand."

Zane's hand shot back like an arrow, and he took two steps back from her. "Got it," he said.

The cameraman stopped messing with the tripod and extended his own hand, his eyes alert. "Jonathan," he said, his round belly like a beach ball under his blue polo shirt, jeans hanging on for dear life by a thick brown leather belt.

"KTUL has the exclusive," Emmaline said. "No one else came."

"Their loss," Kristy said. She pulled her face mask down and let it dangle from one ear so he could see her fake sympathetic smile. She wouldn't shake hands for fear of germs but now she was taking off her mask? People didn't make sense sometimes, Zane thought.

"I know a story when I see one and Zane. Your life is really challenging right now, isn't it?" Kristy said.

"It's definitely been better," he said.

"I'm so glad your friend Emma called," Kristy said.

"It's Emmaline," he said. "And this is my girlfriend, Tiffany. And I guess you met Ballpoint."

"Emmaline. Sorry about that. Nice to meet you, Tiffany. Look Zane, our viewers want to know about you. They want to hear what's going on with you. This overturned conviction has got to be like a nightmare for you and your sister. I can see the floodlights you've installed and the security cameras. Are those new?"

Zane nodded.

"Because of Clyde?" she said.

He nodded again.

"You're going to have to give me some verbal answers when we are rolling," Kristy said with a laugh. "And can we do it inside? It's cold and the noise from the highway, it's too loud."

The highway and the trailer park seemed quieter than usual to Zane, but he agreed it was cold and let her into their home. At the door, Ballpoint waited patiently for the reporter and cameraman to enter before following them in.

"Can he stay outside?" Kristy said.

"We don't have a fence for the yard, so he needs to stay in with us," Verda said from the kitchen, though it was obvious. "I can put him in another room if he's bothering you."

Ballpoint stood in front of Jonathan, tail wagging ferociously, head nudging his hand. The cameraman gave him a good scratch behind the ears and Ballpoint's right hind paw thumped on the step.

"I just don't want a doggie photo bomb," she said. Just then, a pungent aroma crept up toward Zane and Kristy. She wrinkled her nose and waved the air in front of her.

"Sorry about that," Zane said. "He has a little indigestion from his new food." He led the dog into his bedroom and closed the door only to hear Ballpoint whimpering a bit on the other side. "Stay quiet, friend," he said.

Back in the living room, he watched Kristy and the cameraman scan the living room and kitchen, looking for the best angle. Zane fidgeted with his phone, absently scrolling photos without really looking at them. Despite the reassurances of Emmaline and Verda and Angel and Lettie and even Tiffany, he was uneasy about this interview and its repercussions. Though he had to admit, it felt good to do something. Even something as uncomfortable as this interview.

"Can we open these shades?" Kristy said.

Verda and Emmaline started raising the white miniblinds, revealing floating particles of dust in the shafts of morning light.

After about ten minutes of set-up, he sat across from Kristy in their living room, and she tried to put him at ease.

"This story is just shocking to me, and you are living through it," she said.

"Unfortunately, yeah." Zane took a deep breath and tried to focus on Kristy's face instead of the yawning black hole of the camera lens.

"What I should have asked first is how are you doing? Are you holding up okay under all this stress?"

Like she cared, Zane thought. It was all a performance, but he had to play his part too.

"I'm okay," he said. "You just have to keep moving forward."

"Losing both parents is so hard. Especially under the circumstances. But I can see you have good people around you," Kristy said, gesturing to the couch where Verda and Tiffany sat. Out of the corner of his eye, Zane could see Emmaline holding up her phone as though she was recording the interview.

"I try not to dwell on the past too much. I've got my sister to take care of and my brand-new niece so we're busy." Couldn't be any harm in talking about Milly, he thought. It wasn't a secret.

"How did you feel when you heard Clyde Doom's conviction had been overturned?"

"Shocked," Zane said. "Angry. Confused. I thought things like that only happened in the movies."

"It does sound like the far-out thriller movie plot, but this is your life, isn't it? What are you hoping for with tomorrow's arraignment?"

"I'm hoping that the judge will see that Clyde should stay

in prison while he awaits a new trial. The harm he and his brother did to my sister and to me shouldn't be ignored."

"I've spoken to him, Zane, and would you like to know what he has to say?"

Images clicked through his brain. Glassy-eyed Clyde behind the wheel of that red truck, driving him to the shack where they had Lettie tied up. Clyde with a gun in his hand. Clyde laughing like a crazy meth-head. That ridiculous wolf neck tattoo.

Zane nodded. Then he remembered Kristy's earlier admonition that he needed to give verbal answers and said yes.

"He said he has cleaned up his life. He's gotten clean from meth and is working the twelve steps of Alcoholics Anonymous. And that he'd like to make amends."

Zane couldn't stop the cynical smile from erupting onto his face. "Yeah, right," Emmaline said from behind her phone.

Kristy swiveled her head and shot a dagger look at Emmaline. "I need you to be quiet."

"Sorry," Emmaline said.

Kristy turned back to Zane, and he waited for her to follow up. He wanted her to push him on the topic. "You don't believe him?"

"I don't know," Zane said. "That's the kind of thing only time will tell. And I don't want to doubt anyone has had a change of heart, but Clyde did bad things. It would take some convincing for me to think he has mended his ways."

Across the room, Verda sighed and murmured something to Tiffany that Zane couldn't hear. The rumble of an airplane ascending from the nearby Tulsa airport sounded like soft thunder in the distance.

"Are you going to go to the courthouse tomorrow? Will you speak if you get the opportunity?"

"Definitely, both Lettie and I want to go and tell the judge how we feel," Zane said.

"What are you going to say?"

"Just that we think there is enough evidence that Clyde should not get bail. He had a gun. He kidnapped my sister. He concocted a plan to kill her that I stopped him from carrying out. The way things went down, it's reasonable to assume he could still mean harm to us. What happened—" Zane's voice broke a little. "It still affects my sister. And me."

"How do you mean?"

"I mean that it still affects us. We still think about it. She still has nightmares about it. You try to move past it but you can't."

"It's hard to deal with trauma," Kristy said, shifting from a crossed-leg position to stretch her legs out in front of her. "I really appreciate your doing this. I think I have what I need." She rose to her feet and put her hands on her hips. Zane rose too, noticing that the cameraman kept the lens trained on him when he stood up. He got a queasy feeling there was a gotcha coming.

"Zane, I have just one more question for you," Kristy said. A look of anticipation formed on her face, as though she could see the outlines of the full story in Zane's face. "Why did you get suspended from the police academy?"

There it was. Gotcha.

Now it was Zane's turn to shoot dirty looks at Emmaline. How did this reporter even know that? He'd put the whole life of his family on display to the world once again and it felt like there was nothing to be gained but embarrassment.

"Some false accusations about me stemming from that terrible time with Clyde," Zane said. "They have to look into them, that's all. I'm sure I'll be reinstated." Zane tried hard to project more confidence than he felt.

Kristy waited a few beats, pinching her lips as though hoping for more. Zane kept his face still and concentrated on his breath. He wanted to be careful with his words and reactions, to give her nothing. That much he had learned from those terrible years in the spotlight.

"One thing that strikes me," Kristy said. "When terrible things happen, terrible crimes, it seems to me that the victims and the perpetrators are intertwined for the rest of their lives. They think about each other all the time and what happened. Is that how it is for you?"

"I try not to think about him and his brother," Zane said.

"What if he had things to say to you? Healing things?"

"I'd listen," Zane said. "But I have a lot of questions."

"All right, Zane," she karate-chopped her hand, some sort of code that told the cameraman to finally move the camera from Zane's face.

"I'd be afraid, too, if I were in your shoes," Kristy said. "The security lights and cameras, the dog. I get it. We won't show that stuff in the segment."

"They're just smart precautions," Emmaline said. "Whether Clyde gets out or not, there's just more crime these days."

"Weird things happen in our judicial system," Kristy said. "Courts rule this way one day and the other way the next. It's hard to predict what will happen with all that's going on with the McGirt ruling," Kristy said.

"I know that," Zane said. Even though justice had been served once, it still felt like a process subject to whims and judgment calls by prosecutors, judges, and attorneys. His fate decided behind the scenes. A judicial jungle holding out the glimmering promise of justice alongside the fear of life-changing defeat.

"Anyway, I hope you can relax and enjoy the new baby. You've got a lot going on," Kristy said.

The idea of relaxing sounded like wishful thinking. How would he turn his worries off with Clyde's potential release looming? And whoever had relaxed with a newborn baby in the house? He didn't know much about babies but he was pretty sure they needed a lot of attention and care.

"When is this going to run?" Zane asked.

"Maybe tonight," she said. "I'll text you when I know. You've been generous with your time, Zane."

Zane unhooked the microphone from his shirt and pulled the cord out to hand to Jonathan's waiting hand. And with that, the news team grabbed their things and left the mobile home. Zane watched from the small window by the door as they loaded into the van, lost in the feelings of excitement, fear, anxiety, and irritation that crashed in his head. His adrenaline had spiked high during that interview, and he could feel the energy slowly draining from him now that it was over. He might need a nap but he doubted sleep would come.

"Good gravy, did you do a good job," Tiffany said, her voice wrapping him in warmth as her arms squeezed his middle.

"I'll keep trying to reach someone at the Tulsa World," Emmaline said. "And I shot some video of the interview. I'll put a little video out on my Insta and Snapchat. I've got close to twenty thousand followers these days, so maybe someone will share it."

Tiffany poked Zane in the stomach as Emmaline bragged about her fan base. "Most of them are just there for her bikini pics," Tiffany whispered.

Zane turned to face Emmaline, his arm snaking around Tiffany's shoulders to pull her tight, a loving admonition to be nice. "Thanks, Em," he said. "I appreciate any help. Maybe if more people know about what's happening, it will create some pressure on either the prosecutors or the judge."

But he couldn't shake the feeling of dread that came over him when Kristy had talked about the judicial system's unpredictability. With Clyde Doom and with his own suspension, he was caught in a slow-motion tailspin with his hard-won accomplishments, his plans, and his life whirling away from him. Ernest Buckskin would tell him to slow his mind down and do the next thing but thanks to the suspension, he didn't have very much to do other than pick up Lettie at the hospital.

He pulled Tiffany close to him and took a deep inhale of her coconut-vanilla shampoo scent. She must have sensed his anxiety because she asked him if he wanted to go with her to see what a bank would require for a business loan.

"Might as well see what they'd ask for anyway," she said. "Just so I could prove to you that no bank is gonna give me $60,000."

He could see Emmaline working the phone, fingers flying over the screen. He heard Verda open the door to let Ballpoint out of the bedroom, and the dog came flying out, pushing his head into Zane's hand.

"I'm thinking of making chicken fried steak for dinner tonight," Verda said. "A day of hospital food should be erased from Lettie's mind by some good home cooking."

Zane ran his fingers over the velveteen fur of Ballpoint's head, feeling the shape of his skull. Bad things happened to people all the time. But in this moment, all he felt was the love around him. The love in this life he had built from the ashes. This love, these people, made the bad bearable. He just needed to make sure that he protected this at all costs.

Chapter 17
Zane

On the Docket

That Tuesday, Zane and Lettie drove downtown for Clyde's arraignment. Loris and Old Spice had agreed that the hearing was speedily set, an unusual circumstance, but then, ever since the McGirt ruling, things had been different. Zane wore dark pants, a white shirt, and the tie he'd bought at Goodwill for his interview with the Skiatook Police Department. Lettie, just a few days after giving birth, had insisted on attending too, leaving Verda and Angel in charge of Milly. Her slow movement and uncomfortable shifting around shows this was a physical hardship for her. Still, Zane was proud of her.

The Page Belcher Federal Building Courthouse in downtown Tulsa looked like it had been built upside down. A massive concrete ledge jutted out from the flat roof, shading a row of top-floor windows. Beneath that, the tan façade was decorated with a dozen or so scalloped columns covered in metal screens. It kind of resembled a prison, Zane thought. Built in the 1960s, a plaque said on the outside. It was monstrous in size, too, spanning two city blocks between Third and Fourth streets and Denver and Frisco avenues. It looked out of place next to the sleek glass-and-metal architecture of the BOK Center next door.

The street parking lining the courthouse perimeter was full and people milled about on the sidewalk outside. Loris and Old Spice said it was common since the McGirt ruling. Criminal felony cases per judge had tripled in the Northern District of Oklahoma in the time since the decision. Oklahoma judges had put out a national request for federal judges willing to come to Oklahoma and temporarily try cases to help relieve the backlog. For now, cases were being prioritized in which the accused had been in jail for the longest time.

Inside it was crowded, confusing, and disorienting. They stood in a long line to pass through metal detectors, then stood in the lobby reading the directory. People in uniforms and suits walked confidently through the place in the manner that Zane and Lettie remembered from that nightmare time of Clyde and Link's first trials. Zane felt like he was on trial. The waiting. The nervousness that erupted into nausea, the fear of the unknown.

Zane sat on the courtroom bench between Loris and Lettie. Old Spice sat on the other side of Lettie. Even Cal Himmelman and Devante, his friend from the academy, had shown up. Zane was touched by the show of support.

When he saw the face of Donna Lancaster, rage filled his chest. She walked up to the bench where they sat.

"Congratulations on the baby girl," she said to Lettie.

Now Zane's heart hammered like a gun.

"Congratulations on your prison boyfriend's new trial,"

Lettie said, her voice sharpened. "You think he's going to stay interested in you if he gets free?"

Zane kept his eyes on Donna, focusing on her face as she stood there smiling. He took a deep breath and released it slowly. He would not allow this woman to affect him, no matter how hard it was not to jump up and confront her. He needed to stay calm for this to work. He wanted Lettie to stay calm too. Apparently, he wasn't the only one thinking that way.

"Go ahead and take your seat, Donna Lancaster," Loris said.

Donna smiled her simpering smile and backed off a few feet. "What do you think of my new dress?" She glided her hands along the flowy skirt.

"Looks cheap," Lettie said. "But that suits you."

"You would know," Donna said. But the smile vanished from her face, and she stumbled back a bit before turning to take a seat on a bench across the aisle.

Clyde arrived with uniformed escorts and he was all smiles. He wore an oversized white shirt that gaped at the neck and loose blue pants that still showed creases from being folded at the store. He strutted in like a rooster in a hen house, as Verda might say, and seemed to be savoring the moment, looking around the courtroom until he found Donna and blew her a kiss. Zane didn't see Dave or Susie Doom, Clyde and Link's grandparents, or anyone else who looked like they were connected to Clyde. Donna must have brought the change of clothes in for Clyde.

Clyde's attorney didn't fit Zane's mental images of what a lawyer should look like. He was in his mid-thirties with flowing orangey-blond hair in a low ponytail. He leaned his head in to speak quietly to Clyde.

Judge Austin assumed the bench promptly at nine and said good morning. It was an eerie flashback to the brothers' earlier trials Zane and Lettie had testified at. He remembered the drives out to Sallisaw to the old pinkish-brown brick courthouse there, the dreadful feeling of those two brothers watching him testify. Zane tried to remember the name of the district attorney, a potbellied woman with neat, short-cropped brown hair and the easy manner of a rural politician. That easy manner belied a strength and intensity that came out during her questioning of Clyde. She was truly a warrior for justice. It was hard to imagine her being sexually harassed by the judge because she seemed tough as nails, but that's what everyone said happened. And that's why they were here today.

Zane had hoped she would be here, but there was no sign of her. Since the McGirt ruling, either federal courts or Indian courts had to take over the prosecution from the city or county authorities.

The formalities started, first with an introduction that the defendant Clyde Doom was an Indian male and that Lettie Magdite, born of a different father than Zane, was a non-Indian woman. Then the list of counts against him: unlawfully seizing, confining, decoying, kidnapping, abducting, and holding Lettie in Indian Country in violation of the law. Images in Zane's mind played like his smartphone's photo memories montages: Lettie tied up. Lettie with the tape over her mouth. Link and Clyde laughing. A gun in the room.

Next to him on the hard wooden seat, Lettie stiffened and he knew she was reliving the memories too. He tasted the anger and frustration with the system again. Why did people in power, like that sexual-harassing judge, act like that? They already had power. What was it in them that made them seek more of it? An arrogance that they could take whatever they wanted. It pissed him off and here was his innocent sister, suffering the consequences of a second trial and the possibility of this violent man getting out on bail.

"The following firearms and ammunition were found on the property and within the truck that the defendant had access to: A Smith & Wesson, Model 649, .357 magnum pistol; twenty-five rounds of Hornady brand .357 magnum caliber ammunition, a Rock Island Armory Model M200, .38 special caliber revolver, thirty rounds of Hornady brand .38 special caliber ammunition..."

The list read by the judge went on and on, sounding like the contents of a guns-and-ammo store rather than the armory of a small family's compound. The list definitely went above and beyond what anyone would have for personal protection. Surely the judge would see how dangerous Clyde was. Zane glanced over at Donna to see the small smile playing over her lips. She was getting off on the gun and ammo list, the idea of Clyde being a dangerous man. Zane wanted to wipe the smile off her face.

"...intent to kill, injure, harass, intimidate Lettie Magdite..."

Lettie had tears on her cheeks now, streaked with black mascara. He squeezed her hand and found her skin clammy.

"Are you okay?"

"Just a little nauseous," she said. Sweat stains ringed the neckline and underarms of the pale blue knit dress she wore. "I'm fine."

"Please stand, Clyde Doom," the judge said.

Clyde shuffled to his feet as if he was in control of the moment, the chair making a loud squeaking noise as it slid back.

"Do you wish to enter a plea?" the judge said.

"Not guilty," he said.

"The prosecution recommends no bail and that the defendant be remanded into custody," the prosecutor said. "He's a violent offender who terrorized his victim."

Clyde's pony-tailed defense attorney mounted a speech

about Clyde's model prisoner ways, how he had been working through his Narcotics Anonymous steps, gotten clean from methamphetamine, found God. Zane's eyes bored into the back of Clyde's head and he felt like he could read the lies Clyde was telling everyone. Maybe he had gotten clean from meth. Maybe he had found God. But he was still a violent man, and Zane had no doubt he was a threat to him and Lettie.

"No bail," the judge said.

Relief poured through Zane, and he squeezed his sister's shoulders and kissed her on the cheek. Her face said it all. He closed his eyes for a moment as Loris quietly hugged Lettie. This was the moment he had hoped and prayed for. Clyde Doom would be locked away from them, unable to harm his sister and Milly, while he awaited his new trial. And surely he would be convicted once again. A Bible quote Zane came across in his Internet wanderings said something about the way of evil perishing as God watches over the way of the upright and he gave a silent prayer of thanks for the blessed outcome.

Donna watched the marshals take Clyde out of the courtroom then came over to where Zane sat on the bench. "Clyde has a lot of friends, you know, not just me," she said.

"Is that a threat?" Old Spice said. "What do you mean by that?"

"Nothing," Donna said, backing down like a little dog in front of a big one showing its teeth.

"Because threats of physical harm are against the law, too," Old Spice said.

Donna whirled around, pushed the door open, and made her escape, not bothering to reply.

Outside the courtroom, Kristy Diguchi and her cameraman asked a few questions and Zane said a few things about justice prevailing. Lettie didn't say anything other than that she wanted to go home and take a nap. Zane didn't have much to say either. He had been dreaming of this moment, but it was bittersweet. On the one hand, there was immense satisfaction in knowing Clyde would remain behind bars for the time being. But on the other, there were the weirdly unsettling actions of Donna and of course, the fear that this trial would not bring a conviction.

He let Loris and Old Spice joke about the hillbilly security he'd installed around the mobile home and before long he and Lettie were laughing about the silliness of the alligator trap. The laughter felt good and came easily on the heels of such great relief. But something didn't feel right about Clyde's demeanor and Donna's comment. Like they knew something he didn't.

Chapter 18
Lettie

Ten of Swords

The tarot card spread Lettie had laid out before they left for the courthouse had been ominous. One of the worst readings she'd ever done for herself and it was hard to shake the impact of it even now that the hearing was over and the best outcome had manifested.

For that reading this morning, Lettie had chosen a simple layout: three cards representing the past, present, and future respectively. The card that landed in each spot would tell the story of her life during those times. It was a layout her mother had taught her, always stressing that tarot was about showing patterns and likelihoods not about a precise view of the future. After all, anything could happen. Tarot readings were not logical at all but they brought her comfort.

Shuffling the cards brought back memories of her mother in

her recliner, laying the cards out in a Celtic spread on a tray table, talking about the cards and what they meant. Lettie had been so proud of her mother's knowledge. It had been so different from her friends' mothers who mainly looked at their phones or hovered around like helicopters trying to know all the details of their kids' lives. She had enjoyed those times so much and she wanted to have something similar with Milly. Tears welled up as she thought of how her mother would have loved Milly, and she didn't even try to brush them away. Cleansing, she thought, as she braced herself for the question on her mind. "How can I keep us safe in light of Clyde's hearing today?"

When the moon card showed up in the past position, she wasn't surprised. It usually meant confusion and a difficult emotional journey. Certainly, she had had enough of that recently.

The card representing the present was the grim five of pentacles, usually meaning financial problems. Yes, they had those too, what with Zane's job hanging in the balance and a brand-new baby with all the endless things babies seem to need.

But the most worrying card had been the ten of swords in the future position. Swords represented words and action (and often conflict) in tarot. In that suit, the ten of swords was seen as one of the most fearsome cards in a reading because it didn't seem to bring any good news. Lettie always tried to take a positive approach to tarot but seeing the card sent icy shards into her stomach. The ten of swords imagery was bad enough: a man lying face down with ten swords in his back. An unwelcome surprise. A betrayal. A battle lost. Headed for the bottom, either through a rapid fall or slow, painful descent. How do you even prepare for that?

She tried to think of that popular song with the lyrics about what doesn't kill you make you stronger, but the buoyancy escaped her, and she just felt heavy and sad. Even snuggles from sweet Milly and Verda's delicious banana pancakes for breakfast couldn't cut through the foreboding she felt as she got dressed to go to the courthouse.

She hadn't told Zane or Angel or Verda about the reading because she didn't want to manifest the bad energy any more than she already had. If there was one thing she had learned at her young age, it was that sometimes it was better to say nothing at all. Words had power and should be used strategically.

But the arraignment had turned out just about as well as it could, so she tried to shake the negative vibes out of her head as they walked to get something to eat through sparse snowflakes on chilled air. A large flake of snow fell on Lettie's black coat sleeve, and she stared at its mysterious hexagons before they melted clean away. It was not quite cold enough for snow to stick to the ground, but cold enough that she balled her icy hands in her coat pockets and wished for gloves.

Coney Island Hot Weiners was an old-time establishment in Tulsa's arts district, sitting in a pretty red-brick building alongside a Caribbean restaurant. A brightly painted fire truck was parked in front of an equally bright sign reading Coney Island, Established 1926. Inside, the fast-food joint was busy with firemen, office workers, and a few cops drawn to the deliciousness of hot dogs on steamed buns and covered in chili and melted cheddar cheese.

After placing their orders and finding a table by the window, Old Spice said, "Must have been tough for you going through that today, Lettie."

"I did okay," she said and spent a few moments showing

Old Spice and Loris photos of little Amaryllis Lily. They made all the right comments, and Lettie liked seeing how even these tough-skinned law enforcement types got all mushy about a baby. "Some newborns are ugly, they say, but I think she's just beautiful," she said.

"Nothing sweeter than a baby girl," Old Spice said. He played with his phone case on the table for a moment in a way that made him seem expectant, like he wanted to show her photos. She remembered him talking about an adult son who lived in California now, making video games. She wondered if Old Spice was a grandpa yet but didn't want to pry. Luckily Loris stepped into the conversation with a big smile.

"I know you're itching to show some grandbaby photos," Loris said. "You waiting for an engraved invitation?"

"Since you asked," Old Spice said, picking up the phone tenderly as though it was the baby itself. He held up the phone, its lock screen showing a photo of a six-month-old baby, all soft corners and pink ruffles and bright blue eyes.

Then the little girl's photo vanished suddenly, and the trill of his phone's ring startled them all. A name came up on the screen Lettie didn't recognize, but whoever it was, Old Spice deemed it important enough to take the call. He stepped outside for privacy and the three of them took the interruption as an opportunity to dive into the food.

Lettie bit into the soft, steamed bread, through the dark peppery spark of the chili to the salty, rubbery texture of the hot dog. Delicious. Her mother had often taken her and Zane to the Coney-I-Lander on Admiral. It was a different restaurant, owned by different people, but the same tastes, the same junk-food lusciousness.

The Coney-I-Lander on Admiral had an enormous chalkboard with a word jumble on it they would try to work out as they ate. The answer would always be quotes like "A stitch in time saves nine" or "Look before, or you'll find yourself behind." This Coney Island store had black-and-white photos on its walls instead, showing its old location and the founder. She missed the jumble and the nice memories of her mother helping her work out the words but the coneys were definitely just as good.

Old Spice flung the door open wide, walking purposefully through the three office workers chit-chatting in a loose circle by the door. Something had changed in his demeanor. Lettie could sense the energy crackling off him and if that wasn't enough, his face pulled into hard lines of exasperation.

"There's been a development with Clyde you need to know about," he said. "He escaped custody on his way back to prison."

Lettie forced herself to swallow the mouthful of hot dog even though her throat constricted as though hands grasped her neck.

"What do you mean?" Zane said. It was a nonsense question. Lettie knew he really meant "how did this happen" or "tell me this isn't true" because those were the thoughts circling her own mind. She scanned the room for threats, as though Clyde would somehow know where they were and make a beeline directly there.

"It happened on the transport back. Apparently, he had help from a corrections officer named Berry Gathright. She and Clyde handcuffed the officer into the backseat of the transport car and took off in another car parked in front of the Target at the Tulsa Hills Shopping Center."

"They what?" Lettie said. It was beyond belief.

"Gathright told her partner she had urgent diarrhea and demanded they stop at the mall so she could use the facilities. The other officer was a rookie with not much experience. They overtook him easily. It looks like they had this all planned out.

There may be some kind of romantic relationship between this Berry Gathright and Clyde."

"What on earth do these women see in him?" Zane said.

"They're crazy," Lettie replied. "And now is when we run. That's what we should have done from the start."

"Calm down. Let's think."

Loris slid an arm around Lettie and squeezed her shoulders. "Running just postpones problems."

"I've got a baby to think about," Lettie snapped back.

"Tulsa PD is going to protect you all," Old Spice said. "They're sending a car over to the Majestic Trailer Park now. And obviously, everyone's on alert, looking for these two. Usually, fugitives like this are caught quickly."

Lettie stood up and threw the remaining uneaten coney in the trash. Her appetite was destroyed. "I've got to get home to Milly."

The ten of swords card imagery came into her head again: the man on the ground, blood draining out, swords upright in his back, black sky above him. A small glimmer of dawn glowed in the corner of the card, a reminder that there was always a silver lining. Endings bring new beginnings.

But the only ending Lettie imagined was a brutal one, a final conflict between her and Zane and Clyde that ended with someone dead. She wanted to kill Clyde, the lowlife asshole. She felt empty and bereft, wanting to scream and shake Old Spice and Loris and Zane and demand they explain to her why this was happening to them. To her. Again.

How could she not have realized all the bad things would come back to haunt her? How had she been so silly to think that they could put their past behind them and create a beautiful world for Milly? Her eyes filled with tears and she let them flow freely. Zane stood behind her, rubbing her shoulders.

"One moment at a time," he whispered, some of that Alcoholics Anonymous cliché shit he loved so much. "Take a deep breath, count to three, then let it go."

She tried to fill her lungs but the sob in her throat caught the air instead. All she wanted to do was go home and hold Milly in her arms so that nothing could happen to her until this man was back in prison.

Chapter 19
Zane

Devil Inside

That afternoon, Zane sat on the bottom step of the mobile home's entry, Ballpoint's jaw resting on his knee, puffs of warm air appearing and dissolving from both of their mouths. He struggled to find his peace in the scant nature of the Majestic Mobile Home and RV Park. The shimmering of thin wind in the trees, a small brown bird looking for worms in the cold earth, shadows of huge clouds shifting above. A lone car drove by, leaving the smell of fuel in its wake. Inside the Tulsa Police patrol car parked near their home, two officers sat quietly talking, glancing up at Zane periodically.

He still reeled from the news of Clyde's escape and tried to remember as many details as he could about the man and the corrections officers with him when he came into the courthouse. The more he thought about it the more astonishing it became. Two women likely vying for the love and affection of this former methamphetamine addict and violent, unpredictable man. He tried to picture the officer who walked in with Clyde but only got a hazy image of a figure in a uniform. Had Donna noticed anything amiss? A particular connection between this Berry Gathright and Clyde? He had been so caught up in his own emotions he had failed to be as observant as he could have been. His instructors at the academy would be disappointed.

No doubt the situation had changed for Donna. If the rumors of romantic feelings between Clyde and Berry were true, then had Clyde ended his love-after-lockup relationship? Donna didn't seem like a woman who would fade into the background without a fight. She had already taken so many steps to show her loyalty to him. She seemed completely committed to the relationship. Zane got the impression that she would do anything to be with him. He didn't have enough data to know how Clyde felt about her. How had he acted when he saw her at the hearing? Surely Clyde had acknowledged her presence there, but Zane couldn't recall the moment. He remembered assuming that Clyde's civilian clothing had been brought to him by Donna, but now he realized that it could have just as well been his attorney who brought them in.

Clyde had charmed two women into helping him. Zane suspected that Clyde had already worked out some kind of plan to keep both women on his side. After all, he had gotten a corrections officer to throw her entire career away to help him.

She was also the wildcard that could make his run successful. What Old Spice said back at the hot dog joint about fugitives being caught quickly was true, because usually these guys making a break on a transport only had a plan to get free. They didn't often think beyond that moment of escape and they often didn't have money, a change of clothes, or a car to help them make a getaway. Berry had made all that possible. Kristy Diguchi from KTUL-TV had been texting him nonstop, asking for an interview and dropping a few facts she found out. According to her, Berry had sold her house recently, probably to raise money for this excursion.

What did Clyde have planned next? A run for Mexico or somewhere in Central America? Did he envision a life on the run as a fugitive? Or did he have unfinished business with Zane he wanted to conduct? The escape just didn't square right with what Kristy Diguchi had said about Clyde's change of heart. Obviously, his getting sober and finding God had been a scam. Was he truly willing to risk more jail time for this escape? What made it worthwhile?

It boggled Zane's mind. And it brought up the obvious question about what to do while they waited to see Clyde's plan unfurl. Take it one day at a time, as the alcoholics said. Ernest and Loris and Old Spice had said that more than once to him. Do the next thing. Don't live too much in the future.

Sounded simple when they said it.

An hour later, Zane knocked on Leon's door. A television inside the mobile home blared the news of Clyde's escape. The cable news channels were carrying the story now and its potential for an interstate chase.

Leon opened the door and gave Zane one of those half-smiles, half-grimaces. Kind of a "nice to see you but this news is terrible" smile. "How are you doing?"

"Getting along," Zane replied. "I've got a favor to ask."

"Anything." The older man was already nodding his head and leaning forward before Zane made the ask. Zane attributed his eagerness to his interest in Verda.

"I need to get out of here for a bit but I'm worried about

leaving, even with the police here." Zane jerked his thumb toward the parked patrol car.

"You want me to keep an eye out?"

"Actually, I was hoping you could go over there and stay until I get back. Angel and Lettie are busy with the baby, and I would feel better if Verda had someone else there."

Leon's eyes lit up at the mention of Verda's name and Zane found himself thankful for it. His grandmother deserved a second chance at love and Leon seemed authentically smitten.

"Of course. Did Verda ask you to get me?"

"All my idea but she won't hate it." Zane laughed and threw his hands up.

The older man looked confused for a moment.

"She'll be happy to have you there," Zane clarified.

"Good, good. You know, you are something special, Zane."

"What makes you say that?"

"You've faced a lot of adversity for a young man but not crumpled or hardened and become violent. It is not an easy thing to do. I haven't met many people like you, here or in Ecuador. I admire your courage and the way you remain dutiful to your family."

"Thank you. It doesn't feel like I have a choice." There was an edge to Zane's laugh. He didn't know how much Leon knew about his background but assumed Verda had given him the full picture. "You just walk through your life and take it as it comes."

"Not everyone does that. Some people run, some people give up, some people drown it in drugs and drink."

Zane laughed again but even the mention of alcohol made him thirst for its warm feeling down his throat, the slide into oblivion. He never really lost the taste for it.

"I've done all those things."

With a wave of his hand, Leon picked up his keys from a

table by the door. "Enough from me already. You have something you need to do, and I am keeping you."

"No big deal. It's like you said. I just believe in moving on and moving forward."

Zane took a step backward to leave as Leon leaned forward to tap his arm lightly. "You can count on me. That's all I'm going to say." Zane could feel Leon's deep emotion shooting out of his pores and the way he shifted his gaze to some distant point as though not wishing to embarrass Zane with its intensity.

Zane lied to himself that he was driving aimlessly around Tulsa trying to clear his head. But the reality was that he was headed straight for Donna Lancaster's house. Even though it was a terrible idea. Even though he had no plan what to do once he got there.

Afternoon traffic was light on 31st Street and it was a lovely winter day, with no clouds and a slight breeze that had chased yesterday's storm clouds away. He stopped at the QuikTrip for a slushie but changed his mind once inside for something called an "infusion" that was made of Red Bull energy drink and passion fruit, pomegranate, and ginger syrup. He liked it and the unfamiliar flavors zinged a mix of sweet-tart-burn. It was good to try new things.

He turned onto Donna's block of reddish-brown brick houses, teeth gnawing at the thick plastic straw of the infusion. A black-and-white patrol car was parked alongside the curb of Donna's home, and she stood on the dead grass about a foot away from it, leaning forward, her mouth moving and her hand gesturing wildly beneath the loose fur-fringed sleeves of a too-big green puffer jacket.

Zane muted the radio's car warranty commercial and cranked the window down to hear what she was saying.

"He's not stupid, you know!" Donna held up a shaking hand. "Like he is going to come here with this old lady who helped him escape and we're all going to live together like some big happy family."

She stared intently into the patrol car window. The officers must have been trying to reason with her, but Zane couldn't make out the words. He knew they were going to try to de-escalate the situation: "just doing our job" etc. etc. The things the police academy teaches you to say in order to keep conversations calm. A lot of people didn't understand how much effort that took, keeping your emotions in check.

"You'd think I would know about the plan because I'm his fiancée but you got that wrong," she said. "He shows up here with her and he's dead to me."

Zane had let the car roll to a stop about five feet away from where she stood. He wanted her to see him even though he knew that was the opposite of de-escalation. She looked right at him, pointed, and shouted, "Oh this is rich!"

The two front doors of the patrol car opened in unison, and out came two officers in stiff midnight blue uniforms, the kind he had hoped to be wearing one day. Before all this.

"Do you know who that is? Zane Clearwater. Meth-dealing police cadet and the false accuser of my fiancée."

Now it was Zane's turn to try to control his emotions but all he wanted to do was wrap his hands around her neck and squeeze until she shut up. Not good. Calm down, he told himself. Breathe. You wanted to come here for something. What do you want out of this situation?

"Can we help you with something?" the blonde woman officer said, with that polished veneer of unblinking courtesy he had been trying to master at the police academy.

"He came by to threaten me before," Donna said. Spit flew out of her mouth as she spoke and Zane could see her eyes were puffy and red like she had been crying.

"What did you come here for?" The other officer stepped closer to Zane. He was short and bulge-bellied. Short black hair framed his face, which was full of wariness.

"I came by to talk to her," he said, pointing at Donna who stood in place, gaping at the three of them.

"I know who you are," the black-haired officer said. "I've got a lot of sympathy for you. But I think you need to move along. Nothing good is going to come out of a conversation with her. Trust me."

"I just—" Words failed him. He didn't have a plan or a reason to be there, other than that action felt better than inaction. But faced with the two officers and Donna, the adrenaline drained away, leaving him deflated. Fear and worry weren't just mental. These emotions brought a sense of physical weakness with them. And an understanding that he was trapped and helpless and in danger, waiting for Clyde to show up.

"There's a lot of evidence that Clyde and the corrections officer he escaped with had some kind of special relationship," the officer said quietly. "She sold her house recently and cashed out her retirement savings. We're pretty sure they have resources to make a decent run. But we will find them. We always do."

"Hopefully before anything happens to my family."

"I understand. I do. But I think those two are more concerned with staying under the radar than trying to seek revenge. They're probably halfway to Florida or something by now."

Zane hoped it was true, but his gut told him not to get too comfortable with that story. Clyde had proven to be resilient and unpredictable and that made Zane very afraid. He thanked the officers for their time and u-turned the car, returning Donna's middle finger salute to him with a regular wave.

Trembling and a bit breathless, Zane turned the wrong way on 31st Street. He kept driving, to calm himself, and twenty minutes later ended up at the road's end in northern Broken Arrow, beyond the eastern edge of Tulsa. Prairie and pasture dotted with the occasional gas station or convenience store. Not a person in sight.

The phone rang and he slowed the car to a stop along the gravelly side of the road. It was Tiffany. Her smiling face filled his phone screen as he swiped to answer the call.

"I hate to bother you..." she said. He wanted to tell her she was never a bother, but she rushed into a long monologue: flat tire, stuck at bank, needed to get back to the store, didn't have AAA because she'd been cutting back expenses.

"I'll be there in twenty minutes," he said. The opportunity to be useful and help Tiffany lifted his spirits a bit.

He took the Creek Turnpike rather than the back roads to speed his way back in town and arrived at the bank where Tiffany waited next to her car with its deflated front left tire.

He popped out of the car and into her open arms. "We'll get you fixed up," he said into her hair.

"I was in there meeting with the bank manager about the loan and I came out and saw this." She gestured to the deflated tire. "Wouldn't Lettie think it was an omen?"

The way things were going lately with Clyde and Donna and Berry, Zane was more inclined to suspect foul play, but it was a trumped-up fear. The odds that Clyde and his women had given Tiffany a flat tire as part of some grand scheme was ridiculous. Still, he scanned the parking lot for threats but only saw a mustached man walking toward the bank ATM machine, minding his own business.

"Maybe the omen is that when you need help, you get help," Zane said. "Why do people always want to make omens evil?"

"I don't know. Maybe from my years of experience listening to my stepmom give me tarot card readings that always seemed to have a moral about not drinking or doing drugs?"

Zane gave a quick laugh. "Maybe my mom should have tried that. Did it work?"

"What do you think?" Tiffany laughed too, cutting the tension like wind through smog.

He took the jack and spare tire out of Tiffany's car trunk and got to work. He was glad for the chance to do something physical, to burn off some nervous energy, turning lugs. He shouldn't have had that Red Bull infusion drink. It had made him jittery.

"I'm glad you came," she said. "I wasn't sure I should ask you. Like you might want to stay close to home."

Zane carefully placed the first lug nut into the overturned hubcap. He'd once had one roll away never to be found.

"I had to get out," he said. "Plus, the police are there watching."

"So, what was she like? This corrections officer who helped Clyde escape?"

"I didn't take notice of her too much in the courtroom," Zane said. "I couldn't have even told you her hair color until they described it on the news. But listen, I don't want to talk about that. Tell me about the bank meeting. How did it go?"

"The bank loan officer was nice enough, but I got the sense she didn't think much of my background or my business plan. I'd say she thought I came to the bank straight from the delusional Generation Z clubhouse."

"Did she turn you down?"

"No, not straight out. She said she'd look at the files, talk to her manager. She did say the store looked like a good opportunity. That was the positive news."

A smile touched Zane's lips. "That's good," he said. "When did she say you'd hear back?"

"A day or two," Tiffany said.

He looked up at her, winter sun painting her hair a dozen shades of brown. "I'm really proud of you for trying this. And let's think positive thoughts. Manifest the good outcomes, as Lettie would say."

"It's just—" Tiffany stopped talking and cleared her throat as if something were caught in it.

"You okay?"

"Fine." She coughed into her hand. "There was something about the bank officer. She just seemed to be looking right past me. Like she didn't think I could do it. Like she wanted to get on with the next to-do item on her list rather than talk to me."

"There's other banks you can try," Zane said. "This town's full of them."

"I'm just tired of people not seeing me. Do you know what I mean?"

Zane definitely knew what she meant. It summed up how he felt too. People had underestimated him pretty much his entire life. Others looked right past him like he didn't matter, because he didn't have money, had been in juvie, or because he lived in a trailer park. Or lately, because his life had been so profoundly altered by terrible family violence. The bad things stuck to him like a film. Either they didn't want to see him because they thought they were better than him, or because they were afraid of associating with someone like him, someone with such bad luck. From a bad bloodline. Some people probably thought he got what he deserved. But those people didn't know him.

Zane reached out to squeeze her hand. "Of course, I know what you mean. But I see you. You see me. We have each other. Let the rest of the world and their judgments fade away."

Tiffany's brown eyes transformed from the color of hot chocolate to the starched brown of his musty-smelling juvenile hall uniform. That day his mother dropped him off at the Tulsa County Family Center for Juvenile Justice's detention facility and shoved him into a dank cell with a creaking cot and caged windows was the day he realized that pretty much everyone—including his mom—had given up on him. And that it was up to him to decide what to do with this shitty hand he had been dealt.

He served his time, getting sober and earning his GED, each day trying to harness the anger he had at the world into something positive. Some days were better than others.

As Tiffany smiled at him, he glanced back at the tire, not wanting her to see his pain. He was doing everything he could to overcome it.

Her warm voice was comforting. "We have each other," she repeated. She bent her head to touch her lips to his. He tasted the cinnamon sweetness of her lip gloss, smelled a hint of jasmine from her skin as his lips slid across her cheek to nibble her earlobe. He couldn't help himself, despite chilly weather and the afternoon sliding by. He longed to lose himself in her touch. But Tiffany had more self-control than he did, pulling away, murmuring something about the time and how cold it was.

Her reminder crushed the moment, restoring reality to his mind's forefront. A few seconds of blissful relief and then back to the grind. He unscrewed the last bolt with a ferocity that might have stripped the threads had he not stopped himself short.

Tiffany's phone notification jangled. She scanned the bright screen. "Boss man wants to know how the bank thing went," she said. "Should I type the word FAIL?"

"You don't know that yet," Zane said. Then both of their phones went off with the cranky, loud buzz of a government emergency text alert.

"Please shelter in place fugitive at large. 20 white male with 57 white woman. Last seen in red Ford Explorer. Please call 911 may be armed."

Chapter 20
Lettie

Close to Home

The text alert about the fugitive woke up Milly and interrupted one of Lettie and Angel's rare arguments. And it gave her some new ammunition in her arsenal against Angel's desire to leave their home to meet with someone about a Twitch sponsorship deal.

"Look at this, Angel. It's serious. And don't you think it's suspicious that this woman got in touch with you today, out of the blue, to talk about sponsorship? And that she's here in Tulsa?"

"It's not entirely out of the blue, Lettie. She's messaged me before. And of course she's in Tulsa. There are video game companies here. They're not all in California. Ever heard of Atomic Video Games? They make historical games."

"So why does it have to be today? Why not tomorrow or next

week? When this is over?" Lettie bent over the baby's cradle, checking the diaper with a deft, quick stroke. It was still clean. Milly's little pink tongue bulged from her mouth like she hadn't grown into it yet. The girl had her eyes and Angel's round face, and the curve of her lips reminded Lettie of her mother's smile.

"She's only here through tomorrow. And Zane left. Why can't I? You heard what Zane said. It's most likely Clyde and that woman made a run to get out of Tulsa. They're not going to stick around here."

"You don't know how strong Clyde's desire for revenge is," she said. "How can you be sure this video game woman is not that Donna Lancaster with a new angle?" She straightened up from the crib, weariness and dread settling into every bone. "You should stay here with us."

In the silence that followed, a lone siren sounded, seeming to grow louder as if it were coming toward them. Then it turned away. Still, the siren wailed, thin and eerie in its isolation. Lettie walked to the window to peak through the blinds at the patrol car sitting out front to see if it was still there. It was. Inside their bedroom, there was only the sound of their breathing and the low voices of Verda and Leon in the living room.

Angel turned his eyes to the phone and started swiping. "It's the first real money-making opportunity that's come my way, and we really need the cash," he said. "I got excited. I want to provide for our family. Not just be a drain."

Looking into his hopeful face, brown eyes rounded and glowing like polished wood, Lettie understood she was letting fear drive her decision-making. Angel had a point: Zane had left for a bit to drive around. The police were sitting outside the mobile home. Verda and Leon were here. Angel was trusting but he also had a good spidey-sense for people. If he thought the woman and the offer to meet was straight-up, then it likely was. What was the risk in letting him go?

She gave in. "Let me just do some quick internet research on her. It will make me feel better. Can I see the messages?"

Ten minutes later, Lettie had grown more comfortable with the invitation. The woman, Simsie Carver, had a LinkedIn profile that backed up her claims to be doing sponsorship development for a big video game distributor, and her Twitch profile predated the trouble with stalker-creep PeturbabeArgue also known as Donna Lancaster. Indeed, this Simsie had contacted Angel a few months ago, asking him if he was open to doing sponsored content. Though the timing was odd, it seemed legit, and she knew how much Angel wanted this kind of deal. To be honest, they needed the money desperately with Zane on suspension. Verda's Social Security checks were all that stood between them and poverty.

Lettie went into the living room to tell her grandmother the plan.

"I'll drive Angel to the meeting," Verda said as if she had been wanting to get out of the mobile home for a spell too. "Leon, would you stay here with Lettie? Just til Zane gets back?" Her hands went to her hair, soft gray waves loose around her face. "I need to put on some lipstick if we're going someplace lively like the Blue Dome District. I don't want all these young hip folk thinking I'm washed out."

"You look beautiful just the way you are," Leon said.

"We're meeting her at the Dilly Diner," Angel said. "It's pretty casual."

"Still, let me just freshen up," Verda said, disappearing into the bathroom.

.   .   .

Verda and Angel left the mobile home in a mist of baby-powder perfume and hairspray. On cue, Milly began to hiccup, a sweet rhythmic sound. Lettie and Leon watched her face for a few moments. "She's just beautiful," he said. "I have a daughter too. She lives in Hot Springs, Arkansas."

Standing in the living room holding the baby, Lettie realized she didn't know much about Leon. It felt strange and awkward to be left alone with him, but she reassured herself that the police were right outside. As Milly continued to hiccup, she walked over to the window to peek out once again at the patrol car outside. A light dusting of snow fell from the sky and melted immediately on the warm hood of the police vehicle.

"How often do you see her?"

Leon exhaled a long breath. "Not much," he said. "We're not close anymore."

"That's too bad." No matter what, she thought, she would make sure that Milly and Angel were as close as a father and daughter could be.

"Your father's still in McAlester prison, right?"

The question startled her, but she nodded.

"I don't mean to speak out of turn," Leon said, his phrasing reminding her of a dusty, overly genteel aristocrat in a black-and-white movie. "Your grandmother mentioned that you grew up visiting him there. I wish my daughter's mother had done as much for me."

"You were locked up?" Without intending to, she tightened her grip on Milly's tiny form and kissed her on top of the head protectively. "I didn't know that."

"For a short time," he said. "It's no secret. Just not something I'm proud of."

The question of his crime burned on Lettie's tongue, but she knew that inquiry wasn't often a welcome one. That's one thing you learned early on when your dad was incarcerated and your brother was in juvie. People always wanted to know *what did they do? Did they kill someone? Steal something?* The question asked breathlessly, their facial expressions expectant, sometimes contemptuous. As though her father and her brother should only be defined by the worst mistakes they made. Like all they were was their criminal record. She hated it.

There were 38,000 people imprisoned in Oklahoma. Most were for drug use or sales, theft, non-violent crimes, like her father. She had looked it up once, trying to understand why none of her friends had family members locked up. She'd seen that Oklahoma had the highest incarceration rate in the United States, twice that of similar-sized states like Connecticut and Oregon. For every 100,000 people, 639 were in jail or prison. She remembered being in middle school and calculating the numbers. With 650 kids in her school, the statistics showed that probably only four kids in her school also had someone in their family behind bars. She never found them. They probably kept it quiet like she tried to, but she wished kids and the teachers had been more understanding. It wasn't her fault, but some of them treated her like a dirty bandage on their shoe.

Lettie decided not to pry any further into Leon's past, at least not in this conversation. She couldn't promise that she wouldn't Internet snoop though. You couldn't be too careful, and they didn't really know Leon that well, after all. He was relatively new to the Majestic, moving into the lot across the road from them.

"I should turn on Angel's livestream," she said. "I'm going to try to put Milly back down for a little lie-down."

"I'll be right out here," Leon said, gesturing to the couch. He grabbed the remote and flipped the channel to Fox News. His phone chimed and he answered the call with a simple hello, his back to Lettie.

She lingered near the dining room table, fussing with Milly's swaddle as a ruse while nosily trying to overhear part of Leon's conversation. But whoever the caller was, they were doing all the talking. Leon just said "uh-huh" and "yeah" a few times.

She was just about to turn away to set Milly down and get the livestream going when she heard him say, "Yes, I can do that. I understand. Everything is going to be all right." His voice was soft, and it sounded to Lettie like he was talking to a woman. Three questions jumped into her mind. First, was he seeing other women besides Verda? Did Verda know? Or was there a simpler explanation, like another daughter or family member besides the daughter he said he wasn't in contact with. Something about his tone gave her an odd feeling, like something was off.

She continued to pick at the swaddle, and even Milly seemed to be giving her a look like the ruse wasn't working anymore and she'd better move on. Luckily Leon never turned back around and instead settled deeper into the couch to watch television.

Angel was live on Twitch already, the camera lens pointed straight up his nostrils as he got out of Verda's Cadillac, his face framed by dirty grey clouds. She really needed to talk to him about using better camera angles. Sometimes he just didn't pay attention.

"The Blue Dome District in Tulsa gets its name from this iconic building from the 1920s. It used to be a gas station if you can believe it. Over the years, this area has transformed into Tulsa's place to go for nightlife, with restaurants and bars and music venues," Angel said, adopting his best tour guide voice. She was always amazed at the trivial knowledge he had packed away in that head of his.

He panned the camera slowly to show the brick building

topped with a robin's-egg blue dome topped with an ornate finial pointing to the low bank of storm clouds in the sky. The street was empty, dotted with just a few cars.

Angel turned the camera back to Verda, who smiled and blushed and lowered her face, trying to wave the camera away.

"I don't want to be livestreamed," she said with a laugh.

"That's my grandma," Angel said.

Verda stood in front of a red Ford Explorer, holding her purse expectantly. "I don't know what I'm supposed to say on these things," she said.

The emergency alert text had said something about a red Ford explorer.

Lettie dropped out of the livestream, her stomach dropping to her feet. She pulled up the text alert and read it slowly.

"Please shelter in place fugitive at large. 20 white male with 57 white woman. Last seen in red Ford Explorer. Please call 911 may be armed."

Her hands trembled uncontrollably as she tried to swipe back into the livestream stupidly then realized that calling Angel would be more direct. He picked up on the second ring.

"Get out of there now. I'm calling the police."

"What's going on? Slow down."

"Get out of there now, Angel. The red Ford Explorer. Right there. Parked on the street. That's the same kind of car that Clyde and that woman were seen in. Get out of there."

Chapter 21
Zane

Coming Clean

"The alert doesn't have a license plate number," Lettie said into the phone as Zane walked through the front door. She hung up the call and came to him to give him a quick squeeze.

"Zane, thank God you're home. Angel and Verda went off to meet this video game developer, and there's a red Ford Explorer there. Just like in the goddamn fucking alert." She slammed the front door shut behind him and the photo frames on the wall trembled from the impact. On the couch, Leon held Milly and they both swiveled wide eyes toward him as Zane tossed his keys on the kitchen table.

Lettie's rage was a surprise to Zane. Although he knew the situation with Clyde had her on edge, he had never seen this kind of bone-shaking, immersive anger pouring out of her as if a tremendous inner pressure forced it out of her against her will.

Most of the time, Lettie took refuge in her cool world of numbers and logic and computer code, pretending the world could not touch her. He wondered if motherhood had awakened a mama bear instinct that was more comfortable with these big emotions.

But when he heard the story of Angel and Verda's excursion to meet with some Internet rando who said she was a video game developer, he felt angry too. It defied logic and smacked of wishful thinking and faulty judgment. He was surprised Lettie let it happen. Maybe she was too. Maybe her foolishness formed part of this monster anger inside her.

He wanted to act. He wanted to find Clyde and end this, one way or another.

His agitation shifted from protection of his family to a direct confrontation. He was acutely aware that his violent tendencies, the ones he knew he inherited from his father, were emerging. His emotional state made it intolerable to stay in this house and wait. He could not—must not, would not, dare not—allow Clyde to remain a threat to this family. If any of them were to be hurt or die, a part of him would die too, and there would be more burned-out trailers within him that could never again be entered.

Preventative measures must be taken, and not the kind that involved shooting guns or alligator traps. The whole mess of preparation that Loris had helped them undertake seemed like kids' play now. The theatre of home security, making himself feel better through actions that ultimately wouldn't get the job done. Because the only thing that mattered was taking out the threat.

Perhaps Lettie was instinctively aware of Zane's mindset shift, or maybe she just knew him well enough to read his body language and see his muscles and veins straining against the skin, ready to act. Ready to do damage. His worst traits were alive and hungry.

Lettie stared at him expectantly. "Are you going to go over there?"

"Did you call the police already?"

She nodded.

Almost every impulse he had—all the violent ones anyway—screamed at him to get in the car and drive over to the Blue Dome District. But a smaller voice kept whispering not to leave Lettie and Milly unprotected here. The situation was a mess. Clyde on the loose and the people he cared the most about in the world scattered all over Tulsa. Tiffany at the Cell-Phone-Fixit store. Verda and Angel en route home. Lettie and Milly here at the Majestic.

Lettie frowned and her brown eyes darkened with worry, as though she read his mind. She came close to him, touching his arm and then wrapping her arms around him. Zane was so tightly wound he didn't think to hug her back for a few beats until she squeezed him tight. It was as if she thought physical contact would hold him here in their home rather than embarking on some suicide mission trying to find Clyde.

Leon fidgeted on the couch then stood up and started pacing. "The logical thing to do is let the police handle it," he said. "You've got this baby to take care of."

There was a flip side to that argument. Zane knew it and he was pretty sure Lettie and Leon knew it too. "First mover has the advantage," Zane said.

"Right. There's that saying that you should let your enemy move first in battle." Leon said.

"Isn't that from an episode of *Survivor*?" Lettie had been a huge fan of the reality television show for years. She pulled out of their embrace and turned to face Leon, eyes narrowed.

"I don't know. I think it's a martial arts idea. Like the idea of *Aikido*—using the opponent's movement against them. When someone is attacking you, they expect you to resist. When you step back from the fight, you change the rules of the game."

Hot air from the mobile home furnace started blowing through the living room vents with a soft hiss-like breath expelled through clenched teeth.

Outside, a stronger wind moved through the trees like a shudder, stirring a modest flurry of snowflakes the size of dimes. Zane saw through the window that the two officers had gotten out of the car and stood near its trunk, looking down the road that wound through the Majestic. Verda's lemon-yellow Cadillac bumped down the thoroughfare and into the parking spot next to Zane's car. Her car seemed bright as the sun, making Zane think of those baby chicks that, because of their bright yellow fluff, attract birds of prey like owls and hawks and are eaten in a cloud of feathers. The Caddy suddenly seemed like a symbol of their naivete, bad luck, and vulnerability.

Angel and Verda looked unharmed but shaken as they got out of the car. They exchanged a few words with the police officers that Zane couldn't hear and came into the mobile home. A few snowflakes clung to their coats like tiny treasures.

Angel flung his coat off and tossed it onto one of the kitchen table chairs. His usual affable demeanor had gone cold and distant. He stood with his hands on his hips, a scowl on his face, eyes narrowed, face defiant but resigned. Zane had never seen the easygoing young man angry before. Did he not see the danger all around him? Was he truly miffed at missing some meeting that might have even been a set-up from Donna Lancaster? Zane had no patience for his attitude and looked away.

Verda's mood was radically different, the strain on her face vanishing into a wide smile and warm eyes at the sight of Leon standing in the living room. She went around the room, hugging Lettie, kissing Milly, hugging Zane, and saving an embrace for Leon last. Zane noticed that she leaned into him as if drawing strength from his form.

"No one followed us or anything," she said. "I looked in the rearview mirror constantly. I've never been so terrified."

Milly let out a coo and what sounded like a tiny baby laugh, and some of the tension went out of the room as Angel bent over his tiny daughter in the bassinet. "You got something to say, little one?"

"Now that you're all here," Leon said. "Why don't you have a seat? I have something I want to tell you."

Lettie wanted to tell him something. Zane could see it in her eyes, in the tremor that played around her mouth. He moved to her side, but she only said the word "later" under her breath and motioned to the armchair by the couch. Leon cleared his throat with a note of impatience.

As Zane perched on the edge of the chair, Leon removed a flask out of his jacket pocket and took a long pull. Zane could smell the whiskey from three feet away, an alcoholic's sixth sense or something.

Leon shuddered and said, "Before I moved across the way from you, I was in prison. Lettie, I already told you that, and Verda, I told you too but I left out some important parts. I should have been honest about that from the start."

Lettie pressed her hand into Zane's shoulder, an acknowledgment that this was the news she wanted to tell him.

"What are you saying, Leon?" Verda said, starting to get up in a stunned manner. "What did you leave out?"

With a gesture, Leon indicated she should remain where she was, and Verda sat back down. He said, "I wasn't in prison in Ecuador. I did my time here in Oklahoma. Ten months. But there's more I want to say."

The question "what did you do" burned hot on Zane's tongue and his heart was drumming.

Something felt off. For just a moment, Zane felt contempt emanate from Leon beneath his calm exterior. But it vanished as he held his hands out, palms up, in a forgiveness-seeking gesture.

Leon took another swig from the flask and then stared at it for a long moment, bleaker than he had ever seen him. When Verda started to get up again, he said, "No. Stay there. Don't come to me, Verda. I don't want you trying to comfort me. I've got to tell you something."

"All right. Go on."

"Can you understand what it is like to be locked up? The kinds of people in there, the ones with no hope of getting out? The psychological games, the physical violence."

Zane knew. He had spent his time in juvie carving out a reputation as a fighter.

"You make alliances to survive."

Zane came forward in his chair, breathless, electrified. "Which prison?"

"McAlester."

As Zane considered the news that Leon had been in the same prison as Lettie's father and as Clyde and Link Doom, he was temporarily speechless.

"Prison is a crowded place but like a small town. Everyone knows everyone's business. I know what you are thinking, and yes, I did know your papa Roy, Lettie. And Link and Clyde. Word had gotten around that Clyde had been working this guard, building up that bond with her, getting her sympathy. Link let it slip a few times that Clyde was working on an escape. They didn't make any secret of their desire to avenge their father's death, Zane."

Zane's muscles were tense, knotted, and he could not relax

them. As he listened, a fist of fear clutched his guts and squeezed.

That growing dread didn't come from hearing that Link and Clyde wanted to kill him. He knew that.

His inner alarm bells were clanging because Leon had concealed all this for months as he grew closer to Verda.

Why wouldn't he have revealed the connection immediately? He had the feeling when he heard the rest of Leon's story, he would find himself having to make some hard choices once again.

Still standing in front of the television, shoulders slumped, hands fidgeting, Leon said, "Lettie's father asked me to look out for you all. But we agreed I wouldn't tell you why I was here. He didn't want Lettie to be upset. We didn't actually think Clyde would escape. So few people do. It's the prisoner's fantasy, not a common thing."

Zane glanced at the door.

Had Verda and Angel locked it when they came in? He got up, went to the door, and slid the bolt latch in place.

He wanted the action to make him feel better. It did not.

"You should have told us, Leon," Verda said. Her voice was a low, serious rebuke, reminding Zane of his mother's voice when telling him he was in trouble. "It's not right with so much at stake."

"I wanted to tell you so many times," Leon said. "I never thought I would have anything like what we've found together, Verda. It's a miracle, how compatible we are. I felt like we were meant to be together and over time it just got harder and harder to figure out how to tell you about my past. About this arrangement with Roy to take care of Lettie."

Leon's eyes fixed on Verda's, a beseeching brown. Zane found it almost painful to watch. Either the guy was a good actor or he had deep feelings for his grandmother.

"I know. I feel it too," Verda said. "But you could have trusted me enough to tell me the truth."

Zane caught Lettie's eyes to find his skepticism mirrored back. He wasn't the only one with serious doubts in the room. He glanced over at Angel, who had settled into one of the kitchen table chairs. If Zane wasn't mistaken, a few tears had formed around the edges of Angel's eyes, as though he was deeply touched by Leon's story. Or still feeling sorry for himself about his thwarted meeting with the video game developer. Or terrified about what this new turn of events meant.

Leon frowned, looked away from Verda at some distant point, started to speak, hesitated again, said, "Mierda!" and then lowered himself onto the ottoman where Verda had thrown her purse. It slid off, falling to the floor, her keys and phone and a pack of tissue spilling out of it.

Startled, Verda leaned over to push the items back in, her eyes never leaving her boyfriend's face.

Leon took a deep breath. "I want you to hear me out, just listen and don't interrupt, don't stop me until I'm done. Try to understand. I took a step I thought was smart. I made connections with Clyde and Link too. I convinced them I was their friend. Or at least that my friendship—my alliance—could be had for a price. It was a calculated risk, and I approached them, told them that—"

"You what!" Zane trembled with rage.

"Don't interrupt!" Leon said sharply. "This is...this is hard...so let me get through it. I told Clyde that I understood what it was like to have your father killed, that my father had been murdered in a bombing in Ecuador, that I would do anything to make those responsible see justice. That in this awful way we had a connection, and I wanted to help him. I figured if he did actually make good on his escape, he would think he had a friend in me and I could act as a—what is the word?—double agent. Get information from him, protect you all."

"Have you been in touch with him since he escaped?" Zane's voice came out like a low, angry growl that made Ballpoint pick his head up and look.

"Not directly. But his girlfriend Donna has reached out. Asking whether the police were at the Majestic. I told her it was a heavy presence. That there were two cars here all the time. See, I wanted to keep you all safe."

"So did you know about the baby rattle?" Lettie's voice was barely audible. Her mood seemed to have swung to darkness and quiet despair. She sagged against Zane's shoulder, and he reached up to rub her back.

"Listen, maybe I should have told you all earlier. I didn't know what to do. Sometimes it takes a while to understand what the right thing to do is."

"Usually telling the truth is a good place to start," Lettie said.

Zane felt like he had turned to stone. Motionless as a statue, he sat in the chair, listening to his marble heart thump, a hard and cold and heavy sound. He didn't want to hear any more from Leon but he was compelled to listen, to see completely just how fooled he had been. How vulnerable they all were now. Life had taught him not to trust anyone, yet he had let this stranger into their home. Asked him to look after Lettie today while he confronted Donna. He was an idiot.

"Was today a set-up? Angel's voice from the kitchen table was thin and shrill, like a child's. "Was there really a video game developer wanting to meet with me?"

"I don't know," Leon said. "Donna didn't say anything about that to me. I mean, if I'd known it was a set-up, I wouldn't have let you go."

Angel sighed hard and loud, a karate chop of resentful breath.

"These are our lives you're playing with here, Leon," Verda said. She hid her face in her fingers as if she could retreat from Leon's terrible deceit.

Zane wanted to believe Leon's story but he knew that he needed more information to overcome his doubts. "Why would you do all this for Roy and us? What is he to you?"

As tears came to Leon's eyes, he said, "I have a daughter too, just like Roy. And just like you two, Angel and Lettie. A beautiful daughter named Ofelia. Bad people were after me. I have done many things I am not proud of. They took her, did awful things to her, all to keep me in line. Things haven't been right between us since. I suppose I thought I was helping her, in a way, by helping Roy's daughter stay safe. My penance."

"What exactly were you in the penitentiary for?" Verda's voice was ice cold now as though she was trying to freeze her feelings into submission.

"Burglary," Leon said. "I broke into an auto shop to get my car after a dispute over some repairs. Turned out the guy who owned it was a Tulsa police detective. His buddies made sure I got a felony conviction and real time. I served ten months of a two-year sentence there."

Zane felt the need to stick up for the police. "Committing a crime isn't a good way to solve disputes."

"I had a lot of time to think about and regret that decision," Leon said.

"I ought to turn you in to the police right now," Zane said. "Tell them you've been helping this criminal and his girlfriend."

"I don't recommend—"

Raising his voice, Zane said, "What is the difference between the behavior of a woman like Donna Lancaster or

Berry—whatever that guard's name is—and the way you've let Clyde think you're helping him?"

"I haven't helped him. I've done the opposite. I've misdirected."

At that awful moment, Zane's feelings were so complex, so confused, he experienced a fleeting death wish, so vivid and comforting that it made him want to weep. He had no idea how to feel, whom to believe, and most importantly, what to do next. He wanted to get up, unlock the door, burst out into the clean winter air, and run, just run and run, forever. But the heaviness of his feelings made it impossible to even move his feet.

After perhaps a minute during which no one could think of anything to say, Lettie finally broke the silence. "Where do we go from here?"

"Sometimes the only path forward is the path through," Leon said.

"More martial arts wisdom, sensei?" Lettie quipped.

Leon didn't bother to respond.

Zane's mind raced, weighing the possibilities. If Leon's story were to be taken at face value, then maybe there were some options. But if Leon were still lying, the consequences could be deadly.

In the police academy, they learned about body language and how to look for signs of dishonesty. Staring or looking away at crucial moments, grooming habits like playing with their hair or adjusting collars or sleeves, voice getting louder, someone saying "I want to be honest with you" were all mannerisms that could indicate someone was lying.

But Leon had been lying to them for months now, so what kind of baseline did Zane have for his truthful behavior? Not much. He wanted to get Loris's take on this, or Old Spice's but also felt ashamed to tell them he had been so simple-minded. What did that say about his skills in law enforcement?

"You don't understand yet." Leon cleared his throat. "I said Donna reached out. That day she left the baby rattle for you, she came to visit me. To let me know how easily she was able to track me down. I told her I had nothing to hide, so I wasn't worried about her finding me. But she made it clear that Clyde expected me to be loyal to him and not my bunkmate Roy. Not to get any ideas about backing out."

Leon was easily twice her weight and a head taller. Zane couldn't believe that the woman posed any kind of physical threat to Leon. But he supposed that messengers like her came with borrowed authority. You treated her with kid gloves because you knew Clyde was on the other side, working the puppet strings. Plus, Donna had an unpredictable streak, and not knowing what someone was going to do could be the most frightening thing of all.

"She's especially alert and clever," Leon said. "She told me she thought something was going sideways in my alliance with Clyde because she didn't see why I would move into the Majestic and get close to you all. I think she sensed that I was becoming close to Verda. She was not easily deceived. She kept pressing me."

It felt like Leon had circled a noose around them and was drawing it tighter with every word. Zane's instincts were to punch Leon in the mouth. Or Taser him. Then kick him. He reconsidered, thinking that Leon still had more to tell them, and it would be best to stay on his good side for a while. His earlier thought had been right. They should turn this guy into the police. But not quite yet. Zane wanted to learn exactly what he knew and what he said to Donna and Clyde.

"Zane, you know the same as I do that there is no honor in running. And often no success either."

Zane's eyebrows launched into orbit. "I don't need lessons about honor from a liar."

Leon didn't hesitate. "Are you ready to walk through fire to keep your family safe? To meet Clyde head-on and resolve this, once and for all?"

At Zane's silence, Leon added, "You know it is the only way."

Before Zane could say anything more, Lettie jumped up and walked so close to Leon that their noses almost touched. "You are talking about cold-blooded murder, aren't you?"

"I am not," Leon said, backing away from Lettie. "I am talking about getting Zane and Clyde together and we'll bring him back into custody. Zane as the bait."

"Clyde doesn't want to go back into custody," Lettie said. "So when it goes wrong and turns violent, then what? Then Zane has to kill him or be killed?"

"And who's to say we can trust you, Leon? After all this?" Verda's voice was melancholy and weary.

This went beyond crazy, it was insane. Yet Zane felt like he had to do it. He had no choice. Leon's words rang true. There may be no honor in running, but the kernel of truth was that running only kept you living in fear, waiting for the day you were found. Sometimes you had to walk through the fire, not around it.

"Okay," he said. "I'll do this. But you'll come clean to the police about your role in this. No bullshit."

Leon held up his left hand as though God were hovering near the ceiling fan. "I will."

"All right." Zane's misgivings ran deep. Very deep.

What was this man's word worth? Here was someone who admitted to being a liar and a thief, and worse, for acting as a double agent and concealing it from them for all this time. Weeks and weeks. Someone who saw the impact of the baby rattle and the indirect threats from Clyde on this family and said nothing. This was a man who was good at deceit, who admitted to extremely impulsive behavior like breaking into an auto shop. One with a bad past.

It added up to a dangerous and unpredictable combination.

But his own past bad behavior made Zane identify with him on a certain level. It gave him a morbid sense of understanding that would likely astound Lettie, Angel, and Verda. He didn't like it, but he couldn't ignore it. People get in bad situations and try to do the best they can. They made mistakes. They get in with the wrong people. They try to course-correct on shifting sands. Maybe Leon was trying to go beyond those mistakes.

"All right," Zane said again. "How does it go?"

As if the tense conversation had put him on edge, Ballpoint walked to the front door and whimpered as though he had to go out.

"I'll do it," Angel said, not making eye contact with anyone as he grabbed the leash and unlocked the door. The pit bull bounded out as though he was being sucked outside by a gravitational force and Angel padded behind him.

Leon watched them leave. "I know how to reach her, and she'll get the word to him."

Zane got what he meant. "You set up a meeting, pretend to be delivering me to him."

"No, Zane, that's insane. It makes no sense," Lettie said. "And what makes you think they don't want me too?"

Zane looked at her. "I think it's mainly me they have the beef with. I shot Jeremiah Doom. So, I have to do this."

Lettie flexed her jaw, hands on her hips, then turned on her heel as Milly let out a cry.

Zane focused on Leon. "By her, do you mean Donna or this guard who is with him now? Berry? Because if you mean Donna, I'm not sure she's in touch with him. I was just by her house, and she was acting madder than a wet hen about him being off with another woman."

"You went over to Donna's house?" Lettie was incredulous. "Zane, what were you thinking? I'm over here thinking Angel's being silly, now I think I ought to knock both your heads together."

"It might all be an act," Leon said. "That Donna's a crafty one."

"I have a friend I want to bring in on the planning," Zane said. "This woman Loris."

"Is she police? We can't have even the scent of police on this, or it won't work," Leon said. "What is most important is that we set up the meeting, get Clyde in position, and it's back to prison or Clyde can meet his maker."

Leon's offhand talk of killing, like it was nothing, bothered Zane. His inner voice roared at him, advising him: This guy was missing a few moral buttons. Did he have a sociopath gene connecting him more closely to Clyde and Link than he was willing to admit?

Zane had killed his father, without a choice and as a last desperate resort. And he'd wrestled with that decision every day since. His father's face, the circumstances, the doubt, could he have done anything differently? Could he have been smarter, faster?

"No killing. Not unless it's absolutely necessary."

"You know him, Zane. You think he is going to be taken alive?" Leon's gaze narrowed and he sized Zane up as if he were a silly child.

Maybe he was. "I have to try."

"Okay." Leon fished in his pocket for his phone and made the call. "Voicemail." He left a brief message and hung up. "Now we wait."

"No. Now we plan." Zane pulled out his own phone and

scrolled to find Loris's phone number. "We need to control this —where, when, everything."

"Okay, what are you thinking?"

Since accepting this wild plan, Zane had started mapping out different scenarios in his mind, contemplating possibilities and pondering countermoves. His brain circulated through the many things that could go wrong and what they could do to minimize the danger. He laid out for the group what he thought they should do.

Clyde would have to believe that Leon had lured or forced Zane to a site to meet with him. Clyde would be prepared to kill him. That much was clear. There's no way Clyde would have taken this stupid risk of escaping if he didn't have that kind of intent.

On the other hand, hurting or killing Zane only guaranteed him more prison time if he was caught. It wasn't the logical choice and could mean Clyde was operating on emotions and not clear thinking. He might be fool enough to believe Zane would walk right into a trap. Maybe they could use his emotional state to their advantage here. If Zane could harness his own emotions and act coolly and logically, maybe this would give him the edge he needed. Especially if he was going to keep his commitment to not getting anyone killed.

When he finished telling them the plan he'd come up with, Leon and Lettie nodded their approval. Verda said she wouldn't stand in their way but she didn't like it. Angel said he wanted to come along, but Zane shook his head. "Too danger-ous. I can't let you do that."

"Stay here with me and Milly," Lettie said. "We need you, Angel."

Zane used the time to call Loris. If there was anyone he wanted along with him for this ride, it was her. But he hesitated to think of meeting her disapproval of the plan. Would she tell her police friends about Leon's involvement and mess it up? It was a risk he was going to take in telling her.

Doubt gnawed at him as he told Loris what had happened. Was he doing the right thing? What would she say? It felt like hours thrummed by as he waited for her response.

"Let's get the asshole then," she said. "I'm in."

Leon's phone rang. He picked up the cell and showed them the display. A 539 area code. "Probably a burner phone," Leon said. He answered, mouthing Donna's name. He told her where and when they wanted to meet. Listening, he shook his head. Something felt off.

Zane whispered, "What is it?"

Leon shook his head again. Then he said, "All right." And hung up.

He looked around the room, his eyes finally resting on Zane. "We're on."

Chapter 22
Zane

Fear Factor

Donna said there was no way Clyde would meet them at Tulsa's popular Gathering Place as Zane had suggested.

"She said we meet them in an hour at the old Will Rogers Turnpike, in Catoosa, off Pine Street," Leon said.

Zane knew the place. An old stretch of the Interstate-44 crossing Spunky Creek that sat abandoned and desolate about eight miles outside Tulsa. The perfect site for a double-cross ambush and murder, he thought. Didn't the police find a dead body out there not too long ago?

Loris knocked on the front door of the mobile home so hard the walls shook. She had a blue duffle bag with her. "I've got some zip-tie handcuffs, lock picks, bolt cutters, duct tape, pepper spray, and other stuff in here. In the car, I've got two bulletproof vests and some rope," she said as though it were the most normal thing. She laid it gingerly on the floor, her crisp khaki pants and dark shirt crackling softly and whispering as she moved.

"I don't need one," Leon said.

"Wasn't going to give you one. I'm Loris. You must be Leon."

They sized one another up for a few beats, neither extending a hand to shake.

"Verda, Lettie, Angel, I want you all to go out to Uncle Brian and Aunt Tracy's house and stay there til we call you." Loris's low voice made Zane think of a female lion protecting her young. "I don't want you here like sitting ducks in case something goes wrong."

"The police are here," Lettie said.

"You can tell them where we're going," Verda said. "I think it's a good idea to get out of here."

"Me too." Zane wondered if Verda had told Leon about their trip out there to shoot guns. Did he know where the place was? There was no way to ask right now, but he carefully avoided saying anything to give away its general location.

"Call us as soon as it's over." Lettie's tone was pleading, and tears shimmered in her eyes.

Ballpoint suddenly rose and padded to a window. He put his forepaws up on the sill and pressed his black nose to the glass, staring out. Maybe he was only thinking of relieving himself. Or maybe something outside attracted his attention.

Zane squeezed his sister's shoulders and moved to the window to look out. The dog's alert state only served to remind him of the imminent danger they faced. Would they ever truly feel safe again?

Verda came to stand beside him, frowning, and her brown eyes darkened with worry. She hugged him tightly, hard enough that she seemed to be trying to stop time to prevent him from embarking upon this dangerous mission. Behind them Angel paced nervously, his head pulled down, shoulders hunched.

"You have a death wish, that's what this is," Angel said, reopening the debate. "If you go to some abandoned place, how do we know it's not some set-up and that Leon here is a double agent?"

Leon froze at the words, looking down, as Verda shifted and leaned ever so slightly into Zane. Angel didn't seem to notice and continued his monologue, a dark undercurrent ran through his words, a tugging heaviness.

"I've heard Lettie scream in her sleep from nightmares about what Clyde and Link did to her. These aren't normal people. What you're doing isn't normal." Angel worked his jaw as if the right words to persuade them were caught in the joints, but when at last he continued, he just repeated, "Death wish."

"We all have so much to live for," Verda said, gesturing toward Milly's bassinet.

"That's exactly why," Zane said. "And this isn't something we're going into carelessly. We're going to be careful."

Angel stared at them in frustration. His eyes clouded over, seemingly full of apocalyptic visions. "Why? Why did this happen? Why do we have to do this?"

Lettie went to his side to take his hand. "You have to have hope and determination to get through this life. It is the one thing my experiences with these brothers taught me. No one can take hope and determination away from you. You let those two things drive you like a strong engine, even when logic tells you to surrender."

"Hope and determination along with a plan," Zane said.

"And weapons," Loris said.

They were silent, thinking about that for a moment.

"I still don't like the odds," Angel said.

"What do you know about odds?" Lettie said with a half-smile. A joke about Angel's lack of prowess with math that felt out of place and belonging to a happier time, but Zane appreciated the effort to lighten the mood.

"We'll be as careful as a naked man climbing a barbed wire fence," Zane chimed in.

"We'll be all right," Leon said.

"You don't have to worry about us." Zane looked at Verda, Lettie, and Angel in turn, his eyes resting on each for a long moment.

He thought he truly meant what he said. He felt that self-assured. It was the kind of unjustified confidence he had felt many times while under the influence of alcohol, but this time he was intoxicated by a desire for revenge.

Leon slid in behind the wheel of his old blue Hyundai and popped the locks. Zane opened the back door and tossed in his own version of Loris' war bag: the guns, two spare .45 magazines, a flashlight. Loris slid in her bag and a case holding a sniper rifle.

Getting past the two officers hadn't been easy. Zane concocted a story that Old Spice had asked them to come down to the police station and that they were to stay with Verda, Angel, Lettie and Milly who were heading out to the country. He could read the skepticism in their eyes but he kept talking until the sheer force of his words convinced them they were doing the right thing. Or maybe his onslaught of words just wore them down.

Zane's phone rang. Tiffany. He explained the plan briefly to her shocked silence.

"If something happens to you—" Tiffany could not finish the sentence. "This is impossible, crazy, anything can happen.

You've told me Clyde was violent, unpredictable. And you're going to walk right up to him?"

"Nothing is going to happen to me," Zane said, digging deep for the confidence he had felt back at home.

"I'll meet you there," she said.

"Absolutely not," Zane said. "I didn't let Verda or Angel or Lettie come and I won't have you with us. We'll be all right."

"If it's too dangerous for all of us, how is it okay for you?"

She had a point.

"Tiff, please, this is the best way I think. I need to do something, take action, and if it all works out, Clyde is back in prison and—"

"Madder than ever and what if he gets off on his new trial?"

Zane shook his head as if to chase the thought away.

"I'm not going to let him hurt anyone I love again," he said. "I promise you. And don't worry. I'm not going anywhere. I'm going to fight like hell."

"But if something happens."

"Nothing is going to happen to me, but I want you to know how much I love you." Loris and Leon both sat in the car and started fussing with their phones to give the illusion of privacy for Zane's conversation. He took a few steps away from the car and continued in a low voice. "I can't wait to be back in your arms, feel you against me, and know that this danger has passed. Start our next stage: you as a business owner. I think about our future all the time. It is what keeps me focused. I love you with all my heart."

"Zane!" He could hear Tiffany's breath catch in a sob. A heat traveled through his hand from the back of his phone.

He wanted nothing more than to take her in his arms and hold her. Hearing her cry and not being able to comfort her was a sharp, physical pain. He felt adrift on an icy island, helplessly watching Tiffany get smaller and smaller as he floated away, unable to touch her. She was so good and generous and caring and he was putting her through so much.

He resolved again to make it back to her from this thing he had to do.

"Please, just come back safe to me."

Leon drove out of the Majestic Mobile Home and RV Park and headed east on Interstate 44. The afternoon was quiet as the sky filled with soft white snowflakes against an opalescent sky. It looked like the kind of snow that was going to stick instead of melt, coating the world in a soft, clean blanket. The road was wide open.

As Leon drove, Loris peppered him with questions, and he was surprisingly forthcoming about his past. He told them about his childhood, growing up hard in Ecuador, admiring the drug traffickers because they seemed to have it all and the nerve to challenge just about everybody. They were reckless, forceful outsiders claiming money and respect wherever they went.

Opportunities were scarce, so Leon joined up with them when he was thirteen. A bell-ringer at first, using a radio to alert the cartel to police movements, then a drug seller, then managing over a territory of sellers.

That all changed when he and his young daughter went out early to buy bread one morning and they came across a shocking scene: two headless bodies left as a gruesome message by a rival gang.

He started making secret plans to get to the United States with his daughter and wife. But his wife, whose brother and father were in the gang, gave away his plans. To their horror, the cartel took their daughter from them in the night. He still didn't know what happened to her in their hands. She never spoke of it. His wife blamed him, he blamed her, and things got ugly. He smuggled himself and his daughter, Ofelia, to the United States not long after.

Looking at Leon, listening to him tell his story, telling the horrible things he had done over the years, talking about the people he hurt, made Zane want to abort the mission. Drag him down to the Tulsa Police Department. Turn him in for conspiring with Clyde.

"What was the deal with the baby rattle? You knew who sent it, right?"

Leon shrugged. "I thought it was nothing. Saber-rattling, as they say. An empty threat from Clyde's girlfriend. Really, I knew as much as you did."

Zane believed him. Not that Leon knew as much as they did, because it was clear he had way more information he could have shared. His cool deception since that event told Zane he could lie easily and well when it served him. But Leon couldn't have known for sure that Clyde would be able to pull off an escape from prison. "You could have warned us about Clyde's plans."

"I don't know what to tell you, Zane. I thought I was doing the right thing. I thought it was going to work out okay. In prison, lots of people talk about escaping and many also talk about revenge on those who wronged them. Not many get to act on it. I underestimated Clyde and his ability to charm this corrections officer."

From the backseat, Loris chimed in. "If someone wanted to kill you and they were making plans, wouldn't you want to know, Leon? Even if you didn't think they could pull it off?"

There was a long silence in the car before Leon answered. "Probably."

"Do you even care about my grandma?"

Leon's voice lowered and sounded choked with emotion. "Yes. Don't doubt my feelings for Verda. They are true."

They passed the massive Hard Rock Hotel and Casino complex, and Leon exited the highway not long after, pointing the car down the U.S. Route 66. They were getting close. "A friend of mine on the force says that the woman who helped Clyde escape cashed out her retirement nest egg recently," Loris said. "I have this funny feeling about her, like she's in over her head and in some danger."

Zane shrugged. "That KTUL-TV reporter told me she sold her house too. She's been planning this for some time."

"This officer, Berry Gathright, she's fifty-six, Loris said. "Retirement age. A four-time employee of the year with an unblemished record. They say she sold the house at a significant loss too."

Leon took a deep breath. "Sounds like someone who was getting ready to run to me."

Zane snorted. "Did she think she had a future with him?"

"Forgive the blunt question, Leon, but did they offer you any money to help them?" Loris leaned into the space between the two front seats.

"No, not at all." Fibbing must come so easy to Leon, he did it even when there was no need to. But he saw that they didn't believe him. "Yeah, they said they'd make it worth my while, but I haven't seen any money yet. Bringing you to them would be where the payoff was."

Leon's words sent a wave of cold through Zane that had nothing to do with the snow falling lightly on the car windshield.

"Sorry I can't make you a counteroffer. I'm pretty damn broke."

"It's not about the money. I told you back there. It's about keeping a promise."

Zane ran his fingers through his hair nervously. Which promise and to whom? The question nagged at Zane. Was he crazy for signing on to this confrontation? His old boss Gerry at the zoo had told him once he tended to run toward conflict instead of taking his time and getting the full picture. That sometimes this led to unnecessary drama. Had he done that here, only this time running toward danger?

They had arrived in Catoosa just thirty minutes before the scheduled meeting time. "Let's check it out with the little time we have left." Loris's voice was grim and low as her eyes met Zane's.

The abandoned stretch of interstate next to Pine Street had been the western end of the old Will Rogers Turnpike before the Creek Turnpike was extended. For nearly twenty years, the four-lane highway to nowhere had sat empty, unused—a hidden destination for hikers and partiers interested in apocalyptic views of civilization's end. The cracked and buckled road sat like infrastructure bones in a vast and caney creek bottom, flanked by blackjack trees and shrubs, protected not by a fence but by cement k-rails meant to keep cars from driving on the old road. The powers that be weren't too worried about pedestrians apparently. An old guide sign pointed to the East 66 Catoosa exit, flanked by overgrown brush collecting a layer of snow.

The car bucked and jolted as its front tire dumped into a big rough pit that had been invisible before they hit it, and Zane bit the inside of his cheek. Leon turned the wheel hard to the left, slid into reverse, and nursed the car backwards into the buffalo grass. It was obvious that the front end of the car would be visible to passersby, but Zane could see why. "This will have to do." They might need a quick getaway.

Zane's eyes swept the fields on either side of the road. There were no other cars, no houses, no fences, no sign of humans save for the road they drove in on and in the distance, the decaying highway, and its old overhead light fixtures. Fast food wrappers, beer cans, and plastic water bottles pressed against the roots of grasses that had grown long and wild then died to bleached tumbleweeds. Someone had spraypainted the word "RESIST" on a rock. A plastic bag fluttered across the ground, flapping in the soft wind. Nothing to indicate that Clyde and Berry had arrived ahead of schedule, ahead of them.

The snow had stopped. Zane popped out of the car and raised his face to the sky—crammed with clouds, frosted, almost silver in its winter turning—and for an instant, he felt pure fear. This was not a day he wanted to die. Old memories of Clyde and Link and Jeremiah tried to emerge, but he pushed them back. The brave aren't those who feel no fear. They are the people who feel fear and act anyway. He opened the trunk and stared at the contents. Reassured by the presence of Loris's sniper rifle and his own guns, he put his gun on his hip and a spare clip, and slipped a Taser into his coat pocket.

"Where are we going?" Loris asked.

"Toward the old bridge."

Loris swung her war bag over one shoulder and carried the sniper rifle in her other hand. Zane grabbed his bag and watched as Leon pulled an automatic out of the wheel well next to the car's spare tire and checked to see if it was loaded. It was.

Dead grass and broken glass crunched under their feet, and the smell of urine, excrement, and riverbank filled their noses. Zane fought the urge to gag. The ground rose and fell in large folds, pleating the land and keeping the highway out of view until they hit a crest. The field opened up on all sides with a broad expanse of cracked and weather-beaten asphalt, four lanes wide. Donna had said to meet them about a hundred feet in, toward the old bridge.

That's where they headed, and it was spooky.

K-rails and fencing lined the road on the right side, and an old sign warned that two lanes would merge into one ahead. Long white lane markers ended abruptly in bleached-out bushes of wild grass. The snow had already melted off the pavement but still clung to the weeds like frosting. They reached the old overpass over Spunky Creek, covered along the bottom in bright orange graffiti: "Rachel loves Jared" and "J-rod."

"This can work," Loris said.

On either side of them was the creek and surrounding brush with no trails or roads in sight, so Clyde and Berry couldn't sneak in that way. Not without a long hike through the brush. They wouldn't have the time. That meant the entrance from Pine Street would make the most sense and Zane, Loris, and Leon would be able to see them coming.

"Okay," Zane said.

"Now what?" Leon said.

"Wait here," Loris said. "I'm going to scramble up the hill and check the overpass. Make sure there are no other ingress points. And see if I can find a good position."

"Shit," Zane said. "What if they see three sets of footprints around the car instead of two?"

"Already thought of it," Loris said. "I was walking in your footprints in the dirt. It's going to be all right. I've got your back."

"You all know how desperate Clyde is. How violent."

"We've been over it. I'll be right there, waiting, covering you. You talk to him, keep him occupied. Get some space between him and Berry, if you can. I'll come up from behind."

"You may need to take him out fast," Leon said. Even in the cold, sweat ran down his temples.

Zane saw it differently, perhaps too optimistic, but he couldn't stand for planning someone's death in cold blood.

"When he sees Loris has him in her sights, he'll understand it's the end of the road."

"You're a fool," Leon said.

Maybe he was simple-minded. If Zane were honest, he understood there was a good chance that not everyone would walk away alive from this standoff in the middle of nowhere. People who are trapped become desperate. But they more often chose life than death. Was Clyde desperate enough to choose death? What about Berry? He didn't know for sure, but he hoped that the will to live would kick in for everyone. He tried to visualize the end: Clyde back in prison. The image wouldn't come.

It didn't matter. He wouldn't kill anyone outside of self-defense, and neither would Loris. It would be murder. He'd be no better than Clyde and Link and Jeremiah. If he wanted to live with himself after today, he had to try to end this without bloodshed.

"I doubt he's afraid to die," Leon said. "He's driven by a consuming rage."

"It's going to be up to him what happens."

Chapter 23
Lettie

Frame of Reference

Lettie studied the Google Maps satellite view of the meeting place on her phone as Angel drove them out to Uncle Brian and Aunt Tracy's house. The meeting spot was secluded enough but not that far from multiple businesses clustered along Route 66. Less than a mile according to the map. People might hear gunshots. Response time might not be too long. She took comfort where she could.

"The smartest thing to do would be to call the police and have them ready to ambush them," Angel said.

"We have a plan." Lettie added more conviction to her voice than she felt. "I just wish there were more we could do."

Verda gave a half-nod, mirroring Lettie's determination. "What we can do is take care of sweet Milly and make sure nothing happens to her."

Lettie looked at her baby, sleeping sweetly in her car seat.

But something, an old memory, kept her from drinking in her daughter's beauty. She turned her gaze out the window to see a red semi-trailer whoosh by them. Treeless fields and a white sky horizon for miles, in the distance an oil pumpjack dipping and rising. Some connection about Clyde and Link and Catoosa skirted the periphery of her memory, taking her back to deep, ugly memories of the two brothers holding her in that clapboard house, windows covered in blue plastic tarps. How cold it was. Had they talked about having land in Catoosa? Or family? She couldn't bear to think about that time and she couldn't not bear to. Was there something she should remember?

Then it came to her. Of course. Remember that industrial park full of warehouses where the Dooms had taken them? That was out near the Port of Catoosa. She found the area on the map and calculated the mileage. It was just under six miles away, on the other side of the Redbud Valley Nature Preserve. This couldn't be a coincidence, could it?

Her hands started to shake. She zoomed in on the lonely house near the meeting point. From the Google satellite images, it seemed to comprise three structures: a house and what looked like a barn, and another shed. It sat at the end of a long road that Google hadn't seen fit to give a name.

She quickly flicked through the addresses for nearby businesses: a sports complex was in the 22000 block and was a little to the east. A Baptist church just to the west sat at 20600. So, a rough address for the property could be 21000 East Pine Street.

She opened a new Google search and typed in "who owns 21000 East Pine Street" and hit send.

Nothing.

She obviously didn't have the address right. But one of the search results offered up the names of voters registered along

Pine Street in Catoosa. Registering to vote made your name, address, and political party affiliation a public record apparently. She scrolled through the lists of registered voters—mainly Republicans, no surprise if you knew anything about Oklahoma politics—looking for a street address that would match the house she saw. 21270 East Pine fit the bill. Two Independent voters named Mike and Marla Bond in their sixties lived there. But a check back with the map showed she didn't have the right address.

Then she saw the names at 21200. Franklin Gathright. Gathright. The same last name as Berry Gathright, the female corrections officer helping Clyde.

Her body knew it was a match before her mind did, as she forced herself to double-check her work. Terror swept her as she saw the address line up on the map, a cold, dizzying, biting surge, like an arctic blast in her chest and stomach. This location was handpicked because of its proximity to any property that Berry would likely have access to. They were planning an ambush. How had they all been so naïve to think that this location was a neutral one?

She blurted the news out to Verda and Angel, her emotions jumbling the words, so they had a hard time understanding her the first two times through.

Out the windshield, she could see Uncle Brian and Aunt Tracy's driveway on the right. They had arrived. She had to think fast.

She called Zane, but he didn't pick up. He had probably put the phone on silent. Verda dialed Leon only to get the same result. They quickly pounded out texts with the basic information to both men.

"Angel, take Milly in the house and give me the keys," Lettie said.

"You're not going out there, Lettie."

Angel turned the car onto the driveway and toward the house.

"You aren't going to be able to stop me. Look, we're only maybe fifteen minutes from there. I have to try to warn them."

She stretched her arm between the two front seats to show them the map. "They're going to think there's only one entrance off of Pine Street, but since they have access to this house over here, it's not that much of a little hike to come around this way. It could change everything."

Angel looked at the clock as he put the car into park. "Lettie, that meet-up is happening basically right now. You won't get there in time. You don't have any weapons and you're a lousy shot anyway and a new mother. And to top it off, you don't have a driver's license."

Lettie sighed and sunk into the seat.

"I'm not a lousy shot," Verda said. "And my rifle's in the trunk."

Chapter 24
Zane

Buy a Ticket, Take a Ride

Zane watched his breath cloud the air, surprised not to feel the cold. That was the little gift adrenaline spikes gave him today. Leon, on the other hand, was clapping his hands together and stamping his feet, a weird little dance to stay warm or pass the time.

He felt like a silo sitting in the path of a tornado. He gazed up at the steeply sloped swales running down both sides, as though the old road was a river that had cut deep into the earth, leaving high banks. Loris was up there, on the right. Knee-high, yellowy-brown plumes of summer's now-dead vegetation clung to the steep pitch.

He took out his phone. No bars. No cell connection.

"Do you have service?"

Leon shook his head. "Must be a dead spot."

The other man's word choice sent a buzz through the air

that ruffled the hair on the back of Zane's neck. "Maybe it's just temporary. We're not far from civilization."

Leon nodded and slipped the phone back into his pocket.

"Lettie once told me there was some kind of device that could block cellular signals."

Leon kept his eyes on the horizon.

Despite the graffiti, the trash, and that smell of urine by the entrance, Zane had the sense that no one had ventured back here recently other than wildlife.

But what did he know?

He couldn't see Loris but he visualized her, lying in wait above, sniper rifle in hand, trapping them. She was the special sauce that Clyde wouldn't know about. He let the image of her above reassure him.

A disquieting silence fell over the space. Even the wind stopped blowing. He hoped they wouldn't have to wait much longer. Patience wasn't his virtue, no matter how hard he tried.

He started running different scenarios through his head, trying to be strategic, but his efforts were disturbed by images of Lettie's face. He saw her in that awful cabin where Link and Clyde had taken her, duct tape over her mouth, eyes wide in fear. Her lying beside him in that trailer truck, counting on him to save them both. He had done it. Could he do it again?

He thought about what might happen to Lettie if he were to die here. Verda would be her guardian, that much was clear, at least until her dad got out of McAlester. His little sister had already suffered so much loss. What would it do to her if he were to leave this earth? She was strong, but how much loss was too much? The more he thought about it, the more his anger built at the people who were putting them in jeopardy. Clyde. Berry. Donna. Leon. He stared at Leon, his pulse roaring in his ears and his body quivering with fury. What the hell was he doing here?

The waiting was making him jumpy.

This was the path that made sense. Bringing the conflict to a head. Rushing toward it instead of running away. It wasn't his downfall like his old boss Gerry said, it was his superpower. Hadn't that been the theme of every day since finding out Clyde was getting a new trial? He had rooted himself in place for the conflict from the first moment he decided not to cut and run. He hadn't been wrong. Had he?

A sound from above yanked his attention back to the moment.

He looked up at the spot where Loris had set up but didn't see her. He started moving around, looking for her from different vantage points. Nothing.

Then he saw her. She rose from behind a tall weed, hands in the air. Facing her, just about twenty paces away, was Clyde Doom. Where had he come from?

Clyde's gun pointed at Loris. A few paces away, a woman in a tight, red puffer coat stood with both arms out, two hands holding a gun pointed directly at Zane. Her feet were planted in a linebacker's crouch. Behind mirrored sunglasses, her face was pudgy and unreadable.

"You got him?" she shouted down the hill to Leon. Zane felt Leon's hand grab his arm and pull him close. He felt the gun's metal snout against his shoulder as Leon whispered, "We'll figure it out." To the woman, he shouted, "I've got him."

"Is he armed?" she called back.

Zane held his breath as the little voice in the back of his mind whispered about betrayal and dumb ideas. He waited for Leon to yank the gun out of his belt, disarming him. Leaving him vulnerable. But the moment didn't come.

"No." Leon raised his face to the slope. "Who's that?"

"I thought you might know." Clyde's drawl was sarcastic, slow. The voice made Zane clench every muscle in his body. A terrible voice from the past. A voice he couldn't reason with. Zane turned his attention to Berry in an appeal to what he hoped was a remnant of logic within her.

"It's not too late to change course, Berry," Zane shouted at the woman. "You can stop this at any moment. You have the power."

The woman stayed silent, side-stepping down the slope like a heavy-bottomed crab with her gun still trained on Zane.

"Why don't you make sure my *brother* Zane isn't armed, there, Berry?" An ear-stretching snarl came over Clyde's face when he said the word brother. "We need to see what's going on here with our sniper friend. I have the feeling my prison buddy Leon here isn't telling the full story. You know these convicts. They lie so easily."

Berry's foot slipped, sending some potato-sized rocks rolling down the slope before she caught herself.

A rhythmic rattle began, echoing in the still air.

"Baby rattlesnake," Loris shouted at them.

Berry started running down the slope, gun pointed down toward the snake. One shot, then another, unbelievably loud. She fell backwards with the recoil, back arched like a diver and arms spread in futile mimicry of wings, sending out a sharp animal cry of terror. She fell onto the slope and then tumbled head over butt once. She slid face-first down the last fifteen feet, finally coming to rest in the place where the slope met the road, not far from Zane and Leon. A few more rocks rolled in a miniature avalanche after her.

The next sound was a dark laugh. "She rolled like a beach ball," Clyde said. "You all right, there, Berry?" His amusement gave way to a look of exasperation and disgust. He pulled Loris closer, a bully determined to stay in control. He had on dark blue work pants and a buffalo-check plaid coat that strained against his wide shoulders. The collar hid all but the ears of the wolf tattoo on his neck. Black wraparound sunglasses shaded his eyes in the weak winter sun. "Berry, you awake?"

Berry lay completely motionless on the slope, head at a strange angle, face hidden by tall weeds. They all stared at her form, still as a broken porch swing. The left leg of her dark jeans was pushed up to her knee and part of her muscular white calf was revealed. One foot was shoeless, and the missing sneaker lay a few feet above her head on the slope.

Loris's face was a mask of shock, mouth open, hand at her chest. On Clyde's face, the expression was less concern and more calculation and callousness.

Zane felt Loris's eyes on him, and when he looked back at her, he understood the opportunity she saw. The numbers had changed to their advantage.

"You two, go see if she's all right," Clyde said, pointing his chin at her body.

Leon and Zane inched slowly toward the body, scanning the ground and slope for the baby rattlesnake until they reached her. Her sunglasses were bent and hung askew on her face, revealing one closed eye. Her mouth was open as if in amazement at finding herself in this position as if she had been out for a pleasant hike and someone had pushed her off a cliff. Her arm was outstretched toward the gun, which had fallen just out of her reach. Her white sock was turning red with blood seeping from two distinct points.

"That snake bit her. And you know the juvenile ones are more poisonous," Zane said. The memory of the terrible pulse of pain he felt when he had been bitten by a snake flooded back to him. Berry must be unconscious if she wasn't writhing with the pain. Or dead.

"She's breathing," Leon said. Zane studied her chest, looking for a rise and fall but didn't see one. Had Leon drawn the same conclusion that he had? Berry could be more useful to them if Clyde thought she was still alive than if she was dead. He must care something about her, right?

"We need to get her to the hospital," Zane said. "We've started a clock ticking. She could die. Her neck doesn't look right, like it might be broken."

"We're not going to worry about that right now," Clyde said. "And there's a clock ticking all right. Ticking away my time spent in prison, locked up. Ticking away the days without my father. Ticking away the time you have left on this earth."

Berry made a gargling, guttural noise. Her mouth closed and opened, notes of pain unraveling from her.

"Are you okay?"

More gargling and twitching. She tried to move one arm, her fingers trembling spasmodically as if an electric current coursed through them.

"In the movies, wouldn't someone suck that poison out of her leg?" Clyde said.

"I don't think that really works," Loris said. "Your girlfriend there needs medical attention. I am a trained emergency medic. Do you want me to take a look?"

For a long moment, no one moved while Clyde seemed to consider his options. Waiting, Zane broke out in a cold and acid sweat. He unzipped his jacket to let in some cool air and breathed in the stink of dread and despair pouring off his body.

"All right," Clyde said. "Let's go down there."

Chapter 25
Lettie

Into the Woods

Zane's "find your phone" function wasn't working, but Verda and Lettie spotted Leon's car poking out of a turnaround along Pine Street. In between there and the road that Lettie thought led to the Gathright place, a narrow deer trail appeared to run directly into a line of trees.

"Through there," she said. They set out on foot, Verda carrying the rifle like a cattleman warding off coyotes. Lettie carried a loaded revolver in the deep open pocket of her parka. They were as well-armed as they could have been, but she still felt like David with his puny and pitiful slingshot rushing headlong foolishly into Goliath's line of sight.

The snow had finally relented, and the sun had found the courage to exert itself from its low point in the afternoon sky. Shadows were everywhere, wind whispering warnings through the brush. This was either the dumbest thing Lettie had ever done or the most courageous. Maybe both? All she knew was she didn't have a choice. Logic be damned. Everything depended on Zane getting out of this alive.

The grey Camry she spotted in the trees was parked in a funny spot, as though it had gotten lost in the woods. She peered past it and could just make out the roofline of a structure. Were they that close to the Gathright property? She stepped closer to it and could hear the engine fan whirring even though the engine was off. Someone had just driven this car here and parked it. She touched her grandmother's arm and pointed at the car.

"Do you think that's Clyde's car?" she said.

"I don't know but I have an idea just in case," her grandmother said and quick-stepped it back toward the Cadillac, leaving Lettie standing there. She was suddenly struck by how quiet it was in this spot, surprising as they were so close to the road. The silence was so heavy it had brought a pressure with it that she felt on her skin. Graveyard-quiet. They needed to move. What was Verda doing?

A few minutes later Verda returned, making a beeline for the car, rifle strapped around her body like a warrior and something in her hands. Lettie lost sight of her as she went around the passenger side of the car and ducked down. After a few suspenseful moments of Lettie wondering if she had fallen, Verda popped back up.

"Let's go," she said.

"What did you do?"

"Just making a little contingency plan in case they get back to their car."

Lettie scooted around the car to see her grandmother's handiwork. "Brilliant," she said.

They went downward on the winding deer trail where no underbrush and only a few fallen branches blocked their path.

Lettie was already out of breath and in awe of her grandmother's stamina. Just ten minutes after they set out, she glimpsed the concrete bones of the old interstate, weedy and cracked but massive, a scar against the scraggly winter beauty of the creek bed. Piles of leaves had blown down to the creek in the autumn months and over time been slowly saturated into dense, soft masses.

Side by side they advanced as noiselessly as possible toward the interstate along the tree line, eyes scanning the road. No sign of human life.

Ahead of them, a hundred yards away, the remnants of a bridge stood like a concrete ledge. Something moved quickly at the top, catching Lettie's eye. She squinted in the winter sun, trying to make out what she saw. Maybe two figures, working their way down a steep grade from the bridge to the interstate below.

Turning to look at Verda, Lettie pointed. "I think they're up ahead," she whispered.

Her eyes followed the figures down the slope as she and Verda paused in the shadows. Lettie drew her pistol from the deep pocket of her parka and switched off the safety slowly, worried that the click might travel to Clyde's ears. Verda slipped the rifle off the cross-body strap and held it in her hands at the ready.

They marched forward until Leon and Zane's backs came into view, Leon's left hand grasping Zane's shoulder. In Leon's other hand was a gun. Trained on Zane.

"I'm going to kill him," Verda muttered.

Now Lettie also made out the woman's body crumpled at the end of the slope and saw Clyde pushing Loris down the remainder of the slope toward it. Loris fell on her knees in front of what could only be Berry's body and leaned over her. Something had happened to Berry. Good, Lettie thought. One less person to worry about. A famous line from that movie popped into her head, unbidden: May the odds be ever in your favor.

Next to her, Verda closed one eye and put the other to the rifle's scope.

"Clyde's got his gun pointed at Loris. Leon could get off a shot if he wanted but he's acting like he's frozen. And he's got a gun on Zane. That god-damned piece of shit."

Lettie blinked at her grandmother's language. She had never heard her curse before, but if ever a situation called for it, it was this one.

"I need to get a bit closer, that's all," she said.

"You're just going to kill him?"

"I'm going to do what I need to do to get Zane out of here," Verda said. "I don't want to kill anyone. But there are a couple of problems here. I don't know what Leon is going to do. Has he truly switched sides? Is he a threat? I need to think."

"We don't have time," Lettie said. She tugged on her grand-mother's sleeve, and they inched down the treeline, trying to keep to the shadows until they were close enough to hear their voices.

Clyde's voice was the first one to carry to their ears. "You're playing me, lady. She's deader than a doornail. There ain't no medical help that's going to fix that broken neck. You're just telling me that to try to buy time or change what's going to happen here."

"What is going to happen here, Clyde?" Loris's voice was strong and loud. "You going to kill all of us here, even Leon? Leave no witnesses. Then what? You got every cop in Okla-homa, Arkansas, and Missouri looking for you. Where you going to go?"

Lettie's pulse was so loud in her ears it was like a bass drum beating. Clyde was clever enough to have turned the tables and gotten Loris. She had been their contingency plan. But they had one good play left. Lettie's intuition had been right. They were needed here. She wished she had a way to let Zane know they were here without tipping off Leon.

The body of the gun hit Loris's head with a loud smack, and she fell onto Berry's stomach. Clyde glanced down at the two women. A look passed over his face, softening his scowl for a moment. Was that mercy? A swift moment and then the expression was gone, replaced by something inflexible and cruel. In that instant, Lettie knew Clyde would kill them all if he had the chance.

Clyde pulled the hammer back on his gun. He held it stiff-armed, aimed at Loris. The metallic click echoed crisply in the cold, open space.

"You don't need to worry about what my plans are. I can travel light now. No ties."

Loris scissor-kicked at his legs, toppling him off-balance. He shot his hands out to break his fall, gun slipping to the ground as loud gunfire filled Lettie's ears.

Chapter 26
Zane

Fit and Finish

When the shooting started, Zane first thought Leon had shot at him. The other man released the grip on his shoulder and Zane spun away from him, reaching for his own gun in his parka pocket.

But Zane was confused. He hadn't pulled the trigger yet but Leon was somehow on the ground, crying out and pressing his hand against his shoulder. Blood slicked his hands through the bullet hole in the back of his jacket. Zane picked up Leon's gun and shoved it in his own pocket, telling Leon everything was going to be all right. Then he spun around to see who could have been shooting from behind them. Emerging from the trees, was a figure, pointing a weapon at them.

Verda. Next to her: Lettie. They started running toward Zane and Leon. Zane's attention was torn between his grandmother and his sister and Loris and Clyde grappling for the gun as they rolled on the ground, like two kids fighting in a sandbox, a muddle of lurching arms and legs, writhing and cussing.

"Get out of here!" was all he could think of to say to Lettie, which he knew was stupid. He obviously needed their help, but his fear for their safety was so great he couldn't help himself. Then he put it out of his mind and charged toward Clyde like a bull seeing red. This was his chance.

Always the fighter, Loris had unsheathed her knife from her ankle holster and sliced at Clyde's hand, unleashing a red flow of blood.

Zane planted his feet and lined up his shot at Clyde. Loris saw he had taken the advantage and rolled herself out of Clyde's reach.

"You're out of options," Loris said.

A tight smile spread over Clyde's face. "You don't get it, do you? This is about honor. Family honor. Thou shalt honor thy father, not kill him. But that's what you did, *brother*." The word brother smeared out of his mouth like an insult. "You need to pay. I had nothing but time to think about this day. To think about you and what you'd do."

"Oh yeah? What conclusions did you come to?"

Blood dripped from Clyde's hand and onto the gun he still held, a macabre scene along with Berry's dead body and the soundtrack of Leon's groaning, as though they stood in a horror movie set. Loris made her way to stand next to Zane. He handed her Leon's gun.

"I concluded that you wouldn't be able to kill me. You can't shoot that gun at me. You're no real killer. You're a chickenshit killer. Cowardly. Killed my dad when he trusted you because you were so scared of him. But you don't have the guts to do that again. I bet I can just walk to the car and drive off and you won't do a thing."

"You've got four guns pointed at you, Clyde. You want to take that risk that all four of us are chickenshit?"

"I've got some zip ties right here. Clyde," Loris said. "Drop the gun, come down here, and put your hands behind your back." She used her best cop's command voice, but Clyde just snorted.

"That's not going to happen." Clyde gave Zane a determined look, keeping his gun aimed right at him.

"Think about what you are doing." Zane gripped the gun, his finger through the trigger guard.

"I'm not going back there. Not now. And not without doing what I came here to do."

The gun—aimed at Zane—went off.

He ducked and rolled, squeezing off rounds as he did, hands shaking, no sense if any of the bullets hit Clyde. He did not want to kill Clyde. He did not want another death on his hands. But he didn't want to die either.

Zane had no idea how many shots he fired. It happened too fast. Gunfire boomed in his ears, smoke burned his nostrils. When he straightened up, he had his gun out in front of him, both hands wrapped around the grip. And Clyde was somehow moving up the slope, dragging his leg behind him, panting like a rabid dog. He had a bullet hole in his thigh and another on his shoulder, bright red buttons of blood.

A flood of conflicting emotions battled inside Zane. The wounds looked bad but not fatal. Clyde didn't need to die here today.

And Zane wasn't going to die here today either. Not yet anyway. He checked himself for bullet wounds. He didn't feel any pain but knew shock and adrenaline could dull that sensation temporarily. Nothing. He was unscathed, an amazing feat in a crazy gun battle.

He looked at the three women around him. Loris, gun in

both hands like an action movie star, determined. Verda, shotgun raised with its business end ping-ponging from Clyde and Leon, eyes focused like a shark on blood in the water. Lettie, gun hanging from her hand next to her thigh, her body trembling, her eyes were moist pools of sadness mixed with anger. He hadn't wanted them to come here and be mixed up in this. But he had to admit he was glad they came. His grand-mother and Lettie may have saved his life.

He knew none of them took killing lightly. Still, Clyde held a gun as he crawled and dragged himself up the slope, barely maintaining his balance even on all fours. He was dangerous. He wanted to kill Zane. He wouldn't have shown mercy. Or had he? Had Clyde really missed or had he done it on purpose because he had a death wish?

"Let him go. He won't get far with those injuries." Verda kept her eye in the rifle sight and her aim steady.

"His car is right there," Loris said. "We can't let him get there."

"I got that old alligator trap clamped around the tire," Verda said. "He's not going anywhere in that vehicle."

With his adrenaline still pumping madly, Zane itched to follow the man up the slope, grab him by the jacket and punch his face until the anger left him. Instead, he watched as Clyde pulled himself up to the flat ground above the slope and tried to stand up.

"Two wrongs don't make a right, Clyde. I'm like you. I've got a violent streak. I've gotten caught up in it. I killed our father in self-defense. It was a horrible, violent, up-close act, and I live with that every day. The horror of it never goes away. You came here to kill me because you think it's going to help with the loss and the anger. It won't. This can be a new start. Come in with me to the authorities alive. Things have gotten out of control. Don't you want to stop?"

"I'm trying to honor my father." Clyde raised his voice and lifted the gun waist-level, pointing at Zane. But his hand was shaking wildly. "Something you wouldn't understand."

"We can't let you go, Clyde. This needs to end."

"I agree with you for the first time, asshole."

Lettie cried out. "Zane, watch out!"

"Goodbye, asshole," Clyde said.

Clyde pulled the trigger one last time.

Chapter 27
Zane

Full Circle

Clyde was on the ground. On trembling legs, Zane walked toward the slope until Lettie caught him from behind. She wrapped her arms around him. "You're all right, you're all right," she repeated as though on a sound loop.

Loris sat back on her haunches in front of Clyde. "He's gone."

Zane and Lettie stood in silence, without moving, for a long time. Zane tried to comprehend what had happened as his body shook, dispensing the last of his unused adrenaline, but not his guilt. A chill seeped into him.

Another violent death. How had his life led to another violent death? Bad blood ran through him, through his half-brothers, knitting them together in an endless revenge loop. An infinite cycle of pain and hurt. Would Clyde's brother, Link, be the next one to come after them? Would they have to repeat this disaster again?

"You couldn't have done anything different," Lettie said, somehow reading his thoughts as he stared at Clyde's bloody, dead body on the slope. "It was his choice."

Anger rose in Zane along with bile, burning his throat. "My choices led to this day too. The never-ending legacy of this family."

"We haven't had an easy time of it, that's true. But we're good people, Zane. We are trying to live right. I'm proud of us. I'm proud of you. You show me every day how to be strong to deal with anything that comes our way."

"I don't think I can live with another death on my hands. I still see Jeremiah, that day—"

Lettie pulled away from him, grabbing his face in her hands. Her eyes were deep, moist pools of concern. "I don't think you killed Clyde. Me and Verda shot at him too. And you... you... seemed to just freeze when he pulled the trigger."

Zane looked around at the scene, the bodies and blood under a winter-white sky. In the distance, the sound of sirens approaching. Someone had called 911, and the police response was fast.

When the first responders arrived, they checked the three injured people for signs of life—only Leon was breathing and in need of emergency aid. Then the officers started securing the crime scene.

Zane, Loris, Lettie, and Verda sat side-by-side on the edge of the old interstate, cross-legged, guns in a pile several feet away and under guard by a young Catoosa officer. Temporary halogen lights ringed the scene, illuminating the space as dusk began crawling across the sky. Catoosa and Tulsa cops, Tulsa County sheriff's deputies and a half-dozen men and women in blue polo shirts with the CID logo swarmed the scene.

Not much later, Detective Angus Pastor came walking down the interstate and into the glow of the work lamps. Old Spice looked like a deer hunter on his way to the opening day of the season in his bright orange parka.

"You all right, Zane?" Worry swept over his face, but he also looked like he might want to slap Zane upside the head.

Zane said he was fine and watched as the relief on Old Spice's face melted into anger.

"What the hell happened here?"

Zane and Loris spent the next twenty minutes recounting the tale.

When they finished, Old Spice's nostrils were flaring like a dragon's, his breath loud, as he worked to keep his anger under control. Around them, crime scene specialists took photos, made notes, and placed yellow markers near shell casings scattered on the ground. There were a lot of yellow markers, renewing Zane's amazement that he had not been hit.

"Allow me to recap," Old Spice said. "You agreed to go with this man Leon to meet Clyde. Without letting the police know."

Zane nodded. "I had backup."

Old Spice reached for his electronic cigarette and put it in his mouth then took it out again without a puff. A nervous tic. "Don't get me started on Loris here. And Lettie and Verda as your backup. How could you put them in harm's way like this? What were you thinking?"

Lettie cleared her throat. "We just came. He didn't want us to."

Old Spice flicked the e-cigarette between his fingers, as though trying to shake off frustration or anxiety. Zane wasn't sure which one.

"This is a goddamn tragedy and it could have been a worse one. I really question your judgment, Zane. You blindly trusted this Leon, here, and came to meet a violent escapee who wants to avenge your father's death and thought, gee, it'll all work out okay?"

"When you put it that way, it sounds stupid," Zane said. He caught Loris's eyes in the periphery, and she winked at him.

"We're still alive," she said.

Zane shrugged. Old Spice knew him well. The detective was furious now and surprised that Zane had taken such a crazy-seeming risk. But then, people did all sorts of crazy things under pressure, didn't they? After some time passed, Old Spice would understand. At least Zane thought he would.

"So, what's the story with Leon? Did he betray you?"

Zane shrugged again, opening his mouth to answer when Verda interrupted.

"I don't think so," she said. "He was on our side. He just wasn't too quick thinking in the moment."

Old Spice wrote something in his notebook, paused, and stared at them, taking them all in one long glance. Then he shook his head. "You should have called me."

"Clyde got the drop on me as it was," Loris said. "He would have never gotten close if he smelled the cops around."

"We'll just never know, will we?" Old Spice said. "You didn't even give us a chance."

Zane could see Old Spice's point of view. The good news was that a dangerous escapee was off the streets and no longer capable of harm. The bad news was that he was dead, and so was his accomplice, Berry Gathright. It wasn't the ending anyone wanted.

"Can we go?" Loris said. "You know how to find us."

"They're taking Leon to the hospital," Verda said. "I'm going to ride with him."

His grandmother must have read the surprise on his face because she reached over to pat him on the arm. "He doesn't have anyone. It doesn't mean more than that right now. But sometimes you have to be there for people despite their mistakes."

Zane pulled his phone out of his pocket, wanting nothing more than to reach out to Tiffany and let her know he was safe. Only one tiny bar showed on the phone. Cellular service here was shit. He tapped out the message anyway: I'm all right.

Delivered. Three dots on his screen showed she was replying. She must have been sitting on her phone, waiting to hear from him. He was so sorry to have put her through that.

A stream of praying hands emoji popped up on his screen in response. "Thank God." Then: "I love you."

"I love you too." He resolved to show her how much he meant it too, just as soon as he could get his arms around her.

Chapter 28
Lettie

She had fired the gun at Clyde, but so had Verda, so she didn't know if her bullet was the one that felled him. Maybe that was something the crime scene people would figure out. Would someone tell her if she had killed him? Did it matter? She felt like she had. She had the intent anyway, if not the skills. The feeling was shocking and numbing at the same time. She'd never done violence to anyone before.

Suffering did not always bring strength and courage. She may be young, but life had already taught her that much. Sometimes people are knocked to pieces by it. That superhuman adrenaline surge she had heard about—the woman who punches an alligator to save her child or the girl who lifted a car off her father when the jack slipped—didn't arrive today for her with extraordinary physical strength but it did slow down time.

That moment, when Clyde talked about honoring his father, it felt like someone had pressed the pause button on the scene. Everything moved slowly. It was hard to understand, but she felt like time slowed down so much she could see the bullets from Verda's gun floating through the air, toward Clyde. Like they were in a movie, watching a slow-motion action scene.

In that moment, she had a strange realization. When she really thought about it, what scared her more than anything was Zane's death. She was scared for her own life, of course, and deeply saddened that there could be any chance she would not live to see little Milly grow. But losing Zane in this life would be painful. A daily loss. An hourly loss. That love she had for him was a bedrock of her life; to lose that love would be to lose herself. Fear of Zane dying drove her to pull the trigger.

Her mind turned those moments over and over on the drive back to Uncle Brian and Aunt Tracy's house, and she rolled the backseat window down to try to cleanse her mind of the emotions. Now, all she wanted to do was hold Milly and Angel.

"What do you think my chances are of getting back into the police training program?" Zane kept his head turned to the right, watching the open fields rush by.

Loris rat-tat-tatted her hand on the steering wheel of Leon's car and took a sidelong view of Zane.

"You ever thought of operating outside of law enforcement? You don't need a badge to do some good for people. You don't strike me as a by-the-book, color-in-the-lines kind of person anyway."

"What do you mean? Like a vigilante justice provider? Like on that show, The Equalizer? Who would hire me?"

"Plenty of people need help and don't want to involve the police. Or can't get the help they need from the police until something bad happens to them. I make a pretty good living at it."

Loris hadn't asked them for payment that Lettie knew of, but she knew if she had any money, she would have gladly paid for Loris's help throughout this ordeal. Loris's suggestion resolved into a fine-grain picture in Lettie's brain: Zane as a private investigator or fixer, for regular people. The idea excited her more than Zane's current plan of returning to the police academy and moving to Skiatook. All that only if the Skiatook Police let him. There was still that matter of the meth accusation. Zane didn't get it. They weren't going to let him back in.

"I could help you, Zane," Lettie said, "with all the computer stuff. Online research, finding people, that kind of thing."

Zane just sighed. "Just what I need. Another way to put you in danger."

"If you think about it, police officers' work is ninety percent reactive, happening mostly after crimes take place. What if we could do work to prevent them for people? People in situations like us—"

"Lettie, I don't want to talk about this now. I started something with the police academy and I want to see it through. Do you know how many things I've started and not finished in my life?"

"I can only think of one," she said. "Welding school, right? And you had to quit because Mom died and you didn't have the money for tuition once you had to take care of me. So, it doesn't count and neither does the police training program. They quit you, you didn't quit them."

"What you need to focus on is finishing high school," Zane said, his stern tone warning Lettie off from saying anything further. For now. But Loris wasn't fazed.

"I bring it up, Zane because I don't want you to be disappointed. I just don't think you're cut out for the police brotherhood any more than I was. And let me remind you, you asked if I thought they'd let you return to the police academy."

An angry energy jolted through Zane's torso as he shifted in the seat, but he stayed silent for the rest of the ride to the Majestic. Sometimes truth takes a while to sink in, despite people's best efforts to see their lives honestly. Lettie knew about denial as much as anyone. Hadn't she thought that she could evade the law and make easy money with that credit card fraud ring last year? People tell themselves what they want to believe. She knew Zane felt the pinch of hard truth in what she and Loris said, but he wasn't ready to face it. That was okay. They had plenty of time now, with Clyde gone, and Link still in jail.

Link Doom.

She hadn't really thought about what Clyde's death would do to his still-living brother Link. Clyde was cut from the same gene pool as Link: violent, hot-headed, angry. What would stop him from coming after them as well? Now he had one more reason to do so. The thought of Link's reaction to the news of Clyde's death sent her reeling back to her original fear—that terrible encounter with those brothers when they had abducted her.

The fast-approaching dusk dimmed her view beyond the window and transformed the glass into a dim mirror. Her pale reflection trembled like a ghost as the car sped home, reminding her of those movie montages that film directors used to show the passage of time: a woman with a hundred-yard stare, watching the seasons change, healing from past trauma. The tall yellow lights lining the interstate flickered on, and as the car passed underneath each one, she watched her reflection disappear and reappear in the yellow lights. She felt like she would arrive home years older from this journey.

Loris exited the interstate, and Lettie's mind inexplicably

flashed back to the few days she spent at Bible camp with one of her friends. She hadn't thought about that fleeting flirtation with Christianity in years.

There were all sorts of Scripture quotes that had perplexed her that week but none more than "Love your enemies, and do good, and expect nothing in return," as Jesus had said in his Sermon on the Mount. As an eight-year-old consumed with ideas of justice, she had thought it was ridiculously passive and weak. Not the words of a revolutionary, but the solace of a sucker, born to be taken advantage of. It was a harsh view and not one she shared with her friends or the pretty dark-haired Bible camp counselor. What was her name? Mary Ann, perhaps?

But Lettie couldn't help the way she saw the world or her corner of it. And what she saw was that on this earth, people deal with enemies through retaliation and punishment. Mary Ann told them that God—New Testament God, that is— wanted his flock to use forgiveness instead. She did not buy it.

Then and now, Lettie related more to the wrath of God in the Old Testament stories: she wanted Clyde and Link to pay with blood. An eye for an eye. But she remembered perky, sweet Mary Ann saying Jesus brought a different message by dying for everyone's sins. "God's ways are higher than our ways," was one of Mary Ann's favorite expressions. Christians were supposed to follow that impossible example.

It didn't make sense to Lettie, any more than senseless tragedies like those seven little kids who died in that tornado that plowed through an elementary school in Moore, Okla-homa, that year of Bible camp. God would have to forgive her for her hatred of Clyde, Link, and Jeremiah, born of fear. And her resentment too, for why had God allowed these things to happen to her and her brother. God's ways are higher, indeed. So high above her head, she couldn't fathom.

She would not forgive Link or Clyde, not even now that Clyde was dead.

Her reflection gave way to the deep blue and grey twilight and the driveway to Uncle Brian and Aunt Tracy's house. The vision of home and the love inside of it was a comfort falling over her like snow. She was going to hold Milly forever tonight.

Chapter 29
Zane

Million Dollar Questions

He hadn't thought he would see the stars in the sky tonight.

He hadn't thought he would see Tiffany again.

And now he saw both: the stars blinking faintly in the window of his bedroom and Tiffany in his arms. Wind whipping up outside, rattling the pane.

Tiffany stretched beside him on the bed, watching him. Pretty as she was, with her honey-colored skin and thick, dark hair cut short like parentheses around her face, she seemed like a ghost, or maybe a goddess of healing sent to soothe his soul.

"You want to sleep?" she asked.

"Don't know if I can," he said, his voice hoarse and cracked. "I'm tired though."

"You want to talk about it?"

"No."

Common wisdom in Alcoholics Anonymous was that talking about things helped, and maybe it did, over time. But Zane felt too weak to tell the story, too depressed to say all the parts out loud. Maybe someone somewhere would have emerged from a situation like that high-fiving and on an adrenaline rush, but energy had been oozing out of him since they left the scene. Maybe that kind of reaction only happened in action movies. All he felt was trauma and exhaustion.

He started to tell Tiffany how grateful he was for her. He wanted to ask her what had happened with her and the bank and cell phone store. How nice it would be to hear about someone's normal, non-violent day. But his mind misted over, and he drifted into sleep.

When he woke, light strained through the slats of the closed miniblinds, a gray light that told him it must be morning.

Ballpoint had inserted himself in the bed between Zane and Tiffany, the dog's powerful back spooned into Zane's chest like a bony heating pad. Tiffany must have let Ballpoint on the bed because he certainly had never invited the dog up here.

Ballpoint must have sensed his confusion because he swiveled his enormous head to make upside-down eye contact with Zane. His wide pink tongue lolled out like a question mark over his right eye.

"It's okay." Zane gave Ballpoint's chest a few scratches and was rewarded with more nuzzling. Zane would rather it be Tiffany against him, but Ballpoint would do for now. But they couldn't make this dog-in-the-bed thing a habit. The pit bull's breath smelled like the dumpster behind a fish bait store.

Tiffany rolled over and boxed out an arm to prop up her head. "You want me to take him out of here?"

"No."

"I can go feed him, see if he has to do his business."

The last thing Zane wanted was to be alone. "Stay. Tell me about the bank."

Tiffany put a hand on his arm. "Okay. There's not much to tell. Though it's kind of amazing really. I got the loan, thanks to Korey stepping up for me and co-signing. The store's going to be mine."

"But how did that happen? Didn't you say it would take a day or two before you would know?"

She laughed, a merry tinkling laugh that brought a small smile to his lips. There was still joy in this world. He was numb to it but he would find it again. He had no idea why she was laughing though.

"It has been two days, Zane. You've been basically out of it for like a day and a half. We've just been letting you sleep as much as your body wanted."

He was astounded. He'd figured he'd been asleep maybe six hours. Realizing how long he had been out of it, he felt anxious and isolated. "What's going on? Is everyone okay? How is Lettie doing?"

"Everyone is fine. She's resting a lot too. But Verda and Angel are taking good care of her. Your grandmother, she's a rock. I can't believe what a superhero she turned out to be. Well, maybe I can. I think you're amazing so why wouldn't your grandmother be amazing too?"

He didn't want to cry but suddenly two fat drops were sliding down his cheeks. "It was such a stupid risk. And now the blood of another Doom man is on my hands."

"They're saying the shot that killed him came from a shot-gun. Verda's gun."

"That might be worse. She came there to protect me and she wouldn't have been in that situation if—"

"She wanted to be there. You didn't ask her to come. You

told her to stay home. She's a strong woman, Zane. Just like your sister."

Zane reached out to take her hand. Her skin was warm and soft and wonderful. She squeezed his hand back.

"This is what family does. You've seen some pretty awful examples of family bonds with your father and half-brothers, but this—what you have with Verda and Lettie—this is the real deal. The true ties that bind."

"What about Leon?" His grandmother had thought she found love and then been betrayed. Or had Leon betrayed them? He certainly hadn't helped when it was needed most. But he didn't harm them either. Though being neutral in a situation like that was disappointing, to say the least.

"You might want to hear it all from her, but Verda was chewing over the situation for a couple of hours with Lettie and then, sometime yesterday evening she decided the best thing was to go talk to him. He's not under arrest or anything. He's back at the trailer. Verda was there until midnight, according to Lettie."

He shook his head in disbelief. "Wait. So, she's back with him?"

"I don't know exactly what's in her heart, but it seems like she's forgiven him. Maybe there's more to the story than we see. You hungry?"

He was. Ravenous in fact. Tiffany and Ballpoint headed for the kitchen, leaving Zane wondering if Leon had truly been trying to help. Of course, Zane had told the police that Leon had been helping them, for he had enough doubt in his mind to not want to tangle him up with charges. Down there at the abandoned interstate, helpless as a fish in a barrel, Zane had to take a leap of faith when Leon had grabbed his arm and pulled him close, pressing his gun against Zane's shoulder. He had to think fast and go with his gut. Had he whispered a prayer to

God or simply willed Leon to do the right thing when it counted?

Verda hadn't quite trusted him enough. She put that shotgun blast in his shoulder, changing the game. They would never know what was in Leon's heart and mind, or what would have happened if Verda and Lettie hadn't arrived. Maybe Clyde would be alive, and Zane dead. He was mad at Leon still, but in his heart, he believed Leon had the spark of goodness in him. Because he had made Verda happy, however briefly. Because he had tried to help. Maybe he helped in all the wrong ways, but he tried. Zane could relate to that. He'd been in too deep himself a few times like Leon and overestimated his ability to maneuver his way out. He could forgive Leon if Verda could.

Thursday night, two weeks to the day after police academy director Thurman Flentroy had suspended him, the letter from the Skiatook Police Department arrived in Zane's mailbox.

Whatever Lettie had been saying when Zane and Ballpoint entered the mobile home was lost. All Zane could focus on was the Skiatook Police Department logo on the envelope and his own name and address printed on the front. He'd broken into a sweat despite the cold outside—he felt it on his face, beneath his arms. It was almost like that time he was sentenced to juvie for that fight in high school, holding his breath, waiting for the judge to speak.

Tossing the "Current Resident" junk mail on the table, he showed his sister and Verda the white envelope. Lettie's vision was good enough to see it from where she sat at the kitchen table, but Verda motioned him toward her on the couch. She took it from him.

"Want me to read it for you?" his grandmother asked.

"I think I know what it says. I can feel it in my gut."

He took the envelope back from her and slid his hands along the smooth surface of the paper. An unopened letter was a tidy package, but the contents of this one could upend his life. Months of applying to about fifteen different police departments. Feeling the odds were against him. He had even investigated putting himself through the police academy at a cost of seven thousand dollars to try to make himself a more attractive candidate. And then the offer from Skiatook. He felt like a winner, a rare thing in his life.

He ripped the envelope, his forefinger making an ugly gash along the top. As he unfolded the stationery, the words "not truthful" jumped out at him. He gritted his teeth and breathed in through his nose and straightened out the top fold.

Dear Mr. Clearwater,

This letter confirms that your employment with Skiatook Police Department is terminated, effective immediately.

Misconduct: Our investigation into the accusation that you sold methamphetamine in the past has concluded. We determined that the witness providing that information is not credible. We found no additional evidence and noted your denial of direct involvement. However, in the course of this investigation, we have determined that you were not truthful in your application about the full extent of your past relationships with convicted felons. Any employee who knowingly gives false information or withholds required information during the application process is subject to corrective action, including disciplinary action. Disciplinary action may include any range of discipline, up to and including termination.

Payment for your accrued sick day will be included in your final paycheck that includes your suspension pay, which you will receive on your regular payday. You will receive a letter by mail outlining the status of your benefits.

. . .

Zane quit reading and dropped the letter on the table in front of Lettie. It was over. The decision was final, and he wasn't going to nip around the edges looking for a loophole or begging for a position. If they didn't want him, he didn't want them. He hadn't even wanted to work for that podunk town, he told himself angrily, chasing homeless people away from businesses that complained and giving traffic tickets.

"Zane, I'm so sorry." His grandmother's arms were around him and he just hung there, practically draped over her shoulder since she was squeezing him so tight as though to pop the bad news out of his head. She rocked him from side to side with no sign of stopping. He'd escaped death multiple times now, but it could all end now, being squeezed to death by his loving grandmother, her head pressing his nose and mouth shut so he couldn't breathe.

"I'll be all right," he choked out.

Finally, she eased up and then grabbed his hands. "There are better things out there for you." He looked at his grandmother, her smile so like his mother's, and the love and pride that poured out of her was so sincere. He could hardly understand it—what had he done to earn her pride or this unconditional love after bringing her into harm's way? But a grandmother's love didn't have to make sense. Maybe it was time just to be grateful for it.

He felt the tears coming and tried to blink them back. "All I can think is what a failure I am. Stupid mistake after stupid mistake. I probably can't even get my old job at the zoo back." He knew he sounded pitiful and he hated himself for it.

"Snap out of it!" Lettie whisper-screamed the words so as not to wake Milly and rose from her perch behind the laptop.

"The world doesn't want to give you a job. The world

wants you to make something of yourself. Why don't you call Loris and ask her if you can apprentice with her? Learn how to help people in trouble outside of law enforcement? You're good at it. I bet you can make a living at it."

Her words echoed his own to Tiffany about buying the Cell-Phone-FixIt store. But his self-esteem had taken a hit from that stupid letter, and he was in no mood to acquiesce to his younger sister and her well-meaning advice.

"That's an idea," he said, his jaw clenched with irritation at her.

"Don't blow me off, Zane. I mean it. Let me paint a picture for you of why a law enforcement career isn't going to be for you. Imagine you do get a position and one day you're called to testify in a trial against someone who did something really bad. The defense attorney is going to call everything you do into question! Your whole past will become an issue. Don't you see why it's not going to work?"

"What are you, the chief of police or something?"

"I'm just trying to tell you how I see it. It's just like in tarot. The Death card means the ending of something but also a chance for a new beginning. It's okay for some dreams to die. You can make more dreams. Different, better ones. Envision something you never saw before."

Zane's phone buzzed. He reached into his back pocket to grab it, then froze. It was Loris. He read the text message two times, then continued to stare for a moment.

"Did you plot this out? It's a bit much, little sister."

"Plot what out? What are you talking about?"

He read the message to Lettie and Verda.

Zane, I've got a new client and I could use your help. And Lettie's too. Online threats, that kind of thing. Interested?

Lettie's eyes widened with excitement then softened. "I

had nothing to do with that. When the universe gives you a gift..."

Zane put the phone in his back pocket without responding. If Lettie was lying, she sure was convincing. He'd think about it. That was all he could commit to now.

Chapter 30
Lettie

Looking at Us

Lettie had been in bed an hour when Angel finally stopped livestreaming, but she wasn't asleep. She sat up, plumped the pillows into a back brace and motioned for him to come lie beside her. The bedroom was quiet, nothing but the sound of Milly's soft breathing as she slept. That baby came with the gift of deep sleep.

Angel looked tired and bleary from another six-hour stint of video game playing and chatting, but his face still lit up with a smile when he saw she was up.

"Hi."

He wore an Atomic Video Games baseball jersey, one of a dozen the company had sent over for him to wear on his livestreams. Simsie Carver had been the real deal, all right, and the Atomic Video Games' sponsorship was pretty much the best thing to come out of that hellish week of Clyde's escape.

Angel looked adorable and despite the late hour he still smelled delicious to her, citrusy and fresh. Maybe it was the hand soap.

She leaned over to hug him, but it caught him off guard and she wound up poking him in the neck with her thumb.

"Ouch," Angel rubbed his neck where she poked him. "Sorry I went so late."

"No worries."

The nightlight bathed the room in a dim, orange glow. Lettie looked around her at the room they shared: filled with books and computer equipment and baby stuff. Diapers, wipes, blankets, soft toys. The little bassinet where Baby Milly slept, next to their bed.

"How did it go?"

"Long."

"Lots of people tune in?"

"It was decent. Atomic Games reps dipped in and out. Checking up on me, I guess. Anyway, the stream went over 100k views so they're happy when that happens. I'll be glad when this launch is over."

"But you like it? I mean, it's everything you wanted, right?"

"Yeah." Angel nodded, then repeated himself as if just realizing he was living the dream he had held for so long. "Yeah. It's harder work than I thought, coming up with things to say, always trying to make my real life entertaining. And there's so much pressure to be constantly aware of what everyone else is discussing and doing. Sometimes I just want to be real, you know what I mean? Like I can be with you."

"Are you okay, Angel?"

"One hundred percent," he said, but he leaned against the pillow and fixed his eyes on some speck on the ceiling. "Just tired."

She plucked at the loose strings on the chenille quilt, and Angel closed his eyes and breathed deeply. Outside the room, a toilet flushed, and Zane's heavy footsteps thudded down the hall. They both spoke at once.

"I've been thinking—"

"You know what we—"

They laughed and then hushed themselves quickly so as not to wake Milly. "You go first," Angel said.

"No, you."

"I was just going to say we should start a college fund for Milly with some of the Atomic money."

She was touched by how much he cared for their daughter. How much he wanted for her. "You're such a good dad. Who would have known? But what about a college fund for us? We're going to be there in a year."

"You'll get scholarships. I'm sure of it. And maybe I'm not cut out for it. I'm not sure. The way I see it, this Atomic Video Games thing is just the start. I'm going to approach Blizzard and Operose and the Jape Network. I've got plans and I think I need to make this money while I can. University classes aren't for everyone."

"No, I get that. Lots of people in tech dropped out of college or didn't even go. They could make more money right away with their programming skills. I just guess I thought it might be fun but I don't know."

"Expensive fun. Someone told me University of Tulsa tuition is almost sixty-thousand dollars a year."

"I've heard that too. It's ridiculous. Four years of that. You could buy a house outright. In a good neighborhood and everything."

Another silence settled on them for a bit.

"I've been thinking about us, Angel."

"What about us?" He sat up as the noisy furnace kicked on and took hold of her hand.

"You know how you were talking, I don't know, before all

this...stuff with Clyde...you were saying maybe we ought to get married?"

"Yeah, I know." He seemed so vulnerable, his heart locked in his eyes like priceless amber. He was guarding his feelings, and rightly so. She'd turned him down before.

"I suppose I wasn't very open to that and all."

"No, you sure weren't." Angel's shoulders tightened and he looked down at their hands interlaced.

"It's partly about the data, you know. Teen marriages are twice as likely to end in divorce as ones where the two people waited until their twenties to do it. It's just statistics."

"That's what you keep telling me."

"But it's also partly because—as funny as this may sound—I don't want to lose you."

"You could never." He took her hand and led it to his heart. She could feel the thump, thump beneath her palms.

"Hear me out. I mean we're all swept up in this baby bliss, and I've got hormones galore pouring through me. I'm an emotional wreck. I don't want us to do something too fast, so fast that it's not built to last."

"Are you saying what I think you're saying?"

His smile made her feel light-headed. Lettie could feel her own heart quicken, pushing the words out of her lips in a pulse of love. "Can we—can we just say we're promised to each other? That we're going to get engaged when we're eighteen? We'll know by then, won't we? We'll know if we're built to last in two years. Less than two years, even. Then we can do it properly. A big wedding celebration. Me in a white gown. Milly as our little flower girl. You in a tux. The whole enchilada."

Time froze while Lettie stared at his hand sitting on top of hers, waiting for him to speak.

"I'm saying that if the offer still stands, I do want to marry you. Just not today."

She heard him draw a deep breath, then felt him tip her chin to meet his soft brown eyes.

"Oh, the offer still stands." His voice was husky and thick. "Lettie, we can do it today or we can do it fifty years from now. I'm not going to change my mind."

She nestled into his arms and turned to smooth a kiss over his lips. She felt like she'd never lose the thrill of his touch or the spark of joy that his love and steadfastness brought to her. A constant presence in a chaotic world.

As she pulled away from him, she saw the contentment in his drowsy eyes. She thought about the way he looked when she first kissed him, hair windblown, wearing that silly Rugrats T-shirt that was four sizes too large for him. He'd changed her life for the better, tethering her to this world and the magic to be found in love.

As he began gently snoring, she started thinking about the differences between mathematics and life. In the world of mathematical logic, nothing can be both true and false. In life, this happened all the time. Contradictions were everywhere and hardly anything followed cold, rational logic except in her textbooks and in her computer programming. There was a place for her to find harmony between both.

She'd leaned on the tarot for years, wanting desperately to know the unknowable. Then she'd stumbled onto the crisp truths of mathematical logic and looked for certainty there. Both offered solace and insight. But for constancy, she would look to the love she found in her family.

Chapter 31
Verda

Second Chance

What young people didn't know could fill a set of encyclopedias, she thought, lying down beside Leon in his sparsely furnished bedroom, his arm wrapped around her waist, his hand tucked under her side. They didn't know or didn't want to think about, how the desires they felt in their firm, young bodies stayed constant even as those bodies started sagging and creaking and shrinking with age. The need for love didn't diminish with age. It was a lifetime pursuit, growing more urgent as the days whizzed by faster and faster. That's what Lettie and Zane and Angel and Donna and Clyde really didn't understand. Their youth blinded them to just how precious every day was. How precious love was. Love was a treasure worth hoarding, worth hanging onto as much as that tricycle that she'd brought home from the thrift store only to later figure out that Lettie and Zane had tossed it in the dumpster when they thought she was asleep.

She knew they disapproved of her bargain hunting and she agreed with them that the stuff had taken over her old house in Okmulgee. She'd seen that television show about extreme hoarding and knew that could be her, crying on camera about old cereal boxes or moldy yarn skeins she was going to one day turn into a sweater.

She wasn't going to let the hoard build up again. But it had hurt her feelings more deeply than they would imagine that they had tossed away that vintage tricycle. Chipped paint and a broken wheel could be fixed. That tricycle had been built back when people made things to last. Everything now was built so shoddily: clothing, furniture, appliances. Everything built to be obsolete, ready to be landfill fodder in just a few years so you would buy more, more, more.

At her age—really at any point in life—you just didn't toss love away when it came for you. Even if it came with baggage. Even if it demanded forgiveness and a leap of faith. You took it because it might not come another time. She'd already gotten one second chance when her grandchildren sought her out. She wasn't going to ask God for another one.

The next morning Verda tripped around the mobile home as if in a dream. She might be in love, or something close to it. It felt great, a comforting balm to cushion the world's blows. She didn't expect her grandkids to understand.

She told Zane as much when he asked where she'd been all night. "I've forgiven him but I'm not going to ask you to. I'm just going to pray that you consider it."

He had grunted but not rejected the notion outright, so Verda considered that a victory.

The knock at the door interrupted their silence, setting off the Ballpoint alarm. Verda imagined Leon on the doorstep, his appearance provoking an angry reaction from Zane. Surely he knew better?

Reflexively, nervously, she called out, "Who is it?"

No answer came but another knock at the door.

Zane followed Ballpoint to the door and looked through the peephole.

With an angry snort, he whipped the door open.

"What do you want?"

Donna Lancaster stood on the step, looking small and anxious. Verda had only seen the woman in the photos Lettie found on the Internet. In most of those, she was dressed to the nines with full makeup and flowing hair. Young women did amazing things with their hair these days, and the rainbow of dye colors they had to choose from seemed endless. Verda had even considered a pink streak herself.

But today, the woman before her was a wreck, dressed in saggy sweats, blonde-tipped hair back in a greasy ponytail.

"You're breaking the restraining order so back off!" Zane's voice rose to overcome Ballpoint's barking.

She stepped backwards off the step and onto dirt in front of the home. "I come in peace."

Verda stepped up behind Zane. There was an earnestness to the woman's energy that made Verda want to move closer to her, maybe even hug her. Behind her, Leon's home seemed to sparkle in the morning sunlight.

"I recanted that accusation about the meth-dealing," she said. "I just want you to know that."

"It didn't matter. They still kicked me out of the police force."

Donna's arms curved slightly at her sides in a defensive posture. "Ever get caught up in something and lose your mind?

Forget who you are? I thought I loved him. I thought he loved me. I thought he was innocent."

"I don't buy it." Zane shook his head, his arms crossed over his chest. "What do you want?"

"Let her talk a minute, Zane. You don't have to believe her. But let her say what she came to say." It worried Verda to think of this young woman being turned away, what might happen to her change of heart if Zane wouldn't hear her out. It didn't cost much to stand here and listen to her. A few moments.

Donna looked from one to the other. She took a deep breath and continued, fussing with the fake fur trim on the sleeve of her ill-fitting parka. "The police say I could be charged for making false accusations like that. Providing false information. I don't want to go to jail." She began to shiver, shrinking even farther into her enormous jacket. Had Zane not been there, Verda would have invited her in and warmed her up with a cup of tea and a cookie, she felt such pity for her. But Zane couldn't see past his anger. She understood that.

"Of course, you don't want to go to jail. No one does." Verda's voice was gentle. "But actions have consequences."

"They don't have to." Donna leaned forward slightly, barely controlled agitation seeming to leak out of her pores. "I mean if Zane were to put in a word for me. That I was sorry."

Zane held both palms toward her as though warding her away. "Are you kidding me?"

"It's too much to ask, Donna. You helped terrorize us. What we've been through—" Verda stopped when she saw the tears swelling in the young woman's eyes. She looked exhausted. Clyde's violent acts had sent long and tangled shockwaves through their lives, Donna's included. Verda could see the victim in this young woman before them, but she knew all Zane saw was a menace.

"You've said your piece. Now all you can do is go home and

hope for the best." Verda placed her hand on her grandson's stomach and pushed him lightly back toward the kitchen. Then she grasped the doorknob and softly closed the door as Donna started to move away.

Zane leaned into her, his cheek pressing into the top of her head. "I don't want to be so angry," he whispered.

"I know. You have to give it time."

"She's full of shit, I can just smell it."

"Maybe."

"Not just that but—I mean, they'll probably drop the charges. At the most, she'd just have to pay a fine and be on probation for a while. I don't know what she's whining about."

"I get it. You're madder than a box of frogs. You should be. All I'm saying is you don't know what private hells people live in, Zane."

"She made my life hell. Our lives."

"Yes, and you can continue to give her power to make your life hell with anger and resentment, or you can choose another path. It's up to you."

They both knew they were talking not just about Donna, but also about Leon. And Clyde. And if Verda were to trace it all back to the roots, about Jeremiah and Lily and Osbert and all their mistakes and all the second chances they had and didn't have.

Chapter 32
Zane

Take Two

The Cell-Phone-Fixit store was packed to its balloon-filled rafters for the grand reopening. A gold, black, and silver balloon sculpture framed the right side of the door like the bubbly crest of a wave. As Zane parked the car, he could see Tiffany standing in the doorway in a sleek silver camisole and black slacks talking excitedly with a man and woman Zane didn't know.

He walked in and Tiffany wrapped her arms around him almost immediately. He could feel her heart beating fast inside her chest.

"So many people came!" she said. "The chamber of commerce really came through, as did all of Maxine's friends from the Earth Spells store."

Her enthusiasm was contagious. He couldn't wait to

surprise her with the gift. His own heart started pounding with anticipation.

"I love you," he whispered into her hair.

"Prove it," she said. "Get Angel to start livestreaming this. I could use the social boost. But Lettie told him he's supposed to live in the moment tonight, whatever that means." She laughed.

Angel's Twitch following had grown exponentially over the past few weeks, the result of the deal he signed with Atomic Video Games to be one of their featured players on their new historic video game about the rise and fall of the doomed city Pompeii. Zane found Angel and Lettie behind the store's counter. Angel held Milly in one arm and was bagging a phone case with the other hand, while Lettie poked at the tablet that served as a cash register, inventory manager, and customer database.

"Hey Angel, Tiffany says she could use your help over there." Zane pointed in the general direction where he'd left her. "I can take over for you here." He stretched his arms out for Milly, and the baby stared at him with wide, round eyes. He started making goofy faces at her. He'd never felt so much love for a little creature as he did for his baby niece.

Angel handed the bag of merchandise to the customer with a smile. "Okay to go see what she wants, Lettie?"

Lettie rolled her eyes to the high heavens. "Jeez, just go stream already. I give up."

Now it was Angel's turn to smile, though his was tinged with relief too. He cut through the crowd toward Tiffany while Zane and Lettie turned their attention toward the next set of customers.

"How did it go?" Lettie's voice was low as she spoke directly to Zane, then she raised it again to ask the customer how they'd like to pay.

"You wouldn't believe this guy. Or maybe you would. He

was exactly what you'd picture, an unhappy, unhealthy-looking soul living in a shitty apartment. Looked scared as heck when we turned up. Keyboard warrior, real-life scaredy cat. Loris almost burst out laughing, it was so—I don't know—cliché. You know what I mean? Like what you'd expect?"

"Things are cliché because there's truth in them."

"Tell me more, oh wise one."

Lettie laughed. "So, is that the end of the job then?"

"I think so. Unless this guy keeps coming after Loris' client online. Then I'd guess we'd need to take more steps. But it's the same thing we faced with Clyde. The authorities can't do anything unless there's a real, direct threat of violence. And seeing him, I don't know that there is. But we'll keep an eye on the situation."

"Good."

The thousand dollars Loris had paid him, in cash amazingly, sat like a plump peach in his wallet. Back when he was still in the police academy, he had told himself he was doing that training to learn every single skill he could so he could help those in need. Someone who understood the right and the wrong side of the law and could help good people navigate the grey areas in between. The job with Loris, working outside the law, was teaching him just that.

Still, Lettie's know-it-all face was too much. He loved his sister and knew her well. The words "I told you so" were probably choking her to death, growing larger on her tongue. So, he put her out of her misery.

"You were right about working for Loris," Zane said, holding up his hands in surrender. "It was a good idea."

"Printed receipt or email?" Lettie asked the customer, then turned and winked at Zane. "I know that. But thanks for saying it. We've been through a lot, haven't we? Just allow yourself to feel it. All of it. And the joy of today. You believed in Tiffany. Got her to take this huge leap. Then you took one yourself."

"When did you get so grown up?"

"Having a baby makes you see things differently. The world got larger and smaller at the same time. And I see how everything is connected, how good things that happen are a gift. And sometimes the bad things are a gift too, but we don't see how right away."

Zane nodded, then slung an arm around her for a sideways hug. Her hand squeezed his side. "Who's next?"

Leon and Verda swept to the front of the line, smelling of white wine and his grandmother's lilac and baby powder perfume. Leon's light blue shirt had a wet spot on the front which Zane deduced was emitting the wine smell. Accidents happened in close quarters, he thought. Even after all this time sober, the smell still made him want a drink. He pushed the temptation out of his head as Leon laid two antibacterial phone screen covers on the counter.

"You ever use these?" Leon asked. "I was watching a video about all the bacteria that get on our phones."

"I don't know anything about them," Zane said. He realized that the answer came off gruff, so he softened it with a smile. His relationship with Leon was still tentative, even though his grandmother appeared to have forgiven him fully. Zane was just going to have to get used to having Leon around. And that would mean seeing him with compassion and kindness and not suspicion. It was a hard thing to do.

Lettie rang up Leon, giving him the friends and family discount, just as Tiffany climbed atop a short step stool and cleared her throat.

"Attention everyone! Attention!"

Zane gave a wolf whistle and watched as the room slowly

quieted and everyone's attention turned toward his beautiful girlfriend.

"I want to share a few words with you," she said.

"Everything's free in the store!" some joker in the crowd shouted.

Tiffany's eyes narrowed as she turned a comic glare toward the source. "No! What is it with you, Trevor? Let me say something nice here. It's a big day for me."

"Everything's half-off!" the same voice called out.

Zane cupped his hands around his mouth and shouted back, "Let her speak! Let her speak!" Lettie joined in, followed by Leon and Verda, and then many in the room joined the chorus as Tiffany blushed the prettiest shade of rose.

"Enough silliness. Let me just say what I want to say without crying here."

Everyone piped down.

"I was taught from a young age to believe in myself. To believe that I could do anything. But it never really took root in me for some reason. It's not my dad's fault, or my mom's, or my stepmom's—where are you all? Okay, I see you. You've always had my back. I've known it, I've counted on it, but I didn't really believe it. Do you know what I mean? It took someone very, very special to make me really believe in that potential inside me. Zane Clearwater, right there, that man behind the counter. His love and support filled those empty spaces inside me. He gave me the idea to buy this business and the motivation to keep going after it even when it was hard. Even when it seemed impossible. He helped me grow. And I owe him a huge debt of gratitude for making today a reality."

The crowd seemed to embrace Tiffany in a collective hug when she stepped down. A few people got misty-eyed like Zane did. When he worked his way to her, he said, "I don't know what to say other than I love you. I don't want to start getting all slobbery like Ballpoint."

Tiffany beamed like a ray of sun. "You could have brought him."

"And he would have knocked over all your displays, eaten the cut-up vegetables and cheese and crackers, and probably bitten your customers. Trust me, he's better wishing you well from the Majestic."

"I love him despite that. Just like I love you."

Zane's heart and body began to melt. He pulled her closer to him, wanting her support. "Sometimes I think you must be blind as a bat to see anything good in me, but I sure don't want you to get your vision checked. I want to keep you seeing me that way. It makes me try to be better," he said. "I'm going to try and partner up with Loris. So we'll both be business owners. You'll probably be more successful than me."

Tiffany put a finger over his lips to shush him. He could smell the faint crumbs of chocolate chip cookie on her hand. "No negative self-talk."

"I have something for you." He fished the tiny black velvet bag out of his back pocket gingerly, careful as if handling a butterfly's wings.

He handed it to her, and she undid the tie to let the gold pendant necklace fall into the palm of her hand. The 18-karat gold disc had the words BOSS BABE hand stamped on it. She picked up the dainty chain and seemed to stop breathing for a moment.

"It's beautiful. I love it. But is this real gold? It's too expensive!"

"Don't worry about that. I can afford it. But this gift comes with my gratitude to you, for your support and it also comes with a promise: I'm yours and my entire being only wants the best for you and for our life together. I also promise this isn't going to be the last piece of jewelry I buy you."

Smiling broadly, she turned around so he could hook the chain around her neck. Once it was on, he couldn't resist kissing the back of her neck. She nuzzled against him.

He thought of those words someone had spoken at an AA meeting: *on the right path, we are on the side of good and we have all the power of God's spirit behind us.* Those words had given him the courage to face Clyde and not run. And he did feel like he had the power of God's spirit behind him. He couldn't be much in God's eyes other than another sinner but somehow, he was still here to fight another day. To feel ridiculously happy just being near Tiffany, watching Lettie grow up before his eyes, learning how to take care of little Milly with her help and Angel's and Verda's. Seeing his grandmother get a second chance at love, even if he had a few reservations about Leon.

The words Zane's violent, dangerous father had spoken in that Sallisaw bar—*now I know you're my son*—were as far away as the stars and nebulas and galaxies being captured by that new Webb telescope. The words were artifacts from a distant time. Their meaning no longer resonated with him. Why would they? He had moved on, shedding layers, and growing new skin. He was his own man, not his father's. He turned back to Tiffany, feeling the warm electricity of their love extending throughout this room full of friends and family, infusing him with hope and energy for the future.

THE END

Acknowledgments

Thank you so much for making it all the way to end. I hope you have enjoyed Zane's third story and are excited to discover the rest of his journey. If you did, leaving a review is the best possible present for an author!

My most sincere thanks to:

My MFA program writing bestie Marina Crouse for holding me accountable to finishing this sequel and encouraging me with thoughtful texts, regular check-ins, and the occasional cup of coffee IRL. She has a writing coach business so hire her if you need the extra support!

Editor Natalie Cammaratta for her insightful and witty developmental edits to the manuscript. Go buy her book *Falling and Uprising* immediately. She knows how to tell a great story.

Editor and proofreader Cindy Price for her eagle-eyed perspective on missing commas, unclear sentences, and all those little inconsistencies us writers leave in our manuscripts.

My mother Rosemary Lipinski, my sister Laura Kane, friends, MFA writing besties, and family members Darcy Burke, Carol Golyski, Kayla Harris, Ron Kane, Priya Kapoor, Brenda Laplante, Zhenya Matt, Bernie Stillions, Leo Vegoda, and Jill Wicke for their unwavering and enthusiastic support of my writing. I know I'm missing about hundred people here. Your support means the world to me.

My husband Stephen Arakawa for always believing in me.

The amazing TikTok community of #booktok #indieauthortok that reignited my love of books and writing, particularly Millie and Kayla Renee. Yes, Milly in this book is named for Millie in real life. Kayla, you'll get your character in the next book, *Find Him Fast*.

And to the talented fantasy thriller author Caytlyn Brooke, whose casual question "what if one of the brothers got out of prison?" inspired this entire novel. Go buy her book *Among the Hunted* now and let her take you on the adventure of a lifetime.

Find Him Fast

Want more? Turn the page for an exciting preview of the next Zane Clearwater Mystery novel.

Chapter One

Every weekend it was the same. Zane and Tiffany, coming home from a movie or the arcade or dinner, climbed the steps and approached the door of her midtown Tulsa apartment, faced the dilemma of the apartment key.

Tiffany had given him a key to her apartment about a month ago, telling him it was in case she got locked out or left the oven on before leaving town. That kind of thing. But every time they stood outside her apartment door, as he watched her fumble around in her purse for her version, he shoved his hand in his pocket and ran his fingers along the key's serrated edge, wondering if he should leap to the rescue. But her determination to find the key instead of asking him to do the honors made it clear: yes, he had a key but it was her apartment and she'd open the door.

That Saturday afternoon in April, they had been at the Cell Phone Fix-It store that Tiffany owned, building then installing new display shelves. Exhausted from opening boxes and finding tiny allen wrenches and arguing over which piece went where, it was about five o'clock when Tiffany used her key. Inside, she shouted out to Kayla Renee, her roommate, that she was home and Zane was with her, and went to the bathroom.

Zane went to the kitchen to the left of the tidy living room, with its blue L-shaped sofa and about two hundred pillows of all shapes and sizes, for two cans of diet soda, the only kind the women kept in the house. By the time he returned to the sofa Tiffany was standing in front of the television, remote in hand, clicking through options on the streaming service. She found a movie she had seen at least a dozen times and hit play. It was one of her adorable quirks: she liked the background noise and the comfort of the dialogue she practically knew by heart.

Zane handed her a soda and sat. "Ricky seems like a good guy."

"Thank goodness. I don't think I could ever fire the first employee I've ever hired as a business owner."

"You're going to have to get used to that kind of thing, if you're going to be a big boss lady."

"I still think of myself as an hourly employee. It's hard to imagine—"

"You own that joint." Zane clicked his soda against hers. "Here's to you."

A door opened and a woman's voice carried across the space. "Hello, hello and goodbye."

Zane and Tiffany turned to see Kayla heading for the front door. She was a relative newcomer to Tiffany's world and he'd only seen her three times. She was in her early twenties, clad in a black leather jacket, with honey-hued face shaped like a heart and big brown eyes. From what Tiffany told him, she had just gotten her college degree in physical therapy at University of Tulsa and was looking for a full-time job in that field. Meanwhile, she was working the register at Drysdale's Western Wear.

Kayla and Tiffany chatted briefly about a planned trip to the grocery story the next day and Kayla left. Then Zane and Tiffany snuggled up for a bit, letting the movie run in the background while they paid absolutely no attention to it. Before things got too heated, Tiffany pulled away, reminding Zane that she was meeting her dad and stepmom for dinner and that he had promised his sister and grandmother he'd babysit his niece Milly tonight so they could go play bingo.

But in the parking lot he was intercepted. He'd barely made it to the back bumper of his car when a woman's voice said his name and he turned, thinking he'd left something important at Tiffany's like his phone or his brain. But Kayla was walking toward him with a smile on her face. "Do you have a few minutes for me to ask you something?"

"Okay," Zane said. He glanced at his phone for the time. By his best guess, she'd been out here thirty minutes waiting for him. Something was up.

"It's personal," she said, smiling in a pretty but apologetic way, dimples emerging on her light amber skin.

"You don't like me spending the night there," Zane said.

"It's not that! It's not about you. It's about me."

"I've been told that before." His joke fell flat the moment he said it. Kayla was serious and earnest.

"Tiffany said you're a detective."

Zane raised his eyebrows. "Sort of. I mean, I'm working for a woman named Loris Trapper. She's a—problem solver of sorts. Former police officer."

"Tiffany said you were in training to be a police officer too."

"It didn't quite work out." He glanced at the drawn blinds covering Tiffany's bedroom window, wishing she had warned him that Kayla was looking for help. But maybe she didn't know. After all, Kayla had ambushed him in the parking lot.

"But you still want to help people, right?"

"I do."

"I'm looking for someone to help me find my father."

Zane rested a hand on his car's trunk. A million images flooded his mind: the face of his own father, Jeremiah Doom, who had thought nothing of kidnapping Lettie and planning to kill her. Zane, firing the gun to kill him.

"Are you sure you want to find him? How did you leave it with him when you saw him last?"

"I've never seen him. I don't know him. I don't know who he is."

"Some things are better left alone."

There was a pause while Zane waited for her to say Tiffany had told her all about his past but it was going to be different for her. But she just sighed instead.

"Look, I've never told anyone else this. Not Tiffany. Not anyone. But when Tiffany told me what you do—and about your family—I felt like I could trust you." The way she hesitated before saying the word "family" made it clear that Tiffany had spilled the tea on Zane's violent relationship with his father and half-brothers. "I'm not usually wrong about these things," she said.

"You don't need to blow smoke at me," Zane said. "So what's the story then? What do you know about him?"

"I never knew him, like I said. My mother never spoke of him. I don't think she was ever married. I'm not even sure Renee was her real last name. Did you know it's the French word for reborn?"

"It's not an uncommon name."

"Not as a first name, no. But a last name? It's not that common."

"You might be grasping here." His own mother had changed her last name too, from Davis to Clearwater, trying to protect him from his real father. The similarities were giving him the creeps.

"What does your mom say about it? Have you talked to her?"

"I wanted to. But she's dead."

The creepy feeling stayed but Zane's curiosity poked its head out. "When did she die?"

"Last December. Right before Christmas. Carjacking gone wrong, the police said. Someone shot her and left her to die in the parking lot of her office."

Zane remembered the story from the local news. Notable because the crime happened in south Tulsa, a low-crime, wealthy enclave of big houses with wide eaves, shake roofs, and small front yards where Zane assumed video cameras and private security would collect tons of clues on the perpetrator. But the crime was still unsolved. It was also notable that Tiffany didn't seem to know that her new roommate had lost her mother in a violent crime. That told him something about Kayla Renee—she certainly kept her secrets close.

"Did the police get the killer?"

"No. The Tulsa police are still looking."

"What about your family? You have sisters or brothers, aunts and uncles?"

"No. It was just me and mom forever. Really."

His life had been like that too, but he'd had Lettie as a sibling at least. The parallels between Kayla Renee's childhood and his own were too similar to shake off. And he felt compelled to warn her off.

"Like I said, sometimes it is better to let things lie. I don't know how much Tiffany told you about my family but you and I have a lot in common. And trying to find out who my mother was after her mysterious death led me down some paths that I wouldn't recommend. When people who love us, like our mothers, take a lot of steps to conceal their pasts, maybe we ought to trust them," Zane said.

"Isn't knowing the truth better than not knowing?"

"I don't know if you want to hear my answer to that. It's not that clear cut."

"I'm all alone in this world. I thought you'd understand. I might have a whole family out there somewhere. Why wouldn't I want to find them?"

Zane ran his fingers through his hair. "Because maybe they are bad people. Maybe that's why your mother didn't want you to find them. Or them to find you."

"I can pay you," she said. "Isn't this what you do for money? I have some money."

"I work for Loris Trapper, so you'd be paying her. And I don't mean to be rude, but what you're asking is not that cheap to do. It can be a lot of hours of poking around and it may not come to anything. Could be a thousand dollars a week, minimum. I don't know if your paycheck from Drysdale's is going to cover that honestly."

She straightened her shoulders a bit and flashed her brown eyes at him with a little attitude. "I have some money my mom left me. Don't worry about that."

"What kind of job did your mom have?" It was a nosy question but Loris had told him private investigators have to be comfortable pushing clients, or potential clients, for answers.

"She had some kind of IT job in real estate development. Worked at the same place as long as I can remember. We lived in a big house in Delaware Pointe for most of my life. I thought she owned it but I found out after she died that it was a rental from the real estate company she worked for. They let me live there for a few months after she died but that's why I moved in with Tiffany. They told me it was time to leave or pay rent. And I couldn't afford their rent. They wanted like two thousand dollars a month."

"That's a big rent check," Zane said. He still lived with his sister Lettie and her boyfriend in their grandmother's doublewide at the Majestic Mobile Home and RV Park in east Tulsa. With his small salary from Loris, he was still months away from saving enough to rent his own place.

"Will you help me?"

"Let me call Loris, see if I can set up a time for you to come in and talk to us. But be sure that this is what you want to do. That you want to know the truth no matter what. It's not always what you want to hear."

"I want to know." Kayla Renee's eyes flashed again at him and she put her hands on her hips for emphasis too. "I understand the risks."

Zane nodded. They swapped phone numbers and went their separate ways, Zane to his Toyota Corolla and Kayla Renee to a new-looking Volkswagen Jetta.

He sat behind the wheel of the car, watching her drive away and thinking about her parting words about understanding the risks. He knew she didn't fathom the risks at all. But he also recognized her compulsion to find out anyway. The least he could do was try to help her and protect her at the same time.